Select praise for the n[...]

"*The Backtrack* is the perfect nostalgic [...] music taste hasn't changed since high s[...]. It is a love ballad to both pop punk and the people we leave behind."
—Allison Raskin, *New York Times* bestselling author
of *Overthinking About You*

"Bursting with mid-aughts nostalgia, *The Backtrack* is an irresistible take on *what if*. With a cast of lovable, quirky characters and a dreamy seaside setting...La Rosa's newest is the perfect mix(tape) of laugh-out-loud, steamy, and sincere." —Holly James, author of *The Déjà Glitch*

"This is the book of my nostalgic dreams! Erin La Rosa hits all the right notes in this catchy second-chance romance humming with heart, heat, and humor. *The Backtrack* is a perfectly in-tune love story that will be playing on repeat in my mind for a very long time."
—Lauren Kung Jessen, author of *Red String Theory* and *Lunar Love*

"La Rosa has written a beautiful contemplation on what-ifs. Throw on your old band shirts, cue up the music, and get ready for a love story so tender you'll *have* to press repeat."
—Carlyn Greenwald, author of *Sizzle Reel* and *Director's Cut*,
on *The Backtrack*

"A dazzlingly imaginative concept for the ages. Steamy, nostalgic, and often truly hilarious, *The Backtrack* feels like the musical emo love child of *13 Going on 30* and *(500) Days of Summer*, and it turns out that's exactly what the world's been missing. Fans of Elissa Sussman and Ashley Poston will want to scoop this one up!"
—Bethany Turner, bestselling author
of *Brynn and Sebastian Hate Each Other: A Love Story*

"As a reader, it's a privilege to live inside of Erin La Rosa's brilliant, quirky, and deliciously risqué brain."
—Becky Feldman, host of the *Too Stupid to Live* podcast

"A quirky, sexy romp that had me turning pages into the night... Will definitely look for more from Erin La Rosa."
—Kate Quinn, *New York Times* bestselling author of *The Diamond Eye*,
on *Plot Twist*

"[*Plot Twist*] is a true romance lover's romance." —*Publishers Weekly*

ERIN LA ROSA

THE
BACKTRACK

CANARY STREET PRESS

**CANARY
STREET
PRESS™**

Recycling programs
for this product may
not exist in your area.

ISBN-13: 978-1-335-00945-6

The Backtrack

Canary Street Press
22 Adelaide St. West, 41st Floor
Toronto, Ontario M5H 4E3, Canada
CanaryStPress.com

Printed in U.S.A.

Also by Erin La Rosa

For Butter or Worse
Plot Twist

Womanskills
The Big Redhead Book

Look for Erin La Rosa's next novel
available soon from Canary Street Press!

To anyone who has ever wondered "What if?"

prologue

At fifteen years old, Sam Leto knew a few things: humidity was not her hair's friend, she was going to graduate valedictorian of her class and music was life.

"'I Will Follow You into the Dark' was by far the best song of last year." Sam tucked her thumbs into the loops of her jeans, narrowly avoiding the spiky knobs of her metal studded belt. The spider-web chain she'd bought from Hot Topic slapped against her thigh as she walked across the asphalt of the Tybee Island High School parking lot. "It's mesmerizing and so poetic, and Ben Gibbard—"

"What are you talking about?" her best friend, Damon Rocha, interrupted. He threw his head back to get a strand of long dyed-red hair off his forehead. He'd smudged dark black eyeliner all around his eyes to the point where he looked like he was cosplaying as the Hamburglar. She'd told him as much, but in the loving way they told each other everything. They walked so closely that they lazily bumped into each other, as if swaying to music only they could hear. "'Sugar, We're Goin Down' reignited the genre."

Sam blew air out through her lips to suggest her disagreement, then added, "That song is tight, but there are way too many words in the chorus. You can't even hear what Patrick Stump's saying."

"It doesn't matter what he's saying." Damon hoisted his snare drum backpack higher on his shoulder. Night had settled, but the fluorescent glow from the football field lit their way to his car. "They owned that melody."

But Sam knew why Damon was making such a hard push for Fall Out Boy. "You just want me to like Pete Wentz so those dyed red tips make sense." She gave him a half grin.

"Whatever," he said, holding back a smile of his own.

Sometimes they agreed on music, but when they disagreed it was even more fun. And Sam knew she was right about this one. "I read in *Kerrang!* that Ben wrote the song in fifteen minutes. Can you believe that?" Sam looked off, knowing that if she was in a band, she'd be talented like that, too.

"Yes," Damon said. "I believe it only took fifteen minutes, because it's *not* the best song of 2005."

She was choosing to ignore that dig. "What he wrote is totally romantic. To love someone so much that you'd follow them into the afterlife. It's cool, don't you think?" Sam realized she sounded a little ridiculous, but Damon always made her feel safe enough to say anything.

"Yeah, or pretentious." Damon pursed his lips.

"Whatever," Sam mimicked his sullen tone back. Then she jabbed him with the corner of her sticker-covered clarinet case.

The sky was inky-black, and her arms prickled against the brisk air. Fall in Tybee was hard to plan for. The air was almost always balmy, because they were so close to the ocean, but it occasionally cooled down, as it had tonight. Still, she'd nearly sweat through her graphic skull T-shirt as their marching band played Beyoncé's "Déjà Vu" during the football halftime show.

Now, though, they weren't marching across a field lit by hot lights, and she shivered. Damon pulled her in close as they walked. He'd often tuck her under his arm this way. Sam was tall, close to six feet, but Damon always made her feel delicate in those moments. It was something she got unexpected comfort from, but didn't dare tell him.

When she looked up, Damon looked down with the most genuinely sweet smile she'd ever seen. His mouth quirked up as they reached someone's Ford Explorer.

"Hope you don't hate Fall Out Boy too much, because I put one of their songs on this." He pulled a CD sleeve out of his back pocket and handed it to her. His slanted writing and doodles were visible through the clear plastic, and Sam bit her lip.

They were constantly trying to impress each other through music—a kind of unspoken game of who could make the best mixes. And while Sam prided herself on finding obscure bands, Damon had the uncanny ability to put together songs that made her *feel* something. She wanted to listen immediately, but wouldn't show her excitement that easily. Before she could think of something nonchalant to say, he brushed a strand of hair behind her ear.

Sam was taken aback by the gesture and nervously touched the spot his fingers had just left. She'd spent nearly a half hour flat-ironing it that morning, but now it was frizzed and tangled. As her fingers clumsily tried to untangle a knot, her earring fell to the ground. Before she knew what was happening, just as Sam went to reach for her earring, Damon closed the gap between them.

"You look really great." He longingly admired her face. Damon reached for Sam's hand and squeezed her open palm.

She instinctively squeezed back, but her heart raced. Damon and Sam were best friends. They had been since middle school. Yes, Damon was inarguably cute. He understood her like no one else did, and she had already admitted to herself that she had a crush on him…but he was also all she had, in so many ways. Her mom had left her a year ago. Damon was her only friend.

Sam knew that what he was doing might lead to a kiss, and she needed to stop him before he said something that would change them forever. She couldn't lose his friendship, but if he tried to make them more, then she'd have no choice. Because she wasn't going to end up stuck in Tybee.

Before she could find the words, he tilted her chin up gently with an index finger. His eyes locked on to hers as he asked, "Can I kiss you?"

Sam sucked in a deep breath to slow the intense rush of adrenaline that flew through her at his words. Damon wanted to kiss her. And her heart soared at that fact, until her mom's voice broke through.

Don't end up stuck in this place.

That's what her mom, Bonnie, had told Sam right before she'd left. And Sam had taken the warning to heart.

She was getting out, even if that meant she had to leave Damon behind.

As Damon searched her eyes, Sam silently implored him to stop. They could still be friends, couldn't they? If she gave him another few moments, maybe he'd take the words back, or say he'd just been joking.

She waited, but he was waiting, too. And she was going to have to answer him, even if what she said irrevocably changed them.

She took a step away and looked down at her Converse sneakers. She'd have to lie. She'd never lied to Damon before, but now she would. Her lower lip trembled, as unsure of the words as she was. "Actually, I'm not feeling well."

And she didn't feel well. She felt nauseous from this whole situation and the confusion that flashed across Damon's face.

"Oh," Damon said. "Let's, uh, let's bounce, then." He ran a hand through his hair and avoided her eyes.

As Damon turned toward the driver's side of the car, Sam instinctively reached for him. Maybe she should just do what her heart wanted and kiss him. Because what if not kissing him meant he wouldn't want to be her friend anymore?

But then, she also knew Damon. Knew that he wanted to stay close to his family. Knew how much he loved Tybee. And knew that if she didn't break him now, she'd do it when she left.

Sam pulled her hand back and hoped that he could forgive her. She held on to his CD so tightly she was sure it would snap in half, but it didn't. In fact, the CD seemed to pulse in her hand with the throbbing of her heart. As she walked herself to the passenger side of the car, she tried to forget how the light in his eyes dimmed just before he'd turned away from her.

1

Sam Leto's calling in life was flying planes. And unlike other pilots, she still got the same rush of adrenaline each time she pushed the throttles up for takeoff. What she wasn't as good at, however, was playing the "What If?" game with her copilot, Rachel.

"Cabin crew, any updates from the galley? Specifically Row L?" Rachel asked the flight attendants via the cockpit intercom. Her voice bordered on giddy.

Sam waited, hoping Rachel's bet was wrong. The "What If?" game, as their in-flight crew had so aptly called it, was when they paired unexpecting passengers together to see what could happen. What if they moved the chic lady in Row D next to the nerdy cute guy in first class? What if the guy with the noisy cat had a seat change to be next to the single mom and her precocious tween? The possibilities were endless, and the odds of a successful match weren't in their favor. But still, they played the game regularly.

"After the rejected takeoff, we've been in a steady holding pattern," flight attendant Javier relayed.

Rachel grimaced at Sam, but Sam raised a triumphant eyebrow. They'd taken a bet—Sam voted that the match between a tattooed short king and a woman who was Lilly Pulitzer's number-one fan wasn't right, and Rachel bet that they would hit it off. *Rejected takeoff* was code for a rough start, and a *steady holding pattern* meant they hadn't progressed.

"But…" Javier continued.

"Ohhh, there's a *but*!" Rachel clapped. Sam frowned.

"Happy to report that the antics of an unaccompanied minor have brought Row L a friendly runway of opportunity for small talk. They're sharing a snack from the meal cart and, if I'm not mistaken, have exchanged phone numbers via the complimentary cocktail napkins."

Sam's mouth fell open in surprise, then she tightly closed it. She hated being wrong. "Dammit," she said.

"I told you!" Rachel victoriously fist-pumped the air. "You owe me food court fries. What if we'd swapped 3C instead of 2L? This love connection would've never been made."

"*Or* maybe she'll end up in a relationship with this random person and miss out on the *real* love of her life, all because you shoved them together." Sam rolled her shoulders, which always started to hunch when they got toward the end of a long flight.

"Leto, you're in a real mood today." Rachel opened the flight manual and pretended to study the page with their descent route. "First you eat all four of those pains au chocolat, and now you're getting cynical on me. More cynical than usual."

At the mention of the pastries, Sam glanced down and her stomach cartoonishly rippled under her crisp, white button-up pilot's shirt. She loosened her pink leather belt in a sad attempt to fix the situation, but it absolutely didn't.

Rachel gave her the kind of grossed-out expression one might reserve for accidentally touching a wad of gum under a table.

"I'm fine," Sam lied. She was inarguably not fine, and let

out a breath as she sat back in the pilot's seat. Out the window, just past the nose of the plane, was a perfectly blue sky with one fat gray cloud.

"I did plan to share." The nonstop flight from Paris to Atlanta required a little sugar boost—more than the banana in her daily oatmeal could offer—so she'd gotten enough for both of them. "But I'm stressed about the trip is all."

The next few days were going to be hard, to put it lightly, and she hadn't been this anxious in a long time, including the recent emergency landing she'd had to make. The emergency, as it turned out, was a passenger whose support chihuahua had food poisoning from an airport tuna roll.

Rachel gave a gentle shoulder punch that brought Sam back to the present. Rachel was her very best friend these days—not only because they spent hours together trapped in a small room, but because she always knew how to yank Sam out of her own head. "Are you seriously *this* terrified of taking vacation?"

Sam blinked several times. She'd told Rachel that she was finally cashing in some overdue time off with an all-inclusive beach retreat at a luxury resort. Not a complete lie, but...a pretty big one. Because when they landed, Sam would rent a car and drive four hours to Tybee Island in Georgia. And even though Tybee was *technically* a tourist haven—with a stretch of sandy beach, seafood shacks and quaint cottage rentals—it was also where Sam had grown up, and the trip would be anything but a vacation.

She was going back to Tybee—a place she'd worked hard to leave—because her grandma wanted to move into a senior living facility. *A raisin ranch*, as Grandma Pearl had jokingly called it, but Sam supposed was true. Her grandma's memory had started to crack at the edges. The last time Pearl visited Sam in Paris, she'd forgotten the name of the airline Sam flew for, and then misplaced the word for paper towel. And while Pearl had lightly joked about the slips—*I never hold grudges, because*

I have a bad memory—she suggested the transition to a smaller place without any prompting from Sam. Sam wasn't completely sold on the idea of Grandma Pearl joining a retirement home, though, so she was going home to spend the week cleaning out the house and to see if Pearl *really* needed to leave.

The other, more complicated, reason that Sam was so out of sorts was a text from Damon Rocha.

Damon, her childhood best friend whom she hadn't seen since she left Georgia after flight school eleven years ago. The guy who knew everything about who she'd been when she lived in Tybee, and who had tried to kiss her so long ago. That almost-kiss was a moment Sam still lingered on. *What if she'd kissed him?* Would her life be completely different? She thought about that way too much, even though she was a grown ass woman who'd kissed plenty of people since then and could eat four pastries for breakfast if she wanted.

Though that last choice was, admittedly, the wrong one.

Fly safe.

That was all he'd said, but there was so much left *unsaid* that Sam had spent most of the flight filling in the blanks.

Fly safe, because you ran away and owe me one hell of an explanation.

Fly safe, because you've avoided me for long enough.

Fly safe, and I won't be surprised if you bail.

It wasn't that she didn't *want* to see Damon—quite the opposite. She'd wanted to see him for years. He'd been her best friend, and they had so much history together that whenever she thought of her childhood, he was inextricably entwined in it. She wasn't avoiding him exactly, but the way she'd left things between them had been…bad. Like, hugging him goodbye, promising to come back soon and then just not making good on that at all. She'd been scared that visiting Damon would mean more than simply returning to the small city she never wanted to live in again. But now she *was* returning, and he was texting, so there was no avoiding him, or Tybee.

"We've got a bumpy landing." Sam swiftly changed the subject so she wouldn't have to explain herself to Rachel. She'd worked hard to keep her past in the past. "Do you have a dad joke picked out?" She shifted her long legs, which had gone numb from too much sitting.

Rachel raised her pierced brow as she closed the flight manual. "I workshopped this one with Aubry. Ready to hear it?"

Pilots had a high rate of divorce—with too much time away from home, it was no wonder—but Aubry and Rachel were the kind of couple that gave Sam hope.

"If your wife approved this, then I'm all ears." Sam was grateful to hear anything that didn't involve her own sugar-high thoughts of doom. She picked up the intercom and began to talk. "Hello, this is Captain Leto. We're about to start our initial descent into the Atlanta, Georgia, area."

"If you're going to Atlanta, it's a perfect seventy-five degrees," Rachel said into the mic. "There are a few air pockets coming up in our approach, so the ride may get bumpy. Just remember that if the landing *is* rough, it's not the captain or copiot's fault. It's the asphalt."

Rachel turned the intercom off and looked at Sam expectantly. Sam allowed a few beats of silence to build out the tension, then slid her sunglasses down her nose.

"It was good," Sam conceded. "Not as good as the four pains au chocolat, but good."

Rachel sighed, then turned her focus to the instrument panel. "You're gonna miss my jokes, even when you're stretched out on a beach with a cabana boy serving you margaritas."

Sam wanted to tell Rachel that the closest she'd get to a beach would be looking out the window as she boxed up her old memories, but Rachel didn't know anything about Sam's childhood—or what she'd run from. So instead of being honest, Sam swallowed down the sick feeling, either from the pastries or the impending trip—or both—and switched off the autopilot to land the plane.

"This is looking like a rodeo approach," Sam said. There were gusty winds reported, and she'd have to tame the bucking airplane on the descent.

"Your favorite," Rachel said.

And she was right. Sam prided herself on hand piloting the smoothest landings possible even in extreme circumstances. Being able to focus on the landing meant she didn't have to think about Damon, either.

"Been meaning to get us another Superior Airmanship Award." Sam and Rachel had earned the prestigious honor after a flight where there was a fire in the cabin, and they managed a flawless emergency landing. In the forty years since the award started, they were the only women to ever earn the recognition.

"If anyone can do it, it's you," Rachel said. "Let's get you to your vacation in one piece, shall we?"

"Ten-four." Unlike with her personal life, she had no problem focusing on doing her job, the one thing she was truly great at.

When Sam landed the plane, there was a round of applause from the cabin, and she was proud of the reason.

Sam sat in the driver's seat of the rented Mercedes and maneuvered across lanes of highway traffic, sped past lazy rolling hills and drifted into the flatter land near Savannah. Instead of music, an episode of *This American Life* featuring David Sedaris walking the streets of Paris played. She thought the episode would remind her that she had a whole other existence in her apartment in Montmartre, but she barely heard the words as she glanced out the window.

She was struck by how different the area looked. Next to the familiar, distinguished live oak trees covered in moss, were new high-rise, modern luxury townhomes and urban sprawl that she didn't remember being there. The changes blissfully distracted her, and for a few moments during the ride she lost herself completely to the new surroundings. A lot could change in eleven years, she guessed, just as she'd changed, too.

She'd stopped wearing two-for-one thongs from Target—flip-flop or otherwise—for example. Real grown-up decisions had been made.

As the sun steadily dipped lower behind billboards for fast-food stops, she closed in on Tybee Island. A familiar sky-blue hand-painted sign for the town welcomed her, and she rolled the window down. The scent of salt and suntan lotion bloomed in the air like fragrant flowers as she drove through the main street. Despite the fact that it was fall in some parts of the country, in Tybee there were tourists in cutoff shorts and bikini tops strolling the sidewalk past vibrant storefronts advertising souvenirs, beach apparel and ice cream.

It was unnerving how familiar and foreign coming back felt. To recognize the street names, but not the new stores. To have memories of walking across the concrete, but see it replaced with mosaic tile. This had once been the only place she'd known, and now she felt as if she were visiting for the first time. She no longer belonged in her hometown; she was just another tourist. She'd expected to break out in claustrophobic hives as soon as she arrived, but so much had changed that she found herself more dumbstruck than anything else.

Sam turned onto Chatham Avenue, the street where her childhood home was. A handful of original shingle-style beach cottages remained, but were dwarfed by newer modern water-front mansions. This was the street where she'd learned to ride a bike, drive a car and daydreamed about the life she'd eventually lead. Though, as she glanced down the line of the freshly paved road, those memories were like a foggy dream.

She should feel some kind of buzz, like a Hallmark level of warm and fuzzies that tied her to this place, right? After all, she was home. *Home*. There was nothing comforting about that word, though, which felt as heavy as a Boeing 747 on her chest.

That heaviness lingered as she pulled into the sandy driveway of her grandma's cottage, still enclosed by the same chipped white picket fence. She didn't immediately turn the car off, but stared at the blue front door's weathered paint. All she had to do was put the car in Reverse, back out of the driveway and head to the airport she had come from.

But she couldn't run, not this time, because her grandma needed help and Sam owed her that much. The woman had raised her when her mom refused to. So Sam mustered as much positive energy as she could, reapplied her matte lipstick and killed the engine.

When she stepped out of the car, a seagull dropped from the sky, zipping so close to her head that she had to duck. She tried to regain her footing, but the chunky wedges she'd changed into weren't built for the soft sand and she fell into the car door. And as a final punch, she reached a hand up and the blowout she'd had specifically for this trip was beginning to frizz from the moisture.

Ah, yes, it was good to be home.

Sam grabbed her designer duffel out of the back seat and held it in front of her like a protective blanket. She shook out her shoulders and straightened the tie of her pilot's uniform. Seeing Grandma Pearl, whom she loved, would be easy; it was walking back inside a place filled with so much pain that worried her.

Sam walked up to the front and rang the doorbell, but there was no immediate answer. She scratched at her fringe, which stuck to her forehead from the heat, and rang the doorbell again. But after another few minutes, still nothing. Her grandma had always been a fan of daily walks and was likely on one. So Sam bent over and picked up the peach-and-brown-striped conch shell next to the welcome mat. She shook it, and it rattled. Then she flipped the shell over and the spare brass key fell into her palm.

When she opened the door, the salty air was replaced with vanilla candles and lavender detergent—the same clean-and-sweet scent that had always been there. While much of Tybee had changed, some things hadn't, and that truth brought Sam a new confidence. She'd been here before and left. Saying good-bye to this place would be easy, and all she had to do was re-member *that* whenever she began to feel trapped.

"Hello?" Sam waited, but there was no answer, so she con-tinued into the house. Her fingertips trailed along the wall, painted plum and decorated with hanging signs.

In a flip-flop state of mind.

Don't worry, beach happy.

Toes in the sand, wine in my hand.

She couldn't help but smirk at a new one, *Beach, please!*

These small reminders of who her grandma was, and con-tinued to be, stirred a longing that replaced some of the nerves she'd been holding on to. Yes, being home was an out-of-body experience, but Sam wanted to see Pearl and wished she'd walk back through the door already.

As she stood in the living room, her gaze landed on a framed photo of thirteen-year-old Sam, her mom and Pearl stand-ing on the pier near their house, a fishing rod in Sam's hand. Sam picked it up and eyed her adolescent face—a wide smile of braces and white filmy sunscreen on her nose. Too much black eyeliner, blue eyeshadow and an all-black wardrobe. Her knobby knees, which had earned her the nickname "giraffe," were covered in freckles. And then there was her mom, with a blond ponytail and fair skin. Her expression was one Sam had analyzed endlessly: a kind of half smile that wouldn't seem meaningful if her mom hadn't left them a year later.

She put the photo back on the table, and when she pulled her hand away, a clean thumbprint disturbed the coating of dust. Sam swiped another manicured finger along the frame and came back with a thick layer of grime. A knot of guilt wandered into her stomach as she glanced at the table and saw it was also coated. Maybe she'd stayed away for too long.

She hoisted her bag higher on her shoulder and walked down the tiled floor toward a hand-drawn placard, "Sam's Room," which still hung outside the door in glittery bubble letters. She hesitated, but eventually turned the knob.

The room, much like the rest of the house, had not been touched since Sam left, save for some tidying. The twin-size wrought iron bed frame with a dolphin-print duvet was still there, as were the Furby and Hello Kitty dolls resting against the numerous decorative pillows. Over the bed was an Amy Winehouse poster surrounded by CD sleeves for The White Stripes, Muse, Green Day and The Killers. On her desk sat a neat stack of the Twilight hardcover books, alongside a plastic Pizza Hut cup filled with scented gel pens, Lip Smacker balms and a headband with glitter skulls across the top. The corkboard above the desk was littered with tacked-up photos of her intense emo phase…and Damon.

She hesitantly bit her lip as she approached the memory board, but almost instantly landed on a photo taken the night when everything changed. She and Damon were in front of the school bleachers, and his spiked black hair was streaked with red highlights. Sam's overplucked eyebrows and the cartoon skull on her T-shirt were all a *choice*. Sam held up a peace sign and attempted her very best duck lips, while Damon's mouth opened in a genuine laugh.

Despite the fashion that made them relics of the aughts, they both looked happy, and an overwhelming urge to see him laugh that way again flooded through Sam. She took out her cell. Home, she texted Damon. She almost instantly regretted messaging, because where would they start a conversation she'd chosen to end years ago?

Thanks to Instagram, she'd been able to keep up and interact with Damon as if he were an old acquaintance. Over the years, she'd watched as he slowly ticked off all the boxes he'd planned to after graduating high school. He had a house, a job and figured out a style that didn't involve eyeliner and excessive hair gel. She "liked" his posts. He "liked" hers back.

When she decided to come help Pearl, she'd weighed her options: return home, hide and hope they didn't bump into each other; or just reach out and see what happened. And because she was more than a little curious to know if he'd respond, she DMed him. To her surprise, he wanted to see her, too. So they exchanged cell numbers—hers had changed; his hadn't. Damon had grown up, but in many ways still embodied the same indie style. What would he think of Sam?

She pocketed her phone and clenched her jaw. She wasn't sure when Damon would text back, but was surprised by how impatient she was to hear from him.

She supposed the person she should text next was Pearl, but there was a kind of serenity in being alone in the house. Sam hadn't been back in her room in so many years. And while she knew she should change and clean up, she couldn't help but go to the giant map of the world taped to the wall next to her closet. Her flight school acceptance letter and Post-it notes of where she wanted to travel dotted the map. She'd visited almost every one of them, except for Morocco. She tapped the spot with her finger. "I'm coming for you next."

And then her mother's parting words popped into her head. *Don't end up stuck in this place.*

Well, she hadn't ended up *stuck*, as it turned out. Bonnie's warning had served as a kind of challenge that Sam had met and overcome. Not only had she left Tybee, but she'd also become a better, brighter, far less goth-baby version of herself in the process. Still, just the recollection of her mom saying that—how Bonnie's voice had shook with the words—caused panic to rise and lodge in Sam's throat.

Because when it rained, it really poured, Sam's phone pinged with a new text. She checked the screen. Damon's name flashed back like a bolt of lightning.

Damon:

Coming over.

Suddenly, all thoughts of her mom vanished as quickly as her styled hair in the humidity. Those two words made Sam jittery. She was an unwieldy wave about to demolish a child's sandcastle.

Damon was headed to the house and she'd have to see him face-to-face. Now was the time for her to change clothes. She'd been flying all day, then drove straight to her grandma's and probably smelled like an in-flight barf bag. Yes, she'd wanted to dress to impress Grandma Pearl, but the thought of Damon seeing her also stirred up a need to look better than good. She crossed the small space of the room, bent to pick up her carry-on and came eye level with the shelves under her desk.

Her beloved CD player rested on a pair of laughably ancient headphones in the exact spot where she'd left them years ago. Seeing her old Walkman shouldn't have stopped her at all, but Sam couldn't deny that this wasn't *just* a CD player. Her Walkman had become a kind of escape. When she put on her headphones and hit Play on a song, the rest of her reality melted away as she slipped into the music. Her mom and grandma had an epic fight at least once a week—screaming, throwing things and, in general, being terrible to each other. Sam couldn't focus when she could hear them both going at it, but if she turned her music up loud enough, she discovered a new way to block out the noise. And slowly, she realized that zoning out to music gave her space to think about what she wanted: to travel, be independent and never be stuck.

Did she even allow herself time to daydream like that now? Not unless she counted staring at hotel room ceilings in between nonstop flights.

Instead of grabbing her bag, she picked up the CD player. The familiar weight immediately eased the tension Sam had been carrying in her shoulders. The urge to put her headphones on, lean against the wall and let herself slide down to the floor was overwhelming.

"Hello, friend." She put a hand across the top and let it sit there, the way you might give a reassuring pat on someone's back. Her thumb pressed down on the open button. And when the top flipped up, she saw the CD that Damon had made for her, covered in a detailed drawing of the moon and the words *Thirteen perfect songs to play when you need them* written in black permanent marker at the bottom. She exhaled as she traced a finger across his slanted penmanship.

She had never actually played the CD, though. She came close a few times, but couldn't bring herself to hear the tracks Damon had chosen just for her after she'd all but torn them in two. Instead, she upgraded to an iPod Nano, tucked the CD player away and pretended the thing didn't exist.

She closed the player as the doorbell rang. She quickly glanced out her bedroom window and there, in the driveway, was a motorcycle. *Who the hell did Grandma Pearl hang out with these days?* Sam strained to catch a glimpse of the person at the door, which was when she saw the swoop of dark hair—Damon's dark hair.

Ding-dong. Sam jumped away from the window. "Okay, I can take a hint," she said to no one.

Sam didn't have time to change or freshen up. She'd intended *not* to look like hot garbage when she saw Damon, but apparently, her trip down memory lane had other plans. She stopped at the mirror next to her door and did her best to pat down the frizz around her hair. Then, understanding it was a fruitless endeavor, pulled it all up into a high and tight ponytail. When she reevaluated herself in the mirror, there was a bit of improvement. She picked up the CD player, unsure of what to do with it and not wanting to relegate it to the forgotten shelves under her desk again.

The doorbell sounded once more, and she sighed.

As she left her room and made her way down the hall, reality set in. She was about to see *Damon*. He was just a few feet from her. A surprise flurry of nerves swelled in the pit of her stomach, a kind of apprehension that made her dizzy. Just like when they were in high school, and she'd eagerly wait to see him in the cafeteria, or in the parking lot after school. Because being with him was almost always the best part of her day.

When she got to the door, she looked up at the popcorn ceiling and let out a shaky breath. *This won't be weird. This is Damon. A guy you've known your whole life*, Sam told herself.

There was no more stalling. It was time for her to face the man she'd left behind. One quick breath in, then out, and she opened the door.

Her stomach flipped, like a fish jumping out of water. Because while *this* Damon was the same one she'd grown up with, he'd also changed in many ways. His hair, for example, no longer had bright red streaks, but was its natural chestnut hue and fell in a messy way that almost made it look styled. His nose, which she'd never really took note of before, was distinguished and weirdly sexy. Then there was the well-groomed beard, and his tan and toned arms that filled out a forest green tee. All she knew was that he definitely looked better than she remembered.

She stopped at the words *Band Practice Brews* and realized he must've come straight from work, just like her.

Sam didn't say a word, and neither did Damon, but his Adam's apple bobbed as he seemed to swallow the sight of her. Damon cleared his throat and looked at his shoes. When he looked back up, his eyes revealed the same vulnerable expression she'd remembered them having.

Damon moved to close the gap between them and wrapped Sam in a tight hug. His beard brushed against her cheek. She closed her eyes and took in a deep breath, along with the coconut scent of him.

"It's awesome to see you," he said into her ear.

His voice was strong and sure, so different from the teen version of Damon she'd remembered. When she exhaled, she managed to say, "You, too."

And it really *was*. She pulled away, but he kept his hands steady on her shoulders. He squeezed her slightly and licked his lips.

"I can't believe you're standing here, Sam-Sam," he said. *Sam-Sam*, just as he used to call her. "You look…different."

Is "different" a good thing? Sure, she'd lost the dark makeup and traded in her fishnet tights for something more professional. But weren't those changes an improvement?

"You're wearing a lot less eyeliner," she said. She was crummy at small talk. She was about to say as much, but then he clocked the CD player still in her hands.

"Oh, wow, I haven't seen one of those since…" He trailed off, and she wondered if he was remembering the night he tried to kiss her, too. "Well, it's been a long time."

She held the thing up, trying to forget the hurt in his eyes. "I know, right? One of the perks of being home."

"Can I see?" he asked.

The CD he'd made her was still in there. She knew that and, yet, she held the player out for him. As his hand touched the sides, a small electric jolt traveled through her fingers. "Ow," she gasped. She let go of the player, which Damon managed to catch. She brought her shocked finger to her mouth and nursed her tiny wound. "Geez, did you feel that?"

"Yeah." He shook out his hand but refocused on the CD player. "So weird." He turned the player over, then flipped it back and hit the open button on the top. The CD he'd made for her shone up at them. All she knew was that time stopped as Damon stared down at his old drawings. Sam watched him, waiting to see what he'd do.

He looked up at her, and the same jolt of electricity she felt from the player traveled through her again. She shivered. So did he. Then he swallowed, looked back down at the CD and closed the top. When he did, the screen lit up.

Sam stilled, because now that she squinted the screen had absolutely turned on. She was fully aware she might be in for another electric shock but couldn't *not* take a closer look.

She grabbed the Walkman from Damon. "Woah," she said as she flipped the player over in her palms. The screen displayed that the first track on the CD was queued up and ready.

She almost asked Damon if batteries even lasted this long, but something about his expression stopped her.

"What's wrong?" she asked. She'd seen that look on him before, but only once, when she hadn't kissed him back. And now here he was, standing outside her old house and making her feel like she was in high school again.

"I should've started with this, but I got distracted. My dad called me from the hospital." Humberto Rocha, Damon's dad, was a registered nurse at the Tybee Island Emergency Room. Sam immediately knew Damon had bad news. "I wanted to tell you in person. He said Grandma Pearl had an accident."

2

Grandma Pearl, as it turned out, *had* been on her usual walk around the neighborhood, but failed to see a newly formed crack in the sidewalk from the roots of a nearby gum tree. She'd fallen forward, caught herself with her hands and broken a wrist in the process. After four hours in the emergency room, she was back home and sitting at the kitchen table with her arm propped up in a neon yellow cast, like one enormous highlighter.

"The doctor said I have to shower with a trash bag over my arm. Am I supposed to wash my hair with my feet?" Pearl lifted both feet off the floor for emphasis. She was a short, petite and feisty woman, with Birkenstock sandals and faded tattoos that crawled up her arms. She'd taught herself how to boogie board when she was fifty, was the first woman to run for mayor of Tybee—but lost, sadly—and had won a beachside fried shrimp-eating competition in 2003.

Sam's grandma wasn't exactly the cookie-baking, nurturing type that you'd expect from a name like Pearl, but Sam had always liked that she was a bit eccentric.

"Salon de Sam is open for business." She winked at Pearl, but her grandma did not look amused.

"That's not reassuring, considering your hair right now."
Grandma Pearl pointed to Sam's ponytail. Sam reached a hand
up and felt the undeniable halo of frizz. She held back an eye
roll as she smoothed a palm across the top.

Her grandma could also be totally vicious.

"Hey, at least you didn't break a hip." Damon shoved his
hands into the pockets of his jeans, which made his triceps flex.
Sam tried not to stare. "Could be worse, right?"

"Not all old people break their hips." Pearl tsked. Then she
got a little glint in her eye. "But you know who did? Peggy
Clemens. And you know what? She's dead now."

"Jesus, Grandma," Sam said.

"What? It's true!" Pearl threw up both hands, then winced
as she remembered how heavy her cast was. "So, yes, it could
be worse, to your point."

Damon gave her an amused smile. "My mom's going to make
you more food, too."

"Please tell her I'm fine." Pearl's lips closed into a thin line.

"You know Cathy," Damon said. "She's going to insist."

Damon's mom had basically been made in a 1950s lab for
stay-at-home parents, if that lab was also run by vegans. She was
always cooking something for her kids to eat—her tofu muf-
fins were legendary—seemed to be at every school function,
and would bring Sam homemade "chicken" noodle soup at the
first sign of a sniffle. The opposite of Sam's mom.

"I've gotta get back to the brewery before closing. We're always slammed on Saturdays," Damon said as he glanced at his
phone. "Do you need anything before I head out? If you have
questions, you can call. Or text. I know everyone hates calling. I don't know why I said that." He avoided looking at Sam
as he puffed out his chest.

And for a moment, she found herself unable to speak. Damon
used to be such a goofball, which was one of the things they'd

bonded over. He never took himself too seriously, but here he was seemingly self-conscious about an offhand comment.

"We'll be fine," Sam said quickly.

He gave a faint smile, then headed to the door.

"Sorry you came home to a mess," he said low enough for only Sam to hear. "Are you really going to be okay?"

Now *this* Damon was one she recognized—ever protective of her.

"Thanks, but we'll figure it out. If I can fly a plane, I can help Pearl. I think." Sam shot a look at her grandma. The thought of having to clean out the house and assist Grandma Pearl with showers was already feeling heavier than the pressure of flying through an electrical storm.

"I was starting to think I wouldn't see you again." His expression turned somber, and she saw another flicker of the Damon she knew from high school.

"I'm sorry I haven't seen you sooner," she said. And while she thought she was just reciting one of the many lines she'd rehearsed for this visit, she found that she *was* sorry. Because even though they'd only been together for a few minutes, there was a long-dormant part of her lighting up with the familiar warmth she'd always felt whenever she was with him.

He let out a long-suffering breath before the next bit. "We have a lot to talk about."

"Right." Sam coughed as her throat went dry. She should've known better than to think he wasn't hurt. That she could just show up here and not be questioned. Still…could she crawl out of her skin and leave her body? Was that an option? She'd rather be permanently trapped in an airplane bathroom than face whatever Damon had to ask. But she was stuck there, and for longer than she'd originally thought.

Sam pulled at the end of her ponytail, hoping an escape parachute would open up and release her from this moment. None came, though, so she said something to buy herself time. "I'm just a little jet-lagged from the flight and the drive."

"I can imagine." His jaw clenched, which only did him favors in highlighting the dimples in his cheeks. "We don't have to figure everything out right now."

Great. She searched his eyes, waiting to see if there was anything more he wanted from her in that moment. And, apparently, there was.

"Oh, almost forgot." He slapped his hand on the door frame, then turned toward the driveway and waved for her to follow. He took her to his jet-black, flame-decaled motorcycle. He'd lost the red streaks in his hair, but put it on the side of his bike, apparently. He opened the back storage attached to the seat and pulled out a six-pack of beer. She took the pack, and the cold soothed her clammy hands.

Sam pulled a bottle out labeled *Thunder Storm IPA.* There was an ornate image of a beach with palm trees blowing in a gust of wind. "You made these?"

"I own a brewery. That's how a brewery works." He gave her a little shit-eating grin that made her shake her head. "Farrah is the brewmaster, so I can't take credit for the flavors. But I'm the lead on design, marketing and expansion. You'll have to come by and see."

Damon and his sister, Farrah, had dreamed about opening their own bar someday, and now they owned a whole brewery. Their success was impressive, but Sam wasn't ready to admit that. "I don't have a motorcycle, though." Sam pouted. "Am I hip enough to be there?"

Damon playfully rolled his eyes. "You do have this fancy Mercedes. Being a pilot must be treating you well."

She couldn't argue there. Sam made a great living, considering all she had to take care of was herself. She hadn't intended to impress Damon with the car, but…maybe she had. "We've both upgraded our transportation since high school. You with your old Ford, and me bumming rides in your old Ford."

They stood in the thick evening heat, staring at each other.

"I'll text you," she eventually said, breaking the silence.

"Don't call."

"I would never." She smiled, and he smiled back and her silly stomach did the fish flip trick again.

"Good to see you, Sam-Sam." Damon waved a hand, gesturing to the length of her. "The pilot uniform suits you, by the way."

She almost replied, but couldn't. Her nickname in his mouth paired with the compliment made her feel like she needed to lie down, close her eyes and sleep for many days until her brain could process everything the past few hours had brought.

Damon.

Grandma Pearl.

Damon's jawline.

She watched as Damon secured his helmet and revved the engine of the bike, then peeled out of the driveway. This version of him—confident biker dude—while still a bit similar, was also completely new. Part of her wanted to see him again so she could find out all of the ways he'd changed, but the more sensible part of her knew that was ridiculous. She couldn't expect him to just make room for her.

She numbly walked to the front door, closed it behind her and exhaled as her exhaustion finally caught up. She could curl up on the floor and sleep until morning, really. But then there was a rustling from the kitchen, and she knew she needed to check on Pearl.

When she rounded the corner, Pearl had managed to grab a wooden spoon and was attempting to shove the handle inside her cast. But there was *another* item already lodged in there— a spatula.

"Grandma," Sam squeaked as she rushed to Pearl's side. She dropped the six-pack of beer on the kitchen island, then plucked the spoon from Pearl's free hand.

"I had an itch. Don't worry, I got it."

"I can see that. You also got half of your kitchen accessories in your cast." Sam gently maneuvered the spatula out and blinked hard. This was going to be a trying week. Or two? She had to sort out how long she'd actually be staying now that Pearl wasn't supposed to be doing things like lifting boxes or packing up her house. She'd figure out the details with the airline in the morning.

Sam massaged her now-throbbing temple, moved to the kitchen table and pulled out a chair for Pearl. "Just sit and relax. Humbe said you need to give your bones a break."

"I think my bones already had their break, thank you very much." Pearl smiled impishly as she made her way to the chair. "I can still walk and talk. I'm not completely useless."

"I didn't say you were, but I'm here to help. So you need to let me." Sam loosened her pink tie and then eased it all the way off, draping it over the back of another chair.

"Okay." Pearl sat down with a thud, placed her hands in her lap, then looked expectantly at Sam. "Go ahead, then."

Sam was not immediately sure what to do. What would be a win to Pearl? What would someone of her fried shrimp—champion stature be interested in? She grabbed a bottle from the six-pack on the counter and held it up. "Beer?"

Sam found a can opener and popped it, then placed the still-chilled beverage down. "See? I'm helpful."

"So helpful. I'm sorry I ever doubted you." Pearl lifted the bottle to her lips and took a sip. "Oh, and this is so tasty. Speaking of which, Damon's looking good, isn't he? Seems like you both finally grew into your bodies." She kept her gaze on Sam, as if waiting for a reaction.

It was exactly the right moment to put the beer in the fridge and forget the reminder that Damon *was* hot. He was. No doubt about it. He'd physically upgraded from coach to first class, but Pearl didn't need to know all of that.

"Do you want one of the pralines Damon's mom made?"

Sam reached for the sewing tin on top of the fridge. When she opened the lid, it was stuffed with pecan praline candies that smelled like syrup. Sam popped one into her mouth and practically moaned as it melted against her tongue.

Pearl shook her head, but took one just the same. "Cynthia *knows* I have high blood pressure."

"You mean Cathy?" Sam hated correcting her grandma, especially when she knew it was her memory failing her, but she did so, just the same.

"Yes, Cathy, whatever her name is. I swear to God, she sends me a tin every Christmas and pretends like she isn't torturing me. She thinks just because something is made with soy it's a health food." Her grandma took a bite so big she could barely chew through it, but managed to say, "Just one bite won't hurt."

Sam had gotten her sweet tooth from somewhere, after all. There was a substantial lull in conversation as Pearl chewed. Sam fidgeted with her hands and the momentary quiet brought back the questions she didn't have answers for. *What was Damon going to ask me? And why* does *he look so good to me now?*

"Did I hear something about you and Damon seeing each other again?" Pearl asked, as if reading her thoughts.

Sam shot her a knowing look; while her grandma may have been out of commission with her wrist, her hearing was certainly in perfect shape. Sam nudged off her shoes and flexed each foot until her toes cracked.

"I bet Damon didn't know what hit him when he saw you," Pearl tried again. "You used to wear fingerless gloves in the summer, but now you're Pilot Barbie."

"Those were very in style back then," Sam attempted to defend herself. "It's definitely been a long time."

"Yes, it has." Pearl's tone was maybe a bit more chastising than she'd anticipated. But instead of further judgment, her grandma simply said, "I'm glad to have you home."

If ever there was a time where she wished she could hit a

pause button, Sam thought this would be a good one. Because while the sentiment was a simple one, it was impossible for Sam to easily echo the feeling back. She loved Pearl, but she wasn't glad to be home, and she didn't want to disappoint her grandma by pretending to be.

"I'm going to go unpack," Sam sidestepped. She was going to unpack, all right. Not just her clothes, but the conversation with Damon and Grandma Pearl. Plenty of things to unpack all around.

Her grandma stared back, because they both knew Sam was just making an excuse to leave the room. But Pearl eventually gave a resigned sigh, reached for another praline and began to chew. Sam took the opportunity to hurry down the hall. She'd been back less than twenty-four hours and in that time she'd gotten flutters from her high school best friend and become her grandma's caretaker. This wasn't the fake vacation she'd signed up for!

She gladly closed her bedroom door as a text came in.

Rachel:

> How many margaritas have you had? 🍷

What she wouldn't give for a margarita—she'd bathe in one to cleanse the day from her mind. She flopped onto her bed, tossed the Furby to the floor and cuddled the Hello Kitty plush under her arm as she typed back.

Sam:

> Not enough.

Rachel:

> Are you at least wearing your bikini top as a hat?

Sam snort-laughed. Rachel and Sam were *not* party girls. And she'd never been, if the "I Love Dolphins!" sticker on her dresser was any indication. But she appreciated the implication that she could be, and she wanted to delight her friend.

Sam:

I can tell you there's no top in sight...

It was technically true.

Rachel:

omg topless Sam, the beach isn't ready!!!

Sam:

Who knew that a winky face could hide a scream? The truth was that her exhaustion was turning into a kind of sleepwalking, and if she didn't close her eyes soon, she'd simply pass out. But then her gaze met the purple painted desk, where the silvery CD player stood out and almost glowed.

Music was something she and Damon had both loved. They'd analyze the lyrics, CD sleeves and music videos, and bond over which bands had sold out or stayed indie. Music had always been just theirs. Flying was her escape now, but she couldn't exactly hop on a plane. So maybe this was fate giving her a small reprieve from her thoughts. How else to explain the timing?

The CD player still worked. Over a decade later, she'd have a chance to hear the thirteen songs that reminded him of her. When she'd left Tybee, she'd also left behind the music she and Damon had so fervently loved. Listening to any of her emo anthems made her think of him and what might have been. Now, though, she pressed her back against the wall and, as she always used to, slid down until she was seated on the floor with her knees tucked into her chest.

She put on the headphones, and the warm, nostalgic feeling she'd missed when she first arrived finally hit her. Her room and the CD player in her hands—*this* was home. Her shoulders relaxed as she hit Play and wrapped her arms tightly around her shins.

The unmistakable haunting piano notes of Evanescence's "Bring Me to Life" began to tinkle out. She couldn't help but grin, because she and Damon had been obsessed with the ethereal feel of the melody. Of course he'd pick this song for her— he knew how transported she felt whenever they'd listen. And she remembered the story of how frontwoman Amy Lee wrote the song about being vulnerable with her now husband.

As Sam's eyes shut, the music surrounded her and she relaxed back into the bedroom wall. Except, just as Amy Lee sang the first lyrics, the space around Sam grew cold. Goose bumps erupted over her arms. Maybe the AC had kicked in. But then an enormous gust of wind nearly knocked her over.

"Oh, my God," Sam screeched as she caught herself with the palm of her hand.

Though she wasn't touching soft carpet anymore; her hand was on top of something hard. Sam's heart pounded as her eyes quickly snapped open. And then she stilled in a kind of confused horror because, she realized, she was no longer in her bedroom.

3

"What is happening?" Sam's voice was high and tight as her gaze frantically darted around the unfamiliar space. The sky was a wide black canvas dotted with stars.

She turned, but hit her head on the bumper of a car. In fact, she was surrounded by parked cars. And when she looked up, she saw an Islands High School Soccer Champ sticker.

I'm dreaming. She'd put on her headphones, fallen asleep from her long day of travel and now she was in the middle of a dream. Which was actually annoying, because the last thing she wanted to think about was high school. How could she make herself snap out of this?

The CD player rested in her lap, and Amy Lee sang about being numb and needing someone to wake her up. *Yeah, well, you and me both, Amy,* Sam nearly shouted. She tore the headphones off but could still hear the faint piano notes floating up from them. This was *definitely* a dream.

Except, as her chest tightened from her rapid breathing, it didn't *feel* like she was asleep. The way she was aware of her twitching fingers at her side, the rub of the ground beneath her and the welt forming on the back of her head, made it all seem like she was wide-awake and somewhere else.

Sam screamed, a kind of guttural cry for help, so loud that by the time she was done, her throat was sore. When had she ever had a dream where she actually felt pain? Other than when she'd flown free of charge by riding in the jump seat, fallen asleep and cracked her head on the coffee cart when they'd hit unexpected turbulence. But this was different, because as she rubbed her stinging throat with her fingers, she wasn't waking up.

Footsteps across the pavement snapped her back to attention, and she hid behind the car, but not so much that she couldn't see who was coming. And as it turned out, *she* was the person coming. More specifically, her *younger* self—fifteen years old— with shoulders slightly hunched, her Converse sneakers dragging, wearing baggy jeans and a skull tee from Hot Topic. It was the same outfit she'd worn in the marching band photo above her desk. And, to hit the point home, teen Sam—alternative Sam—carried a clarinet case covered in band stickers. She wasn't scowling, exactly, but most definitely brooding.

"What the—" Sam was sure her frown was so intense it might end up stuck there. She pinched herself to wake up, but the spot on her forearm hurt. She ducked lower behind the car, and her heart raced with dread of the unknown.

Is this a concussion?

Can you die from vegan pralines?

Shit. It's cold. Why didn't dream-me wear a sweater?

The thoughts stopped, though, as she discovered that trailing behind fifteen-year-old Sam was fifteen-year-old Damon, with his spiky hair and shiny black button-up shirt. Sam almost gasped but covered her mouth as she watched Damon pull her high school self in close for warmth. Damon, with his liner-rimmed eyes, looked down at Alt-Sam with the most genuinely sweet smile she'd ever seen. Sam blinked hard, willing the images to end, but she was still stuck.

Maybe the CD player was so old that it'd leaked battery fluid and now she was lucid dreaming? Did battery fluid do that? Clearly, she was passed out in her childhood bedroom and hallucinating; how else to explain why she was seeing the night that changed everything and nothing?

Still, there she and Damon were. Sam's stomach sank, because she'd burned this moment into her memory and relived it so many times already. Seeing it again, and so sharply, didn't exactly give her a happy feeling.

She watched as Damon's mouth quirked up and how, when they got to the Ford Explorer, he brushed a strand of hair behind her ear.

As he did, her earring fell to the ground. Adult Sam instinctively reached up to her own earlobe, but she wasn't wearing earrings. She hadn't worn that set—moonstone studs, her mom's—since that night. She'd kept the one remaining earring but had never recovered the fallen one. Now she watched as Alt-Sam bent to search for it on the ground. But it was Damon who picked it up and tucked it into the front zippered pocket of her clarinet case. Alt-Sam didn't seem to notice at all.

Was that where her earring had been all these years?

And before Alt-Sam could find out, Damon closed the gap between him and her younger self. Sam knew what he was about to say.

"Hope you don't hate Fall Out Boy too much, because I put one of their songs on this."

Damon reached into his back pocket and pulled out a white CD sleeve. He handed it over, but Sam knew which CD this was—the exact mix she was now listening to.

Sam moved closer to hear the conversation clearly, but they didn't notice.

"What is happening!?" she shouted.

Sam threw her hands up and sighed in exasperation. Fine. *Fine.* She was stuck watching this incredibly strong hallucination-dream-memory. Sam crossed her arms and hugged herself. Staring at her old marching band photo had probably brought this on. She should've known better than to pilot a long-distance flight and drive straight over to Grandma Pearl's without any rest.

"You look really great." He longingly admired her face.

Damon's hand reached for younger Sam's and squeezed her open palm. Then he tilted her chin up gently with an index finger. His eyes locked on to hers as he asked, "Can I kiss you?"

"Ah, God," Sam muttered to herself. *This* was the part of the memory that really hurt—when Damon had been so vulnerable, and she couldn't reciprocate. His expression had hope, while hers had dimmed. And she remembered what came next. Poor Damon.

Teenage Sam hesitated, the same way she had all those years ago. She'd wanted to kiss Damon. He was adorable, like if Ezra Koenig and Pete Wentz had a baby. But with Damon, she'd known that if they kissed they would no longer *just* be friends. He would expect more. She had a plan to leave Tybee and, deep down, she also knew Damon wasn't going to leave with her.

So she'd faked being sick and asked him to take her home. They never spoke about it again, and their relationship hadn't bounced back to the normal level of best friend status they'd once held for each other.

Sam waited to hear the lie—*Actually, I'm not feeling well…* There was a long stretch of silence, save for the background music still playing from the headphones in her hand as Amy Lee yell-sang the climax of the song.

And then, instead of lying to Damon, Alt-Sam gave a slow but certain nod that made Damon lean down and cup her face with both hands. Their lips met. She pulled him in close as Damon backed her up against the hood of his car, in what was, honestly, a very smooth move. He quickly removed his snare drum case, and her clarinet, as their bodies pressed tightly together.

Then he gently traced the line of her cheekbone with his thumb as she scratched through his hair with her painted black nails.

What in the teenage hormones is going on? Adult Sam uncrossed her arms, cocked her head and watched as history rewrote itself in front of her. "Huh," she said.

Maybe she'd been playing the "What If?" game too much during flights, wondering *what if* they'd ever tried being together. Though she didn't *love* that the blue roll-on body glitter her younger self had put all over her arms was now covering Damon's shirt. That would be a dry-cleaning nightmare.

Adult Sam got so close that she snapped her fingers next to them, but they didn't respond. The rules of dreams were confusing. She circled, but it was like she wasn't even there, or maybe they were just so focused on the make-out that they didn't notice. The sound of their lips meeting—of Damon's low growl in his throat—was honestly not her thing. She put the headphones back on to let the music drown out the saliva swapping. The last line of the song came through, where Lee carried the word *liiiiiife* out until her voice went hoarse. Sam closed her eyes to let the last notes sink in but as she did, the air felt warm again and her eyes abruptly shot open.

The CD player had turned off. The song ended and silence filled her ears. There she was, back in her childhood bedroom—dream over.

Sam tore off the headphones and accidentally bumped her head on the wall she'd been leaning against. "Ouch." She hissed as she rubbed at the tender spot. Maybe *that* explained how she'd hit her head on a "car bumper" in her dream. She'd likely just bumped it at this same spot on the wall as she nodded off.

She hastily pushed herself up, grateful to be awake. The CD player and headphones *thunked* to the floor. "Okay, yeah, wow." She cracked her neck. "That was strange."

She held a palm to her chest and tried to concentrate on the present. She was still in her bedroom. And, yes, she'd had a fantasy about kissing Damon, but that didn't have to mean anything. So what, the dream had been super intense? Jet lag could do wild things.

She smoothed a hand down her pilot's shirt. Her hand shook, though, and she clenched and unclenched her fist to try to stop the movement. "Nothing to get worked up over."

Flying nonstop from Paris to Atlanta, along with the stress of her trip and the nostalgia of being back in her house, had all conspired to make her so exhausted that she'd fallen asleep and dreamt about what could've been. And, to be honest, she'd often wondered what would've happened if she'd stayed in Tybee, or kissed Damon. Not because she regretted where she was; it was just a kind of curiosity that popped up whenever she thought of him. So she'd had a kind of fantastical dream about Damon that felt way too real.

Sam slipped on an old sleep shirt. Probably her subconscious was sending a message that she had unfinished business with Damon. So perhaps the easiest thing to do *was* to just see him again. He might ask her questions—no, he definitely would—but she needed to ask him some, too.

And maybe it was all just a bit too much, because her eyes started to close on their own. Sleep. She desperately needed sleep. Lack of sleep was what had brought this weird hallucination on in the first place. She put her head on the pillow, closed her eyes and wondered if she'd have another dream of him.

4

Sam *had* fallen asleep, curled up on top of her bedspread, like some overly tired house cat. But she was woken up by a rather loud and boisterous set of bagpipes playing an army call. Further adding to her confusion was the come-hither expression from the Legolas poster tacked to her wall. She reared back and away from his icy-blond perfection, which caused her to accidentally roll off the twin bed and land on the floor. She winced from the instant pain in her shoulder, sat up and rubbed the sore spot. Which is when she saw that a mere foot from her was the CD player.

Her hand reached for it, almost out of old habit, but stopped when she noticed the smell of butter wafting up to her room. It was a sense memory so familiar that she already knew what her grandma was cooking, but her grandma wasn't supposed to be doing things that required two hands. Sam pushed herself up and bolted down the hall to make sure her grandma wasn't about to burn the house down.

In the kitchen, Pearl sat at the table in almost the same spot where Sam had left her the night before. Only this time, the bagpipes created the sort of illusion of a built-in dramatic soundtrack. Sam glanced out the window to see Byron, a neighbor she hadn't thought about in over a decade but who, apparently, still liked to greet the morning wearing a green kilt and playing army songs loudly in the sand.

"Sam!" The voice of Jessie Tran, her grandma's next-door neighbor, startled her. Jessie and Pearl shared a common love of dirt bike races and comparing rotisserie chickens from local grocery stores.

Jessie was at the stove and wiped her hands across the apron she wore before wrapping her in a hug so tight that Sam thought she might lose consciousness. Jessie had dyed black hair cut into a short bob and long nails painted neon orange that had remained the same color and length as they were when Sam was in high school. "Did Byron wake you up?" Jessie practically had to shout over the noise.

"What would make you think that?" Sam joked back.

"Huh?" Jessie replied.

"Yes!" Sam shouted. "Yes, he did!"

The bagpipes came to a miraculous halt. Outside, Byron saluted the rising sun and marched his way back up toward his beach house.

"You look like a raccoon who gorged at a dumpsite. What happened?" Grandma Pearl asked. All Sam could do was grunt in response.

To be fair, she hadn't washed her face or showered before passing out—two important things she should do sooner rather than later. She tried to flatten her hair with the palm of her hand. "I need a shower, obviously."

This day wouldn't be her best.

"I wouldn't have recognized you." Jessie grabbed Sam's shoulders and gave her an appraising glance. "You used to remind me of Wednesday Addams with all the black, but look at you now, the spittin' image of your mama, isn't she?" Sam's gaze

darted to Pearl, who pursed her lips in response. But Jessie just
kept on going. "And those legs! Tell me these aren't the longest
legs you've ever seen, Pearl?"

"She didn't get them from me." Her grandma cough-laughed.

Sam's mom and grandma were on the shorter side, so she'd
gotten her long legs, allegedly, from her dad. She hadn't known
him, and didn't have strong feelings about him either way, but
she'd have the occasional reminder, like when her height became
a topic of conversation.

"Speaking of legs, I was worried you'd learned to crack eggs
with your feet," Sam said, deftly switching gears.

"Your grandma said she wanted to make your favorite breakfast, but needed a hand, literally." Jessie returned to the stove to
flip the eggs.

"I managed to unwrap the butter, but cracking the eggs was
not working." Pearl brought the coffee mug to her lips, and
Sam was relieved there were still some things her grandma *could*
handle.

"When I came in, there was eggshell on the fridge door handle," Jessie added.

"Don't ask me how it got there." Her grandma held up her
wrapped arm as if in defense.

Sam's *favorite breakfast* was fried eggs and toast with massive
tabs of butter. It was the only thing her grandma could make
that was actually edible.

Jessie scooped a fried egg from the skillet onto a waiting plate.
"Here," she said, handing Sam the plate. "And help yourself to
coffee."

Sam took the plate and then opened the closest cabinet in
search of a coffee mug, but instead she found bowls. She opened
the next cabinet only to find spices and flour. This was the
house she'd grown up in, but she didn't know where the mugs
were. Eventually, Jessie took pity and grabbed a mug from the
one cabinet she hadn't opened.

"Thanks," Sam said.

"Pearl's been bragging about you all morning," Jessie said.

Sam's mouth cracked into a doubtful smile as she looked to her grandma, but Jessie just continued, "She says you get to fly first class when you travel, and there's free champagne?"

"I fly in the jump seat," Sam corrected. "But sometimes if there's an extra spot in first, they'll let me sit there."

"The only first class I've ever been to was the first pottery class at the Color Me Mine studio downtown." Jessie grabbed a piece of toast from the oven and put it on the plate. "So your first class is exciting, is all I'm saying."

Jessie slid the plate of food in front of Sam; an expectant smile played across her lips as she rested a hand on Sam's shoulder. "You ever think about moving back to Tybee?"

Without looking up to meet Jessie's eyes, Sam said, "I live in Paris, so, no," then took a loud bite of her toast. Her *no* sat in the room like a whirlpool, sucking in all the air and life and good smells and leaving behind the uncomfortable and unapologetic crunching of Sam eating toast.

"Well," Jessie said in a twang so thick it sounded like *whale*. She pinched Sam's shoulder, which made her accidentally bite her own tongue. Maybe she deserved that, honestly. "We sure are glad to have you home."

"Yes, we are," Grandma Pearl echoed. She picked up the toast and took an equally loud bite. "I was getting sick of flying to Paris, truth be told."

"You were not." Jessie gave her a half smile.

One of the ways Sam had avoided a return trip to Tybee was by flying Grandma Pearl out to Paris each winter. They'd celebrated the holidays in a charming French hotel, eating baguettes while walking along the River Seine and drinking endless Bordeaux.

"Now that I'm done playing chef, I'm going to let you two

catch up." Jessie lifted the apron over her head. "And, Sam, can I paint you while you're in town?"

Jessie was a local artist who worked with watercolors and was known for her eclectic nudes. She'd done several of Grandma Pearl that were hard to unsee.

"Excuse me," Pearl piped up. "Sam's here to help me because I'm old and feeble, not pose for a painting."

"I'm old, too," Jessie said. "Old and in need of a model with those legs. Think about it." Jessie pecked Sam on the forehead. "I can't pay you anything, but I make a mean sangria."

"Will do." Sam gave a half smile as Jessie walked out the front door.

"That woman won't stop until she's painted every fuzzy Georgia peach in this town," Pearl said. "And I'm not talking about the fruit."

"Grandma," Sam chided, though she also loved this unabashedly naughty side of Pearl.

"You know I'm right," Pearl said through a mouthful of toast, and the two Leto women ate until they'd cleaned their plates of the buttery perfection.

It was just after nine in the morning when Sam and Pearl took the last cups of coffee out to the beach. The sun was already high—Septembers on Tybee were just as hot and humid as the dead of summer—and the air had warmed to a point where sweat started to form along the line of Sam's spine. Sam briefly stopped when she saw three Adirondack chairs fitted into the sand underneath a generous overhang that provided some shade. There was one for Sam, Pearl and Bonnie. She'd assumed her grandma would've at least gotten rid of the third chair by now, which had always sat like a ghost next to them.

When Pearl sat in her designated chair, she tilted her head back and let the warm morning sun cast her face in a healthy glow. A small smile spread across her lips as she closed her eyes.

"Isn't this the most amazing feeling?" Pearl asked. "The heat and the waves. I come out here every morning."

Sam stared out at the waves gently rolling in, and then quickly getting sucked back out to sea. A handful of terns dotted the shoreline and their spindly legs ran from the water as they searched for their morning grub. Was this the most amazing feeling?

Grandma Pearl saw paradise when she sat on this beach, but the waves crashing into the shore stirred up a kind of restlessness in Sam. Being in the blinding sunshine, but feeling a ball of dark dread in her stomach, made her feel off-kilter. Tybee Island was the place her mom had run from, and where she'd abandoned Sam.

But still, this was her grandma's home.

"That retirement center is not on the water, you know." Sam settled herself into the chair. Pearl loved the ocean, and this house and her Adirondack chair. There was no reason for her to leave. "Are you sure you want to move?"

Pearl squinted through her sunglasses. "I'm getting old, Sam. And you're all the way in Paris."

Old people wore muumuu dresses and ate applesauce for dinner at three in the afternoon while watching *Yellowstone*. They did not go for daily walks and drink beer and make jokes about their best friend's obsession with painting naked women. "Eighty is not that old," Sam said.

"A lot has changed since you've been gone. I can't keep up with this place."

And Sam couldn't help notice the small tremor in Pearl's good hand as she raised the cup of coffee to her lips. Then she remembered the layer of grime she'd found on the living room table. And the fact that her room was still fully intact, and perhaps not just because Pearl was sentimental.

Sam had to squint to look over at Pearl, who'd had the good sense to put on a hat. "We should just explore all of the options." She leaned back in the chair and dug her toes in, letting the sand swallow them whole.

Pearl raised an eyebrow. "I don't want you to think everything is on you to handle. I called Bonnie."

Bonnie. Sam's mom. "You called her? Why?"

"I'm leaving the house she grew up in. I figured she might want to know." Pearl sort of half shrugged, but also wouldn't meet Sam's eye. Probably because she didn't want to see the flames burning there.

"Well, what did she say?" Sam finally asked.

"She didn't pick up. I left a voicemail. Told her to come get her things. But you know Bonnie."

"No, I don't know Bonnie. I haven't seen her in eighteen years." Sam's fingers fisted her ponytail in frustration. She knew Bonnie wouldn't show up—she never did—but her mom didn't deserve a phone call from Pearl.

"You okay?" Pearl asked. "If I'd known you'd get so upset, I wouldn't have told you."

Sam gave her a hard look. "Yes, you would've. You're terrible at keeping secrets."

"That's true." Pearl settled back into the chair.

Sam tried not to fixate on the fact that Pearl had called Bonnie, and she stared out at the ocean and did her best to find the sound of the waves soothing. Her attempt at calm, though, was short-lived.

"Morning to ya, Pearl!" a high-pitched voice called out.

Sam squinted at the lean and tanned figure close to the water's edge. "Is that...?"

"Alligator Alice." Pearl finished her thought and gave a wave to Alice. "Can you believe *she* hasn't dropped dead yet?"

Alligator Alice was nicknamed such because she was constantly out for a walk in the sun and, as a result, her skin was leathery with just as many cracks.

"Not really, no," Sam said, genuinely in awe that this person from her childhood was still around and mostly unchanged, save for some updated wardrobe.

"So, what's on the agenda today?" Pearl asked. "I know you've probably made a list already."

Sam was the kind of type-A organized that meant she had a physical and digital running log of her to-do list. But she'd put off coming up with any firm plans for cleaning out the house, mainly because she'd hoped she wouldn't have to. "I'll start going through my bathroom," she eventually said.

"Don't touch mine unless I'm there. I don't want you throwing everything out." Then Pearl perked up. "Hey, do you still have those Beanie Babies? Aren't they worth money now?"

Sam stood, put a hand on Pearl's shoulder and readied herself to walk back into the house. "We'll see what I can find."

What she found was a hair crimper, cucumber melon Bath & Body Works hand cream and about two dozen half-empty bottles of Urban Decay nail polish. And that was just in one bathroom drawer. Sam grabbed the coffee mug she'd filled with water and three cocktail-size ice cubes and drank the whole thing down in one luxurious gulp.

The little rush of cold fluid fueled her on to the next drawer, but when she pulled it open there was a tube of roll-on body glitter. She picked it up and the shiny blue looked suspiciously similar to the one she'd seen Alt-Sam wearing while making out with Damon.

Her jaw clenched and she dropped the glitter into an open trash bag. It was so ridiculous that she'd had an exhaustion-induced dream in the first place, but even sillier that she'd noticed the body glitter. She was an aughts cliché of a person, clearly.

She stared at the tube in the trash and tapped her foot. She should just go to the brewery. Damon told her to come check it out, so that was a perfectly reasonable and friendly thing to do. Only, the brewery was Damon's territory—a place where everyone would know him. She'd be the odd person out, the way she always had been in Tybee. But maybe she'd have to accept that when she was here, that was the role she'd play.

"I can casually pop by to see him," she said as she looked through the open drawer. She pulled out black hair mascara, Proactiv toner, Herbal Essences shampoo and a mood ring, all of which she threw into the trash. In some ways it felt like a nostalgia crime, but also if her CD player was making her hallucinate, who knew what an ancient mood ring could do.

"We'll be old friends, catching up," Sam said to herself in the mirror. "We can do that."

"Are you talking to me?" Pearl called out.

Sam rolled her eyes. "No, just myself."

"Knock it off and get back to work," Pearl said.

Sam brushed some dust from her fingertips. She'd finish cleaning out the bathroom and then get ready to see Damon. She could do that.

She opened the next drawer and grimaced as she pulled out a scrunchie covered in fake blond hair. "Fashion was really something back then."

"What's that?" Pearl called out again.

Sam bit her lip as she threw the scrunchie in the trash and got back to work.

As Sam drove down the stretch of sandy road that served as a kind of beachy thoroughfare—with the water unobscured on her right, and restaurants and shops on her left—she rolled down her window. The cars in front of her drove the twenty-mile-an-hour speed limit but the crosswalk blinked her to a stop. A gaggle of teen surfers in board shorts ambled across the road carrying bodyboards, with one even stopping to tie a lace on his sneakers. As a soft breeze blew into the car the light changed, and Sam drove along the path. The sign for Band Practice Brews came into view, lit up in neon with a massive guitar dangling from the corner.

She pulled into the crowded parking lot and past an actual line out the door. There were groups of people in cutoffs and tank tops, cargo board shorts and floral print button-ups. Which made Sam realize that she'd maybe overdressed. Trying too hard to impress someone she *didn't* have feelings for. But it was too late now—no time to change. She'd just have to own her heels, silky slip dress and blow-dried hair.

When she walked in, there was the bar itself, which was a rich mahogany with a mirrored back, and bar stools that swiveled. High-top tables lined the walls, and a few corner booths with sleek leather were particularly inviting. There was a wall accented with shiny hanging guitars, while the other walls displayed a few photos of Damon and his family. The photos ranged from fairly normal to borderline absurd: a photo of him fishing with a beer in hand was next to one of his sister, Farrah, in a hospital gown, cradling her newborn while Damon handed her a beer. Though she had to admit, the guy photographed well. She stopped at a particularly enticing photo of Damon as he leaned against an open truck bed with his triceps bulging. A firm hand landed on her shoulder.

She turned and there was Damon in black semifitted jeans, a dark gray tee and a leather jacket. His hair was styled so it spiked up a bit in the front, and his beard had been trimmed from the day before into a respectable shadow. He hadn't overdressed, but anyone could see that he was a step up from the guy just behind him in camo shorts and flip-flops. And why was the sight of his shirt tucked in just in the front making her want to untuck it with her teeth?

"Hey." He wrapped her in a hug so warm and tight that if she'd been a stick of butter, she'd have melted. "Didn't think I'd see you so soon."

"I probably should've called." Sam attempted to make a joke but, as she said the words, she realized she *really* should have.

"I actually *only* accept calls." He pressed a palm into the bar, then handed her the nearly full beer in his hand. "Here, give this a try. It's a sour beer we're testing. You'll either love it or hate it, but I'll enjoy the look on your face either way."

"Oh, I don't really drink beer." She still held the bottle, though, not sure what the hell to do with it. "I'm more of a wine gal."

Damon squinted, as if unable to process what she'd said. "I've met your type, but do me a favor and take a sip."

Sam's level of enthusiasm must've shown on her face, as Damon laughed and said, "You never were all that good at hiding how you *really* felt."

He lifted his own beer and she lifted hers in solidarity before taking a sip. She braced for the impact of hops and bitterness but found there was a tart cherry and peach that lit up her whole tongue and fizzled on the way down.

Her eyes widened as she swallowed. The label on the bottle read *Sour Good*, and she had to admit it was. "I like it," she eventually said.

"Phew, I was worried your jet-setting lifestyle had turned you against some of the finer offerings we have here in Georgia. Come on, let me give you a tour." Then Damon's hand landed on the small of her back and she stiffened as if she'd never been touched by another human being before. Damon pulled his hand back. "Oh, sorry," he said.

Sam had never thought it possible to die of humiliation but well, her cheeks were so hot that she was certain she might explode. She shook the stiffness off. "No, I'm sorry. I'm not used to that." Maybe the beer was already hitting—she'd had a day of cleaning out half-used body glitter tubes—but the goose bumps trailing up her arms gave her pause.

Coming here wasn't a good idea, not only because she found

herself leaning into Damon as he led them outside, but also because she just couldn't ignore the way her body reacted to him.

And that draw caused her to slightly trip as they stepped out the back doors. Damon caught her so she was tucked into his side. When she looked up, he was backlit by the bistro lights strung in careful waves above them and highlighted like an otherworldly being. She stared for probably a beat too long.

"Probably not the best place to wear heels," he eventually said. "But you managed to not spill the beer, which is impressive."

She wordlessly slipped off her shoes and walked barefoot past him, trying to muster the confidence she'd come in with, and failing.

The space was dotted with teak chairs surrounding firepits, creamy white sand and two beach volleyball nets. There was also a small stage pressed against one side of the wooden fence, where a live band was doing a mic check. Damon nodded to a server who quickly cleared off a high-top table for them.

"Is it nice being the boss?" Sam asked as she settled onto a stool. "I don't think I've ever nodded at someone and had them read my mind."

"It's not as glamorous as it looks. Half the time, when I nod, I just have to go and explain what I want. What kind of raw deal is that?"

"Good help is so hard to find." Sam looked away and took a sip from her beer. Maybe it was being near Damon, or the heat, but the drink *was* growing on her. Though she still felt a little stiff, like she wasn't totally sure how to act around him.

"Cheers." Damon raised his glass and she raised hers. "To you finally coming home."

His *finally* could've meant nothing or everything, and she wasn't sure if he was holding on to some hostility, or just trying to be friendly. Still, their glasses clinked, and she took a quick sip. Damon tilted his beer bottle toward his mouth, and she watched as his lips wrapped around the glass.

"Farrah will be sad she missed you. She doesn't work Fridays. She has kids, or something like that."

Sam gave a half smile, then kicked her toes in the sand and sent a shower of the stuff toward Damon. His mouth opened in shock, but then he kicked some sand back at her.

"What was that for?" he asked.

"Farrah was way cooler than us. I doubt she'd even remember me."

"She'd never forget you."

Heat spread across Sam's chest. Not because Farrah remembered her, but the way Damon had phrased it.

"I'm impressed." She waved the beer bottle to the space around them. "When you said you owned a brewery, I didn't realize the whole town knew about it, too."

"It's not *all* me. Sundays are seafood boil night, and there's a Fall Out Boy cover band." Damon pointed to the stage, but Sam practically gasped.

"Oh, no," Sam said. "That means we're old enough to have cover bands of our favorite people."

He gave her a side smile and, as he did, the unmistakable rumble of an overhead plane engine broke through. Sam spotted a fighter jet, likely on its way to training, and a little part of her calmed at the familiar hum from the sky.

"I used to hear planes, look up and wonder if it was you flying them," Damon said.

Sam was not blushing exactly, but knowing that Damon thought of her in those moments was a bit of a boost. "You could've messaged me to ask."

Damon bit his lower lip, as if holding something back. Then he said, "But could I have called?"

Sam burst out laughing at the same time a pocket-size woman wearing hospital scrubs hugged Damon from behind. He turned and his expression changed into something altogether warm. Her sneakers had a streak of gold glitter on each side, her hair was long and dark and parted down the middle without any evidence of frizz, and her cheekbones were so high you could safely rest a latte on one. Then she got on her tiptoes, fluttered her wildly thick lashes and kissed him on the lips, and he kissed her back, and Sam blinked as she watched in confusion. Who *was* this person?

"I didn't know you'd be here tonight," Damon said as they broke apart.

"I got off early." The woman's eyebrows rose expectantly as she turned to Sam.

Eventually, Damon turned to Sam, too, and said, "Sam, this is Marissa. She was a grade above us in high school."

"Marissa?" Well, of course the guy riding a motorcycle who had those attractive veiny forearms and owned a wildly successful brewery had a Marissa. Why wouldn't Damon have a cute little hamster to kiss? Only, he'd gone and put his hand on the small of Sam's back. "Marissa," she said again, but much quieter and almost to herself.

And then, the Polly Pocket chimed back with, "That's me!"

5

Sam's thoughts whirred like the engine of one of her massive planes. Damon had a girlfriend. His arm was wrapped around her, and Marissa glowed the way only someone truly adored could. Sam should be happy for him; she *should*.

"It's fantastic to see you!" Marissa said enthusiastically with no hint of unease. And when she extricated herself from Damon and went to hug Sam, her face awkwardly fell in between Sam's breasts. Even sitting, their height difference was substantial. But Sam's nose was just above her head, and the woman smelled like fresh soap and mint in a way that was energizing.

God dammit.

Sam's eye had begun to twitch, and she held a finger to her lid as she replied, "Oh, my gosh, same!" But her tone was flat and fake, and she immediately worried Damon had noticed.

"Marissa is a surgeon at the hospital where my dad works." Damon filled in the blanks. "He set us up on a date."

Marissa beamed at the description as she saddled herself in a chair between Damon and Sam. Suddenly, Sam became the third wheel on her surprise catch-up with Damon. This really hadn't been how she'd imagined the night going.

"At first, I didn't know who Damon even was. I was like, Damon Rocha? Doesn't ring a bell," Marissa said with a laugh.

Sam squinted. Of course Marissa hadn't known who they were—Sam and Damon had been total loners. He was the Romy to her Michele, minus the back brace.

"Yeah, I guess we were kind of hopeless." Sam softly smiled and shifted her legs under the table. Her bare foot grazed Damon's jeans and the friction she'd felt from his hand on her back earlier returned. But instead of letting her foot linger, she quickly pulled it away, and Damon shifted, too, probably to avoid any future touching.

Why was she getting flustered from being around them? Damon and Marissa were clearly happy, judging by the way Marissa smiled at him like the fucking sun shone out of his ass.

Be happy for them, Sam told herself. *Smile, dammit.* And so she did.

"What kind of surgery do you do?" Sam forced herself to ask. She avoided eye contact with Damon completely, even though his gaze was on her and she was drawn to look back as freely as she did in that weird high school dream she'd had.

"Sam?" Damon's voice cut through her thoughts and she shook her head as she looked up.

"Oh, uh, yes?" Somewhere between Marissa describing her job as a thoracic surgeon, and Sam remembering her Damon dream, she'd zoned out.

"The seafood boil. Your homecoming dinner." Damon pointed to a long picnic table covered in a white-and-red checkerboard cloth that stretched the line of the back fence. Servers poured massive steaming pots of seafood and potatoes onto the table, and the smell of salt and fish reached them almost instantly.

Sam's anxiety had reached a bit of a fever pitch, with a leg that jittered so quickly her chair shook. Her inner need for control broke through and told her to just load a plate and stress eat her way back to happiness.

"You don't have to tell me twice." Sam forced herself up from the table and made her way to the lobster, fresh shrimp, sweet corn on the cob and melt-in-your-mouth fish. She loaded up a disposable bowl until the edges burned her fingers from the hot buttery grease. When she arrived back to their high top, a fresh beer waited—one of the perks of dining with the owner, she supposed. Sam ate without thinking, wanting to fill the void in the pit of her stomach.

As she ripped shrimp out of their shells and popped them into her mouth, she chewed and let the salty heat soothe her. When Damon returned with Marissa at his side, Sam took a wooden hammer from the center of the table and hit it hard against a lobster tail.

"Not sure what that poor lobster did to you," Damon said as he twisted a crab leg and cracked it in half with his hands. "But remind me not to get on your bad side."

"You made me wake up at four in the morning so we could wait in line to get Green Day tickets, and I still wasn't mad at you. It'd take a lot to get on my bad side at this point." Sam caught Damon's eye and, for a moment, it was just the two of them again.

"These seafood boils are basically therapy," Marissa interrupted. When Sam looked over, she grinned. "If you're not sweating while eating, then what's the point?"

Though, Sam noticed, Marissa was decidedly *not* sweating and also *not* beating the ever-loving hell out of shellfish. Instead, she picked up an ear of corn and took a ridiculously demure bite.

The cover band stepped up to the mic. "Hey there, we're Fall Out Troy, and I'm Troy," the lead singer said into the mic. "And yes, I'm aware it was a bit egotistical to use my own name, but I couldn't help the pun perfection."

Relieved to hear someone else talking, Sam quickly changed her line of thought. "Marissa, were you into emo music, too?"

"I'm more of a pop girl myself," Marissa said, wiping her fingers on a paper napkin. "Taylor Swift. Britney. The Spice Girls. I never really got into grunge."

Sam's nose scrunched. "Would we call ourselves grunge?"

"Emo for sure," Damon said.

"Your red-dyed tips were absolutely not grunge, and took forever to dye," Sam practically had to shout over Fall Out Troy's rendition of "My Songs Know What You Did in the Dark."

"And to wash out, unfortunately." Damon ran a hand through his non-dyed hair.

"Damon!" A surfer bro wearing board shorts and a puka shell necklace slapped Damon on the back.

"Myles." Damon turned and they did a very choreographed hand bump that Sam would never entertain being able to pull off. "Do you remember Sam, from high school?"

Lord, did everyone from their high school hang out here? Myles took in the full length of her in a way she wasn't entirely comfortable with.

"She wore all black back then and a lot of shimmery eyeshadow." Damon's fingers danced around his eyes, as if that would somehow emphasize his point.

Sam stared at Damon in horror. Was that really how Damon remembered her?

"Um, you're one to talk. You smudged your eyeliner *on purpose* and cut your own bangs," Sam said.

"She's got you there, bro!" Myles covered a laugh with the back of his hand. She remembered Myles, who'd been the opposite of emo, with trucker hats, popped collars and multiple Livestrong bracelets.

"She was also the tallest girl in our class," Damon offered.

There was uncertainty, and then some recognition sparked in Myles's eyes. "Oh, shit, I remember you now. You were Damon's spooky girlfriend."

"We were just friends," Sam and Damon said at the same time, maybe too fast and too furious.

"You look so different, like a fancy statue." Myles thoughtfully gazed at her.

"Thank you?" She had no idea if "fancy statue" was a good or bad thing.

"Weren't you like a vampire or something?" Myles asked, quite seriously. "Like, you drank people's blood?"

"What?" Marissa asked, but she looked a bit *too* amused by the accusation.

Sam tried not to roll her eyes. "I was really into the *Twilight* books, and then someone started a rumor that I liked to visit the graveyard and dig up bodies. Because I'm a redhead, and we're—"

"Soulless vampires," Marissa finished the sentence for her. And something about that irked Sam.

But she did her best to hide her emotions. "It happens to the best of us." Sam lifted the beer to her lips, suddenly self-conscious about the reminder that she was, well, a loser in high school.

"I heard you left Tybee and joined a cult." Myles frowned. "Are you still in the cult?"

"No, I'm not still in the cult." Sam bristled. "I was *never* in a cult, to be clear."

"Shouldn't you be wearing one of those flowing robes if you're in a cult?" Myles, apparently, was hard of hearing.

"I'm not in a cult!" Sam shouted at the exact moment Fall Out Troy ended a song. Her declaration sailed over the crowd and they all turned to look directly at her. "Jesus," she mumbled to herself, feeling her cheeks flame. "I'm a pilot."

"Sam's back home for a bit, but she flies all over the world," Damon said. "She's traveled more than all of us combined." He sat back and sipped his beer, then wiped his mouth with the back of his hand, all while never breaking eye contact with her.

Was Damon…impressed by that? Just stating a fact? She wished she could read him the way she'd used to.

"Rock on," Myles said. Then he leaned toward Sam and whispered, "I won't tell anyone that you're a vampire. That can be our little secret. And let me know if you need a tour guide while you're home."

When he pulled back, he smiled, but Sam flashed her teeth just to up the ante. He seemed to flinch, which was really more satisfying than it should've been. She couldn't believe this guy had accused her of drinking blood and *then* thought hitting on her was a fair next move.

"Great to see you." She gave him a gentle shove away from her, which didn't seem to faze him in the slightest.

"Damon, give *Twilight* girl my number!" Myles called out over his shoulder.

As he walked away, Sam turned to Damon. "Myles? Wasn't he on the soccer team? He was…popular and mean."

"Yeah," Damon said, then took a sip from his drink.

"He was always nice to me." Marissa shrugged and sipped her beer.

Sam ignored her, wanting clarity from Damon. "So, what, you're friends?"

There was the Damon whom Sam remembered from high school, and then there was this strange reality, where Damon was dating a cheerleader and best friends with the popular kids.

"Myles is cool now."

"Myles is *cool*?" Sam mimicked. "Didn't he almost get expelled for tagging the gym? And didn't he misspell the word *freshman* in said graffiti?"

She was not trying to make fun of Myles per se, but she also wanted to remind Damon that he wasn't the only one who remembered things.

"People can change," Damon said. Sam disagreed.

"Unless you're still in a vampire cult?" he finished.

Marissa giggled at Damon's joke and, despite herself, Sam had a hard time hiding the grin that crossed her face. She supposed she deserved that friendly dig. "On that note, I think this vampire is going to head home. I need to get in my coffin before the sun comes out and reveals my glittery skin to the world."

"Really? It's early. The band's just getting warmed up."

"Yeah, you should stay," Marissa said. Judging by the way her nails dug into Damon's arm, though, she didn't really mean it.

Sam pushed herself up from the table, and all of the buttery food and sour beer finally made themselves known. Damon had called this a homecoming dinner and, in a way, Sam wanted to go home more than anything. "Marissa, maybe I'll see you soon?" Sam tried to give what she hoped was a friendly expression.

Marissa took the bait, because she left Damon's side, threw her arms around Sam and hugged her with the kind of intensity usually reserved for children greeting puppies. "It was *so* wonderful to see you!"

And Sam hugged her back, because there was nothing else to do in that moment. But her gaze locked on to Damon, who watched them both, and she wondered if he was just as thrown by all of this as she was.

Be happy for Damon, Sam kept repeating to herself. *Be happy*. But she wasn't. She felt a numb kind of sadness that almost shut her thoughts down entirely.

When she got out of the car, the street was quiet, save for the loud hum of crickets that filled the air and surrounded her. Grandma Pearl had left the porch light on, and Sam found that acknowledgment of her presence a small comfort.

Once she was back in her room, Sam peeled her dress off, the scent of butter embedded in the fabric. In her dresser drawer, she found an old pair of flannel sweatpants and a worn Urban Outfitters T-shirt that read, "Getting Lucky in Kentucky." She was 100 percent sure she hadn't known what that phrase meant when she'd bought it, but she did now as she tugged it over her head. She sat on the edge of her bed and massaged her temples. With her grandma's accident, the house and re-learning who Damon was, her first full day in Tybee might as well have been a full month. If every day was going to be like this, she wasn't entirely sure she could keep up with the pace.

The responsibility of landing a plane safely was absolutely less intense than the interpersonal muddiness she was having to wade through. Not only had she been roasted by Damon and his *new* bestie, Myles, but she'd also hammered a lobster claw so aggressively she was fairly certain she'd nearly splintered the table.

Coming back to Tybee was supposed to be easy, in that she had moved on from this place and the people she'd grown up with, Damon included. She'd arrived and expected to really confirm that leaving had been the right choice. After all, she'd built a great, big, exciting life for herself. She lived abroad. She traveled the world. So why was the only thing occupying her thoughts the heat of Damon's palm on the small of her back? This was a guy she'd turned down so many years ago, yet he somehow still had a line directly to her. But he'd found someone else in Marissa. It wasn't like Sam was expecting him to pick up where they'd left off in high school—in fact, she'd hoped for the opposite: that Damon had forgotten the way Sam ended them when they were fifteen. So how come she was so jealous?

She was determined to just sleep the night off, but couldn't help clock the CD player on the floor. Looking at the thing was a blatant reminder wrapped in a bow of how she'd once been the center of Damon's world—the person he made mix CDs for—but now she wasn't. Marissa was.

She regretted not throwing the Walkman and Damon's CD out along with the collection of black nail polish, because like a moth to some funhouse flame, she reached for it. Her first thought was that she just wanted to hear one more song that

Damon had picked for her. Damon was no longer hers—and really, never had been. But seeing him with Marissa rubbed salt in a wound Sam wasn't even aware she'd had.

Maybe it was ridiculous, but wouldn't listening to another track be a safe way for her to relive their friendship? Her day had been so chaotic that she almost felt hungover from the lack of control, but if she could sit and listen to a song, that might help her relax, just as music used to when she was a teenager.

She was also wildly aware that by indulging this urge, she might sink herself deeper into the Damon quicksand. But she let that thought come and go quickly as she sat on the bed and put the headphones on. Wallowing was apparently her next item on the night's to-do list, and after an evening of watching Damon and Marissa, she needed a break. She didn't know what was queued next as the screen lit up; she just wanted to hear a song Damon had chosen specifically for her.

"Okay, Damon, let's hear it," she whispered as she pressed Play.

6

As the screen lit up, she let her body lean against the wall. Electric guitar gave way to drums as The Darkness's "I Believe in a Thing Called Love" began. She and Damon had scream-sang these lyrics so many times on their daily drive to school. It was a song about falling head over heels for someone, and just pure fun, as if Damon had carefully curated this knowing what her future self wanted. She let out a relieved sigh and closed her eyes but, as she did, a *whoosh* of air surrounded her. She was suddenly weightless and then dropped—the same feeling as being at the top of a roller coaster and taking the plunge down. She wanted to scream but found herself unable to. Eventually, the fake ride stopped, and she opened her eyes just as a loud bell sounded nearby.

Her shoulder landed against a row of metal lockers as she hurriedly pushed herself to standing.

She stared down the length of a sanitized hallway and realized she was back at the scene of the crime: high school. But instead of being outside in the parking lot, it was daytime, and light streamed through the windows highlighting a school banner that proudly celebrated a 2007 basketball victory for the Tybee Typhoons. Once again, Sam was no longer at home, but seeing some other version of her life. She forced herself to breathe and quickly removed the headphones just as The Darkness began to sing about wanting to kiss every minute and hour of the day.

Maybe she was having another lucid dream. Or her CD player was a portal to a different dimension. Either way, she bit her tongue to stop from screaming.

She'd been in terrifying scenarios while flying, and there were three things she always told herself to get through those: *Stay calm. Don't panic. There's a way out of this.*

But when she eventually stopped biting her tongue, the words, "No, no, no, no, no," kept coming.

Whatever was happening couldn't be good. No one would believe her if she said that every time she listened to her old CD player, she found herself back in high school. Hell, even she didn't fully buy that, and she was living it. Her hands fumbled as she tucked the headphones around her neck.

The classroom doors flung open and teenagers began to flood the hallway like a plague of locusts. She grimaced at the sight of JanSport backpacks covered in iron-on patches. There were denim miniskirts, Ugg booties, super low-rise jeans, newsboy caps, shrugs that tied in the front, spaghetti strap tank tops worn over T-shirts, Von Dutch hats and the unmistakable scent of Axe body spray.

She watched the parade of clothing nostalgia march by and pressed herself against a locker. What would happen if she touched or bumped into someone? Would she be a phantom they could walk through? She reached a hand out and gasped when her fingers vanished into a passing girl's bubble-hem tube-top dress. She pulled her hand back, still perfectly intact, and gaped at it. But while she was in the middle of a brain melt, no one even seemed to notice she was there.

Why was she *here* in this moment? She glanced around and,

as if timed, Alt-Sam—Teen Sam—walked out of a classroom
about a head taller than most of the students. Her hair was in
a ponytail with two thick strands pulled out, framing her face,
classic aughts style. A pair of headphones covered her ears, and
her furrowed brows made her look less than friendly.

Alt-Sam came to the locker directly next to Sam and deftly
input her code. The music playing through Alt-Sam's headphones was the exact same song from The Darkness. Sam moved
out of the way right before Alt-Sam accidentally flung the
locker door open and whacked her in the face. Taped up to
the wall of her locker was a *Twilight* book cover surrounded by
glow-in-the-dark vampire fangs.

Alt-Sam opened her backpack, took out a heavy textbook—
chemistry, woof—and swapped it with another one. She also
grabbed a can of Dr. Pepper that rested on top of her books
and slammed the door shut.

"Geez, let's take it easy now," Sam jokingly said, but of
course wasn't heard. Something flashed across Alt-Sam's face
as she opened the notebook in her hands, dark and dreary, like
a cloud settling. Sam glanced at the page and saw the angry
scribbles she'd doodled.

Those doodles were as familiar to her as a first language.
Sam was a straight-A student, but once her mom left she'd also
found it hard to concentrate. Almost like the teacher's voice
sounded under water instead of right in front of her. And the
only real thing that kept her focused was the doodling—her
control issues needed an outlet, after all.

Damon came next to Alt-Sam, a backpack slung over his gray
hoodie, and his bare chest visible under a blue-and-black-striped
tee. His hair was gelled, except for his straightened bangs. He
was all emo punk perfection.

"Hey." Damon's voice cracked, not from pubescent growth
but, it seemed, from nerves. He gave a shy grin as Alt-Sam pulled
her headphones off. Her whole face lit up.

Well, well, well. Their make-out session must have been better than good to elicit that kind of a smile.

Damon reached for Alt-Sam's hand, but she pulled away.

"Oh, sorry." Her teen self scratched at a spot on her forehead. "You think I'd be used to that by now."

"Is it okay though?" Damon cautiously reextended his hand and Alt-Sam glanced at it.

"Yeah..." She trailed off, maybe hesitant, but laced her hand into his just the same.

"Woah, look, the freaks are mating!" A guy in a soccer uniform hooted as he pointed at them.

Alt-Sam tried to pull her hand back, but Damon held on tighter.

"Show us your fangs!" the jock called out pointedly to Alt-Sam.

Sam's jaw dropped as she realized the jock was Myles. Her tongue traced a line across her teeth. She had perfectly average canines, but the dig was most certainly about the *Twilight* obsession. "For the record, there's nothing wrong with being a freak. In twenty years, that *freak* will own his own bar, and the other freakishly tall one will be a top international pilot. One of a handful in the country. And you'll still be *laaaaame.* Am I right?" Sam held her hand up for a high five, but none came.

She high-fived herself.

The jock was tugged down the hallway by a teammate, but still managed to laugh as he walked off.

"Yeah, that's right! Keep walking!" Sam shouted.

"It's always been us versus them." Damon leaned in close to Alt-Sam. "Ya know, you *could* be my girlfriend now."

"Girlfriend?" both Sams said at the same time.

Damon flicked the thick bangs out of his eyes, and Alt-Sam's lashes fluttered as she stretched up toward him. They kissed. Nothing extravagant, but even Sam could feel the pull they had on each other.

"You look good as a couple, I have to admit." Sam held up her hands in surrender. "Aside from the straightened bangs, Damon, I'm happy for you both."

Damon and Alt-Sam pulled apart but stayed locked on each other. Hell, maybe having Damon as her boyfriend would've made high school slightly more tolerable. Sure, she'd hated Tybee High and practically fled after getting her diploma, but maybe Alt-Sam could make it through each day without wanting to pull her arm hairs out one by one.

Damon gave Alt-Sam a sweet kiss on the forehead as the warning bell sounded for them to get to their next class. He walked off, and Alt-Sam watched him move away through the crowd. A hopeful smile played on her lips, so different from the somber expression she'd had minutes earlier.

"Don't let Myles get to you," a small girl in a cheerleading uniform said to Alt-Sam. "Hold on to that one."

The girl looked familiar—gorgeous dark hair, thick lashes, petite and peppy…

Marissa.

As soon as the thought came, everything around Sam went black. There was another fast and unexpected *whoosh* as she fell forward and away from the high school hallway. She blinked in the faint glow of her purple lava lamp and realized that the vision had ended. She was back on her bedroom floor, just where she'd left off.

She eyed the CD player in her hands. No matter how much she tried to calm herself down, her breaths came out like she'd run a marathon. She carefully placed the player on the floor, tucked her knees into her chest and stared at it.

Something very strange was happening. It was possible she'd fallen asleep again but…what was this? And for reasons she didn't understand, Sam was seeing a life beyond her actual memories, a world where she'd kissed Damon, and her high school self was different as a result.

Perhaps the easiest solution was not to put the damn headphones on again. That way, whatever *was* going on would stop. The whole thing would be a nonissue, so long as she didn't engage. Sam unwrapped her arms from the pretzel she'd knotted her body into and reached for the player. She flipped it over, opened the battery lid and removed the batteries. Sam closed the battery chamber with a satisfying click.

There. Done. Nothing bad would happen.

Only, when she flipped the Walkman over, the screen lit up. The next song was queued and ready to be played, with or without the batteries.

7

Sam owned a demonic CD player that operated sans batteries—drifting off wasn't easy. She'd spent a lot of time trying to see if there was some other energy source—there wasn't—then taking the CD out, popping it back in and making sure she wasn't imagining that the screen was just back to normal, and queued to track three. If her CD player worked without batteries, what the hell did that even mean?

She was at the start of a horror movie, obviously. Or it was one of those viral news stories where someone discovered a McDonald's Big Mac from forty years ago, still perfectly preserved. Though, when she'd googled *old cd player works without batteries*, the only thing that came up were people asking how to hook a CD player to their car radio, or if CD players needed batteries.

Hers, as it turned out, did not. So she'd spent time pacing the floor and muttering to herself. Then taken a shower. Then went on YouTube to look for *haunted CD players*, which yielded a few fake, but albeit funny, videos. There was also the general, ever-present feeling that she was on the verge of getting sick. Like, barfing-from-confusion kind of sick.

There was a chance that both songs were just vivid dreams brought on from the stress of the trip and the unending nostalgia. But there was really only one way to be sure. She had to listen to another one.

She warily placed the headphones over her ears, positioned herself on the bed and tried to take deep, calming breaths. Maybe if she was relaxed, nothing would happen. Stress hallucinations were probably a thing. Though, after a few quiet minutes, there was no calming the low current of apprehension that pulsed through her. So she decided to just hit Play.

Muse's sharp electric guitar strummed as "Supermassive Black Hole" began. This had been one of her all-time favorite songs, and not *just* because the lead singer, Matt Bellamy, had said it was about how women were the center of the galaxy and you couldn't help but get sucked in by them. The pulse of the beat, paired with Bellamy's throaty voice, was just sexy.

Not to mention it was used in her beloved *Twilight* movie.

It would've been fun to listen to, if Sam wasn't suddenly suspended in midair while the synths and electric drums blasted through. When there was something solid beneath her again, she breathed in the smell of popcorn and blinked against the low lighting. Muse's song boomed from an overhead speaker and she stiffened in the itchy non-stadium-style movie seats. Which is when she realized that she was in a movie theater, watching *Twilight*. Sam's hand instinctively reached up to cover the shocked noise coming out of her as the iconic baseball scene played, and Kristen Stewart told Nikki Reed that she'd struck out.

Sam tore the headphones off and turned around. Her gaze landed on a girl cuddled up to a guy in the row across from her, and a flare of color from the screen highlighted the long red hair of Alt-Sam.

This wasn't real. It couldn't be real. But this was now the third time and it was starting to feel impossible that it was just a dream. She pinched herself, *hard*, and bit her lip in pain. She wasn't waking up. People didn't feel pain like this in dreams.

Sam dropped her face into her hands and let out a whimper. When she looked back up, Damon was whispering in Alt-Sam's ear. Damon said something that made Alt-Sam just barely look away from the screen. "Huh?"

"You're gorgeous," he said louder, so the people nearby— mainly Adult Sam—could hear.

"Shhh," someone in the audience hissed at them.

"Yeah, shhh, I'm trying to watch the movie," Alt-Sam said as she elbowed Damon.

"This is the third time you've seen it," Damon said.

"Shhh," another person from the audience said.

"Ugh, fine. Will this shut you up?" Alt-Sam turned to Damon and pulled him in for a kiss.

"Not saying you two should get a room, but like…" Sam said to herself. "Have a little respect. Robert Pattinson and Kristen Stewart won an MTV Movie Award for this."

Alt-Sam moaned Damon's name and then—well, the guy started to get handsy. The unmistakable way they pawed at each other made it clear that the movie *they* were about to star in might be rated R.

"I'll give y'all a little privacy." Sam backed away across the popcorn-scattered floor and down the aisle that would lead her to an exit. She was almost out of the room when a guy with a flashlight strode down the aisle. He shone the flashlight on Alt-Sam and Damon, as bright as a spotlight.

"Oh, God," both Sam and Alt-Sam said at the same time.

"Can I help you?" Damon asked, a mix of embarrassed and alarmed. He straightened and there was the bloom of a bright red hickey on his neck.

"Sam! Girl! Hickeys?" Sam slapped a palm over her forehead and sighed.

Damon wiped his lips with the back of his hand as Alt-Sam scrambled off his lap and into her own seat.

"What's going on here?" the man asked.

Adult Sam puffed out her cheeks. "I think you *know* what's going on here, sir."

The man's jaw tightened. "Both of you. Outside. Now."

Sam's eyebrows rose so far up they hurt, but Damon and Alt-Sam obediently stood from their seats and made their way toward the exit.

Damon ran a hand through his hair and glanced over to Alt-Sam, who shoved her hands into the pockets of her low-rise jeans. She shifted in her Converse sneakers as Damon pushed open the doors to the theater, and they both walked out into the night, hand in hand.

"We just got kicked out of a movie theater," he said with a smile.

"It's not funny." Alt-Sam nudged him. "We didn't even get to the prom scene."

Damon playfully brought her in toward him and began to slow dance with her. "We can practice for *our* prom. My moves are way better than Edward's." Damon dipped Alt-Sam low and held her close.

"Prove it," Alt-Sam said with a grin.

As Damon leaned in to kiss Alt-Sam, a *whoosh* of air surrounded Sam, along with total blackness, and she was quickly yanked out of the moment.

As Sam landed back in her spot on the bed, her eyes shot open and she breathed in and out with a new heaviness. Whatever was happening was worse than confusing. It was disorienting. These weren't real memories—at least not the way Sam remembered them. She and Damon *had* gone to see *Twilight* together—she'd been excited about the movie for months. But unlike Damon and Alt-Sam, they hadn't been cozy at all. She'd loved the movie, but there had also been tension between them. The movie had come out over a year after she'd rejected Damon, so when Edward and Bella shared their own first kiss on screen, she'd felt like they were watching what they'd never have. She couldn't speak to how Damon had interpreted the moment, but she inferred from the way he crossed his arms and avoided meeting her eyes that he was deep in thought, at a minimum.

Now, though, there was a different timeline where they were a couple. She and Damon were happy. And what exactly was she supposed to make of that?

8

When the bagpipes sounded that morning, Sam was not fast asleep. Quite the opposite—she was at the kitchen table and watched as old man Byron trudged through the sand in his kilt, admired the sunrise briefly and then began to play. A few minutes later Alligator Alice power-walked past and waved to Sam through the window.

"You'd think Alligator Alice and Byron would have had a conversation at least once, but I've never seen her stop for a chat." Pearl moved to the coffeepot and flipped it on, so the slow and steady bead of filtering took over the room.

"Maybe they don't need words." Sam stood from the kitchen table. She opened the pantry and grabbed bread and a jar of peanut butter. "They have an unspoken language."

Sam smeared thick scoops of peanut butter onto two slices of toast—one for her and one for Pearl—and then plated them. She brought the plates and two mugs of coffee to the table.

When Pearl sat, she winced.

"You okay?" Sam asked as she set the plate down in front of Pearl. "Want me to get the pain medicine?"

"I have some here." Pearl reached into the pocket of her worn cotton robe and pulled out the prescription bottle. She popped open the lid and tapped a pill into her palm. She swallowed it down with a sip of coffee.

"I got a recommendation for a rehab specialist from Mr. Rocha. I put in a call to them, so I should be hearing back on when to schedule your first appointment."

"Isn't it a little early for details?" Pearl lifted the toast to her mouth. "At least let me get my wits about me."

Sam sat across from Pearl and wrapped her hands around her warm mug of coffee. Who would drive Pearl to her appointments when Sam was back at work? Maybe Jessie could, or Damon. She'd have to figure that out, too, before she left.

"I can see your wheels turning. Always worrying. I'll be fine, you know," Pearl said through a bite.

"I know you will. You always are. Which is why I think we should consider postponing the move," Sam said. "You just broke your wrist. It's kind of a lot to move on top of that."

"It took you over a decade to come back home," Pearl said. "I don't know if I have another decade in me. We need to do this while you're here."

Sam tried to hide the frown that creased her brows. The thought of Pearl not being around in ten years wasn't possible. She was aging, yes, but she wasn't *old*. Her grandma would be here. In this house. That was just how it had to be. Tightness rose in her chest. Pearl was the only family Sam had. What would she be without this small lifeline?

"I'm not dead yet," Pearl said. "Don't look so put out."

That word *dead* made Sam cringe. Of course she knew that death was part of life, but her brain wouldn't even allow her to go there. "Can we talk about something else?" Sam asked.

"Sure. How about you tell me why you were up so late?"

Sam sat back in her chair. "You spying on me?"

"I had to use the bathroom in the middle of the night. Your

light was still on." Pearl took a quick sip of coffee. "What's eating you?"

Sam scratched a spot on her head. She *could* try to tell Pearl the truth. Or some version of it. No, she couldn't word vomit this early in the morning. But maybe there was something she *could* ask. "Have you ever, um…" Sam wasn't actually sure how to start a conversation about a hallucination from a CD player. Trying to form a sentence in her head that didn't sound completely unhinged proved hard.

"If you're asking if I've ever been with a woman, the answer is yes. A handful." Pearl held up her hand and started to count off fingers, apparently adding all the women up. "Maybe four? Or three? Hard to remember."

"What? Grandma, no—" Sam's thoughts stopped and stalled with the revelation that her grandmother had slept with more than one woman. Though she wasn't entirely surprised; Pearl often made comments about Helen Mirren that were borderline harassment.

"I see how uncomfortable you get when I ask if you're seeing anyone. And when I mentioned Damon, you practically slid under the table. You don't have to hide who you are from me. Love is love, or whatever they say." Pearl looked out the window again.

"I'm not…" Sam shook her head. "This isn't my coming out moment, okay?"

"Okay." Pearl turned to face her. "Then what's got you so tied up in knots?"

"Is the house…haunted or something?"

Pearl narrowed her eyes.

"Like, has anything weird ever happened to you? Something you have a hard time explaining?" Sam spoke quickly before she chickened out.

Her grandma took a luxurious sip of her coffee. "Life is weird, honey, and I've lived a lot of it. Can't say I've seen a ghost, though."

Her grandma clearly had no idea what she was talking about, which was when Sam decided that the only way out of this situation meant getting back to working on her room. The sooner Sam got to cleaning, the sooner she'd be able to forget everything she'd seen, past or present.

"Never mind," Sam eventually said. "I'm just jet-lagged. What have you got planned for the day?"

"I'm going to take a cup of coffee out to the beach. Get dressed. Go for my morning walk. Then lunch with Jessie, followed by my nap. Sunset stroll. The usual. Care to join?" Pearl pushed herself up from the table with a little extra effort.

"Maybe at sunset," Sam offered. Though she had no intention of doing anything other than cleaning. "Grandma, shouldn't you rest? What did the doctor say?"

"You were there," Pearl reminded her. "He said to wear a trash bag when I shower."

"He also said to rest," Sam pushed.

Pearl waved her hand, as if wiping away the comment. She made her way toward the back door but stopped to knock on the door frame with her cast. "Hopefully, you'll find something good while you're digging through all of these old memories."

Sam was sure she wouldn't, but kept that thought to herself.

When she returned to her room, the first thing she clocked was the CD player on her bed. The thing was obviously evil—just like the board game in *Jumanji*, causing dozens of rabid monkeys to be released into the world. Only in this game, she'd be sent a baker's dozen memories of 2000s fashion crimes. Sam opened the box of trash bags on her desk, draped a black bag over the top of the CD player to keep it from leaking fumes, then gently kicked it under the bed. She'd figure out where to dispose of electronics later, but for the moment she'd focus on cleaning out her desk. It was undeniably where she stored the majority of things she didn't know what to do with.

The top was covered in felt stickers that were so old they'd basically fused to the wood. Sam had done her homework there, doodled in her notebook and stared out the window waiting for Damon to show up. Now all she wanted was to empty it out so she could donate the whole thing. She opened the delicate metal handle of the top drawer to reveal boxes, dividers and a hot pink Caboodle loaded with markers instead of makeup. Why had she hoarded over twenty pens, receipts from thrift stores and concert stubs? There was a box filled with a random assortment of trinkets: a Morrissey rubber bracelet, Magic 8 Ball, a single red-and-yellow-striped-toe sock, three Delia's clothing catalogs, a half-empty bottle of Clinique's Happy perfume and a laminated Blockbuster Video membership card.

Sam held on to the card, turning it in her hands as she remembered going to the local store with Damon every Friday, picking out a movie and ordering pizza. A weekly ritual they'd had, and maybe the only real routine from her childhood. Their Fridays together made Sam feel like she only needed one friend: him. The Blockbuster card was compact and easy to carry. She could slide it into her wallet, if she wanted.

But holding on to things was tricky. Yes, she could keep this laminated card, but what about the other items? She didn't have a place to store her memories, not if Pearl moved. Her studio apartment in Paris barely had enough room for her bed, let alone an overflowing CD collection. As she closed and tied off a trash bag, she fully understood these items would disappear, along with her room and the memories it carried.

The rumble of a motorcycle snapped her out of her thoughts—Damon. She stood just in time to see him pull into the driveway.

Well, what did it matter if she was sleep deprived and a touch manic? She pinched her shoulder blades together. This wasn't a big deal. He was stopping by, albeit unannounced, and she could handle a brief interaction. This was *just Damon*.

She opened the front door and tried not to be fazed. But there was his dark hair, the confident way he leaned against the door frame, and then he spoke.

"I brought ice cream." He lifted the brown paper bag with the word *Mermaids* written in elaborate cursive across the front. Sam had worked summers there, and some deep Pavlovian response filled her mouth with saliva; she could almost smell the sugary waffle cones.

"Don't tell me." Sam took the bag.

"Cookie dough ice cream, two scoops, extra gummy bears," Damon said. "I don't know how you eat this. The gummies get hard as rocks."

"That's the point." Sam pulled the container out of the bag, opened the lid and sniffed the sickly sweet vanilla and cream. She popped a rogue gummy into her mouth and began the business of chewing it back to life. "You have to warm them up until they become half a gummy, but it's all worth it because they're *gummies*."

Damon's eyes widened. "The guy working the counter could barely hide a gag when I ordered it, so it's not only me who's judging you, just to be clear."

"What did you get?" Sam had already made her way to the kitchen and pulled out two spoons.

"I ate a burger at the bar." Damon pulled a chair out at the kitchen table and sat. "You know me, more of a savory than sweet person."

Why was she mildly delighted about that phrasing, *you know me*? Yes, she *did* know Damon, didn't she? Sure, they hadn't ended up dating in real life, but they'd been best friends, and maybe they could be close again. Sam decided to sit, too.

"Pearl stopped in for an early lunch and told me you could use some sugar," he added.

"Mmm," Sam said at both the ice cream and the fact that Pearl had probably meant this as a bit of a double entendre. She handed Damon a spoon, and he carefully scooped a bite without any gummies. He brought the spoon to his mouth, and she tried not to stare as his lips wrapped around it. She shoved a spoonful into her own mouth and looked away.

Sam didn't want Damon to have any inkling that she was attracted to him, even though she very much was. But when she looked back, he licked his lips and watched her. She wondered briefly if he was having similar feelings. But then he asked, "How's the cleaning coming?"

Well, if he *had* any attraction to her, he wouldn't be thinking about Clorox wipes. She raised the cup of ice cream. "This is the fuel I need to finish my room," Sam said. "Thanks for bringing it."

How long would he stay? How long would she have to stare and wonder if his mouth tasted like sugar? She was fairly sure she could go a stretch without Damon noticing any longing in her eyes. But still…she couldn't pretend forever.

"Need any help? I have a bit of time before I head back."

A bit of time sounded like fifteen, twenty minutes tops. And after a sleepless night, she wouldn't mind him lifting the trash bags out of her room and carrying them outside. She wouldn't mind seeing the way his arms looked when he did that, either…

"Sure." She took one last bite of her ice cream, left it on the counter and walked down the hall. Damon followed, just like he used to when they were kids. Except now, the smell of his coconut shampoo and the vanilla from the ice cream shop made her want to turn around and get a spoonful of *him*.

When he came into the room, he eyed the band posters first, then her corkboard. He stopped at a picture of himself.

"It was pretty metal of me to match the rubber bands on my braces to my red-tipped hair." He licked his teeth as he stared at a photo booth shot of them from the high school fair. "Metal pun intended."

"They were a good look. Almost as killer as the shiny shirts

you used to wear." She nodded to the marching band photo—
the one they'd taken the night of their almost-kiss. She wondered if he ever even thought of it.

"I'm offended that you didn't mention my studded belts, but
oh well." He shrugged. "You, on the other hand... Looking at
you now, I don't think anyone would guess that you were an
emo chick in high school."

"An emo chick?" Sam parroted back. Something about his
tone when he'd said that gave her pause, like maybe he missed
the black lipstick and heavy liner. "Emo is a state of mind just
as much as it is a style."

"Are you telling me you're still secretly into Evanescence?"

Her mouth opened as "Bring Me to Life" started in her head,
along with the bizzaro vision she'd had of them kissing. "Anyone who doesn't like Evanescence is lying, obviously."

"Oh, obviously." He grinned. They shared one of those tense
and knowing moments they kept having. Luckily, Damon broke
it for them. "What's left to clean?" he asked.

Sam sat on the ground and slid open the bottom drawer of
the desk, which was heavy with photo albums. "I don't really
know what to do with these." She took one out and opened
the front, and the plastic sheet covering the first row of photos
wrinkled with her touch. Baby photos of Sam being cradled by
Pearl, and her mom smiling tightly next to them. Even then,
when Sam was small and helpless, Bonnie hadn't known how
to be around her.

"You don't want to keep them?" He sat next to her on the
floor and took another album out of the drawer.

"I don't have a place to put them," Sam said. She didn't want
to tell Damon that her only solid ground was, size-wise, the
equivalent of a dorm room. "And I'm not sentimental." She
wasn't, really, not about her mom, at least.

Damon flipped open the album in his hands and there was a
photo of them at Damon's thirteenth birthday. He'd had a family
pool party and wore board shorts. Sam was in a one-piece cov-

ered by an oversize Daffy Duck shirt. They both held up peace signs, and Damon's teeth glittered back with the unmistakable metal braces he'd hinted at earlier.

"Can you believe we weren't popular in school?" he asked.

"We weren't?" she joked back.

"Okay if I keep this one?" he asked, but he'd already tucked the photo into the back pocket of his jeans. He wanted a memory of the old them. A photo of Sam and Damon when they were best friends. Something about that made her chest warm.

"You can digitize these, you know," he quickly followed. "Get rid of the bulky album, but have them on your laptop, or whatever. You don't want to forget how well ballet flats paired with cargo pants." He held up the photo album and, as he did, a little booklet fell onto the carpet.

Sam reached for it at the same time as Damon, and their fingers met. Damon pulled back, but the spot he'd touched burned. She tried to ignore the sensation by pulling the little book close to her chest to inspect. When she turned it over, there was Damon's handwriting. *Sam's Travel Bingo Card*. He'd drawn an airplane, an island and a detailed rendering of an Egyptian pyramid. When she opened the card, there was the bingo board where Damon had outlined specific travel goals Sam had shared with him.

See the Aurora Borealis
Swim under a waterfall
Hike Machu Picchu
Watch the ball drop in NYC
Gondola ride in Venice
Oktoberfest in Germany
See cherry blossoms in Japan
Rent a fancy bungalow in Bora Bora
Get to the top of the Eiffel Tower
Walk the Great Wall of China
Go on a safari

Explore Casablanca
Photos at the Hollywood sign in LA

There was a star sticker sheet taped to the inside so Sam could mark each item off as she accomplished them. Her fingers traced the lines of the bingo squares as she tried, and failed, to think of something to say.

"You're speechless, I see. Is it because my drawing of the Eiffel Tower is borderline phallic?" Damon asked. "My artistic efforts were never as good as yours."

Sam laughed, relieved he found a way to take any humiliation out of the situation. Because the truth was that this gift from Damon had meant so much to her then, and it still meant so much to her now. He was maybe the one person in her life who fully indulged her dreams of traveling, but she'd pushed him away.

Eventually, she met his gaze, and his dark hazel eyes surrounded by even darker lashes locked on to her. Damon carefully undid the star sticker sheet and handed it to Sam. "I think it's time to fill out this bingo card."

She took the stars and stared at them, so wishing she weren't borderline hungover from the lack of sleep. Instead, she peeled off a sticker and placed it on top of the *See cherry blossoms in Japan* square. "That was one of the first places I took a proper vacation to, maybe seven years ago. The trees get filled with these gorgeous pink overflowing blooms, and the buds fall off and float down the Meguro River. I thought of you when I went there." She had thought of Damon, but hadn't reached out because, apparently, she was truly chicken at expressing her feelings.

"Good," he said. She looked up, and a satisfied look passed across his face. Though, just as quickly as it had come, it vanished. And maybe she'd imagined the whole thing, but she couldn't shake the feeling that Damon *liked* the fact that she'd been thinking of him.

She went through the rest of the bingo card and shared when she'd seen the bucket list item, along with fun anecdotes. Step-

ping in donkey shit as she hiked Machu Picchu was a particular
hit in terms of making Damon laugh.

When the card had been filled, minus the Casablanca square,
she refolded the card and placed it on top of the desk. "I obviously can't get rid of that until I fill the whole thing out."

"Not unless you want a life not lived." Damon stretched
out his legs, and his jeans brushed against the side of her knee.

She wanted to lay her head on his thick thigh and fall
asleep—both because she was tired and because being near
him reminded her that anything was possible, which was how
he'd always made her feel. "I remember when you made this
for me. It put all of my goals in one place, and I was so worried that I'd never get to check any of them off," Sam said. "I
didn't want to prove my mom right."

"Your mom was never right about you," he quickly replied.
"She never knew you."

But you knew me, Sam wanted to say.

"Have you heard from her?" Damon gave a gentle look.

Her mom hadn't reached out, not to Sam or Pearl. Sam leaned
back and let her head rest against the side of the bed frame.
"Bonnie's really committed to never seeing me again, so…"

"Did you ever try to find her?"

Not many people in Sam's current life knew the story about
how her mom left. And when they got close to asking, Sam de-
flected. She readied herself to do the same now, but something
cracked open, and the truth slipped out. "I did hire an inves-
tigator once. A few years into flying, when I had some extra
money. I had this idea that I could find her and tell her I was a
pilot, and she'd be proud. Maybe even want to talk. The woman
I hired found her in Clearwater, Florida—this little town, bigger
than Tybee, but kind of exactly the same. She was working the
front desk of a hair salon and rented a one-bedroom place close
to the beach. It was like she'd left here for something nearly
identical. Just, you know, without me and Pearl."

Sam's voice cracked at the memory. "I'd occasionally call the front desk of the salon, just to hear her voice when she picked up the phone."

She cleared her throat, and Damon's hand found its way to her knee and gave her a squeeze. "She's a shitty person. That's not on you."

Sam nodded but didn't look up to catch his eye. She hadn't opened up to anyone about this ever. She was surprised that all it'd taken was a cup of ice cream, but then again, there had been extra gummy bears.

"My mom, on the other hand, is having a barbecue tomorrow and told me it was rude that I hadn't invited you and Pearl."

A small smile crept across Sam's face. The Rocha family was notorious for their elaborate barbecues. "So you're still not going to extend the invite, huh?"

"Not unless you agree to wear your old Doc Martens and do a karaoke duet of a Paramore song with me, no." He leaned back into his palms, and the muscles in his biceps popped under the weight of him. She couldn't help but stare for a beat too long; she was only human, after all.

"Unfortunately for you, I love to crash parties. What time?"

"Two." Damon wiped his hands across his jeans and pushed himself up from the floor. Sam was tall, but she looked up at Damon and felt infinitely small compared to his broad shoulders and wide stance. The darker circles under his eyes told her he was tired, though from work or something else, she wasn't sure. "I should get back. Those beers don't pour themselves."

"So noble, your job."

"The Lord turned water into wine, but someone had to make the beer." He hesitated, and they stayed locked on each other, not saying a word.

Damon shook his head, as if to unlock himself from her. He stopped at the door frame, then turned slightly. "Don't throw out any of my mix CDs. Those are going to be collector's items someday."

"I'd never," she said with a tight smile, and he walked out the door.

Oh, if only he knew all of the trouble one of those CDs in particular was causing.

Sam nibbled her bottom lip. Here she was, in her childhood bedroom, and she'd just watched the man of her visions walk out the door. He was in the past, but he was also so very present.

She went to put the album back in the drawer, when she spotted something shiny in the jewelry dish next to the pile of albums on her desk. She picked it up and inspected the lone earring. Her mom's earring. This was the one she'd lost the pair to.

She swallowed down the realization that there was one other way to confirm that what was happening was real. Her clarinet case was somewhere in this room. She hadn't known where her earring had vanished to all those years ago—she'd been too caught up in the moment—until she watched Damon pick it up and tuck it into her clarinet case. If she found the earring still there, she'd know that what she saw was not a hallucination.

She got on her hands and knees and looked under the bed. There was the small walk-in closet, and she opened the door and pulled the metal chain that turned on the overhead bulb. Within a few seconds, she saw the case. She easily pulled it down, covered in dust as well as band stickers. In her vision, he'd tucked an earring into the front pocket. She unzipped the pocket and reached in, sure she'd find nothing.

But as her fingers slid back out, the tip of her index finger snagged on something sharp. Her eyes widened as she felt around the inside and fingered the unmistakable round stone earring and sharp backing. She pulled it out and pinched the earring between her index finger and thumb, so hard that it hurt.

9

This time, putting the headphones on was easy. The earring was like a sign that she needed to listen to more songs if she had any chance of understanding what was happening. Because as far as Sam could tell, she was being given the chance to see the answer to her biggest what-if about how her life could've been if only she'd kissed Damon that night.

Why this was happening was another mystery entirely. What Sam knew was that she had a magic CD player that transported her to an alternate version of the past, and each vision lasted the length of the song that played. Shortly after the song started, so did the vision, and when it ended, she was back to reality.

So she decided to treat this one differently. She knew what she was getting into, roughly, and needed to take in as much as she could before the song ended. She'd already listened to three out of the thirteen songs, so she'd make the most of the ten left.

She hit Play and closed her eyes as the quick strumming of The Offspring's "Want You Bad" began. The song was, as the title suggested, about a guy who *really* wants the person he's obsessing over.

Oh, sweet sassy hormones, Sam thought as the rush of air swept in along with a big drop. But she didn't have time to revel in the weightlessness, because as soon as she landed in her new destination, she'd only have the time remaining on the player. She opened her eyes and glanced down—three minutes and five seconds left.

When she looked up, there was vinyl flooring beneath her feet, a stadium bench under her, and the squeak of rubber soles hitting the ground. She was in the gymnasium of her high school, and when she turned around, there was Alt-Sam hunched over a papier-mâché garland.

"Valentine's Day is less than a week away."

Sam snapped back to the front where Mr. Meyer, the PE coach, stood with a clipboard. He walked toward the group as he said, "How's my decoration committee doing?"

Ah, yes, Sam remembered volunteering for the Spirit Committee—basically a group of students who did free decor labor to celebrate holidays. She was a straight-A student, but thought more extracurriculars would improve her chances of a scholarship to flight school. The fact that it was only a few weeks of commitment sweetened the deal.

"Jeremy, put the iPod away, please." Mr. Meyer nodded to a brick of an iPod sitting in a kid's lap. Jeremy took off his headphones, and Sam heard "Want You Bad" playing through them before he turned the iPod off and tucked it into his backpack.

"We could use some snacks," a slight girl with bronze gladiator sandals and a matching headband chirped back.

Mr. Meyer tapped his foot. "Copy that. Requests?"

A small chorus of answers came back, "Famous Amos!"

"Dunkaroos!"

"Doritos!"

"Fig Newtons!"

He jokingly placed his hands over his ears before turning and heading to the vending machines in the hall just outside the gym.

Okay, focus on the details, Sam told herself.

"Vampire girl!" There was Myles, the soccer jock who'd gone on to become Damon's close friend. He jogged over to the bleachers. Alt-Sam looked up and scowled.

"Pass me my water bottle," he shouted to her.

A girl in a velour tracksuit turned to eye Alt-Sam. "It's right next to you," she said.

Alt-Sam shrugged. "Vampires don't help assholes, as it turns out."

All six foot four of Myles pouted, like his feelings might actually be hurt. "Did you just call me an asshole?"

Alt-Sam rolled her eyes as she looked up at him. "Did you seriously call me a vampire?"

Myles stared at her then, but Alt-Sam just stared right back. Eventually, he reached behind her and grabbed the water bottle.

Okay, so in this life we have quite the backbone. A door slammed shut, and Damon's unmistakable spiked hair popped into the gym.

"Your boyfriend's here," Myles said, almost like it was an insult.

Alt-Sam ignored Myles and stood from the bleachers, walking toward Damon. "What are you...?" she started to ask as Damon handed her a brown bag.

"My mom made that vegan brittle you like," he said. "I saved you some."

"Thanks." She gave him a peck on the cheek. "Did you get out of detention early or something?"

Ah, Damon and his knack for getting into trouble. While Sam had always been about following the rules—school was one of the few stable places in her life—Damon didn't like being told what to do. He seemed to get off on riling the teachers up, and averaged at least one detention a month for what Sam thought of as fairly silly things. He'd once gotten a detention for skipping class to get a Crunchwrap Supreme from Taco Bell. "It was funny," he'd said at the time, but Sam just thought he was bored.

"I didn't go to detention," he eventually said.

Alt-Sam's mouth opened to say something, but he interrupted her. "Don't be mad. I just wanted to see you."

"Your mom is going to be pissed when she finds out you skipped." Alt-Sam unwrapped the brittle and broke off a corner. She spoke as she chewed. "And you better not tell her it was to see me."

"I was actually thinking you could duck out early, too. We could... I don't know. Go somewhere." Damon raised a mischievous eyebrow.

"Jesus," Sam said, trying to recall a time where she'd ever been this desperate for someone. "The hormones are strong in this one."

The first time she'd ever kissed a guy was when she was twenty-two, but not in this timeline, where things were moving so fast she could hardly keep up.

"Mr. Meyer is trying to get snacks from the vending machine that always breaks. He'll be there for a while. He won't even notice you're gone," Damon tried again.

Alt-Sam softly smiled as she took another bite of brittle. "I don't know. I volunteered. I should stay." She glanced back to the group, where an a cappella version of "Single Ladies" by Beyoncé was being sung. "We haven't decided on florals for the Say You'll Be Mine pep rally yet."

"Come on," Damon said. "Tell them pansies, my mom's favorite, and you can skip the sing-along just this once."

Alt-Sam tucked a strand of hair behind her ear, revealing a fresh bloom of a blush across her cheeks. "Okay," she said.

"Let's go." Damon took her hand and led her toward the exit.

Sam swore she saw the hint of a smile cross Alt-Sam's lips. She looked at the CD player and watched the numbers tick down from seven seconds. She took a deep breath in, braced herself for the plunge and closed her eyes.

When Sam came back to the room, she wanted to get out as many details as she could before she forgot. She went to her desk and pulled out a Lisa Frank notebook she hadn't yet tossed—she didn't have the heart to put Hunter the Leopard into the trash. She opened to a clean page and started writing everything she could remember from the playlist.

SAM AND DAMON'S MAGICAL PLAYLIST

Track One: "Bring Me to Life" by Evanescence. Otherworldly song about being understood by another human. Tybee High parking lot. Questionable amounts of eyeliner. Alt-Sam kisses Damon. Missing earring is found.

Track Two: "I Believe in a Thing Called Love" by The Darkness. A bop about being head over heels for someone. Alt-Sam and Damon are officially dating. Myles continues to disappoint. Marissa didn't have an awkward phase in high school. JanSport backpacks are timeless.

Track Three: "Supermassive Black Hole" by Muse. Inarguably the best song and movie scene pairing ever. Damon and Alt-Sam make out during *Twilight* and get kicked out. One too many hickies.

Track Four: "Want You Bad" by The Offspring. A banger about a bad boy wanting to corrupt a good girl. Myles gets owned by Alt-Sam. Damon skips detention. Alt-Sam skips her extracurricular. I miss Dunkaroos.

Sam scratched her index finger across her forehead. There had to be a bigger point to all of this beyond showing Alt-Sam's life with Damon, right? But none of her notes added up to any grand realization. There did, however, seem to be a connection to the songs and what she'd seen. When she'd listened to "Bring Me to Life," she'd watched as Damon and Alt-Sam lit each other up, metaphorically speaking. And "I Believe in a Thing Called Love" paired well with Damon asking Alt-Sam to be his girlfriend.

Unless the realization was simple: she'd made a mistake in letting go of Damon. Because, while she didn't love Alt-Sam ditching Spirit Committee meetings, her other self was having way more fun than Sam ever did in high school.

But that would mean the life she had now wasn't where she was supposed to be—even though she loved flying, and her little apartment and her adventures. Was the CD showing her that she could be even happier, if only Damon was folded into everything? Was that even an option anymore?

Maybe she'd missed some important detail in the other visions where she hadn't paid close attention. Going back for a relisten made sense, given her experiment. The CD player was next to her, and she hit the back button, but the display stayed stuck on the next queued song. She hit the next button, but it wouldn't skip to the next track, either. Okay, so she couldn't revisit the visions. Well, she was definitely going to chalk this up to more possessed CD weirdness.

Sam brought the notebook onto the bed and stared at the page. She could listen to another song. But how would seeing herself so deeply entrenched with Damon, when he wasn't anywhere close to her now, help? And if she was right about the CD player trying to point out her biggest mistake, would she even be able to fix it?

She put the notebook and CD player on her desk, more than a little annoyed at herself, yes, but at the playlist, too. She shouldn't be defensive, but all of a sudden she felt attacked for her choices and the suggestion that they were the wrong ones. Yes, she'd wondered what would've happened, but she'd also assumed she'd done the right thing by *not* kissing Damon.

Was rage sleep a thing? Because she wanted to rage sleep hard. Or, at least pretend to sleep so she'd have an excuse not to touch the player again. So she got ready for bed, flipped the lights off and closed her eyes, willing her brain to think about anything but the past.

10

"Are you Amish?" Pearl asked.

Sam had not slept well. Instead of sleeping, she'd spent most of the night telling herself to go to bed but was unable to do so because she just wanted to listen to more songs on the CD player. And now she was finding a parking spot in front of the Rocha house, and she couldn't be totally sure—lack of sleep, and all—but her grandma seemed to be asking a bizarre question.

"What?" Sam watched the backup camera as she parallel parked.

"Your sleeves are down to your wrists and your dress has a collar," Pearl clarified.

"You'd rather I dress like an ad for Margaritaville?" Sam countered. Pearl was festive in a Hawaiian shirt that matched her neon cast. "This is from Paris. It's Parisian."

Pearl pointedly yawned. "What it is, is a hot one. You'll get swamp pits. Don't come crying to me when you're swimming before you've gotten into the pool."

Pearl opened the car door and got out. Sam looked down at her outfit. She'd put this on to feel confident. The dress was chic. It hugged her curves. It made her feel sexy. And she'd be lying if she said that she didn't want Damon to see her that way, especially after the visions she'd had that suggested they were better together than apart.

She wasn't able to explain that to Pearl, though, so she'd just take her chances with the swamp pits and hope for the best.

As soon as she got out of the car, a dog the size of a bag of airplane peanuts came bounding out the front door toward them.

"Is that Rusty?" Sam asked and slammed the car door shut. She held a bouquet of pansies. Yes, Dream Damon had told her they were her mom's favorite. And yes, she'd bought them specifically to see if he'd been right.

"No." Pearl pursed her lips. "This is Rusty 2.0. We don't much care for each other as you can probably tell."

Indeed, the dog—which was almost a copy-and-paste replica of the miniature pinscher Damon had grown up with—got out multiple barks and growls at Pearl. Pearl, for her part, growled back, which forced the dog to turn its attention to Sam. Much to her surprise, the dog quickly mounted her calf and began a long and luxurious series of thrusts.

She regretted her decision to wear a dress that didn't cover all of her legs as she tried to gently shake the dog off.

"Making friends already, Sam-Sam," Damon called out.

She managed to forcibly remove the dog, though Rusty 2.0's tongue hung out and his gaze remained fixed on the spot he'd violated. "Yeah, well, they say the South is super friendly!"

Sam quickly walked away from the dog. She gave Damon a hug and lingered in his embrace for perhaps a beat too long. To be fair, their bodies fit together and being wrapped in his arms was even more satisfying than finding the perfect carry-on bag that stowed easily under a seat.

"Everyone's out back," Damon said as he pulled away. "Are those for my mom?"

"Indeed." Sam lifted the flowers in acknowledgment.

"She'll love those," he said.

"Would you say they're her favorite?" Sam asked.

But a bark from the dog broke off her question. Pearl swatted at the tiny, vicious thing with her handbag.

"Pecan!" Damon's tone was so stern that the little dog quit
nipping at Pearl's sandals. Then Damon held out his palm and
added, "Slow."

And it was the damnedest thing, but the dog slowly walked
to Damon and booped his palm with his wet nose.

They followed Damon through the front door, across the
living room and toward the back patio. This had been her second home in high school, but unlike Pearl's place, Cathy and
Humbe had made upgrades.

"Humbe got rid of the La-Z-Boy?" Sam asked.

"Cathy did," Damon corrected. "She redecorated using only
small businesses. But don't worry, he found a place for it in the
garage. And on weekends, he opens the door, lights a cigar and
reclines the hell out of that thing."

"A La-Z-Boy of one's own," Sam said. "Did she keep your
room a museum, too?"

"Unfortunately, my velvet black light posters have been replaced with tasteful bookshelves. Apparently, my room made
for a great home office." Damon opened the sliding glass door
and a wall of noise greeted them: big booms of laughter and
the samba music Humbe loved to play.

Sam stepped off the patio and onto the grassy lawn where
the scent of spiced meat cooking on the grill surrounded her.
There was the perfectly round pool she and Damon lived in
during the summers, the tire swing Damon used to push her
in and the long picnic table where the Rocha family gathered
for weekly dinners with Sam as the honorary plus-one.

"Sam!" an overly excited voice called out. When Sam turned,
she saw Farrah, bounding toward her. Farrah's rich black hair
was pulled into a high ponytail that swished as she jogged over.

Sam couldn't help but smile; Farrah was Damon's older, and much cooler, sister. They'd both idolized her, and she occasionally gave them a ride to the mall or school. Even now, Farrah wore cutoff jeans and a linen cropped shirt that looked effortlessly stylish.

Sam wrapped her in a tight hug. She was so relieved to see a friendly face that she completely forgot the rest of the party around them. Which is why she didn't notice Cathy approach from the side.

"There's our little valedictorian!" Cathy grinned. Much like everyone Sam had left in Tybee, Cathy had aged. Her hair had gone completely silver, and she kept it in a neat, cropped bob. There were deep lines around her eyes and forehead. And as she walked toward Sam in her chambray jean skirt, even her movements seemed slower. Sam wanted to stop time and go back to the Cathy she'd known before.

Sam started to get emotional, so she cut her feelings off and moved toward Cathy.

"I brought you pansies." Sam held out the bouquet.

Cathy's mouth fell open. "Oh, my favorite! Did you tell her I love these, Damon?"

"No," he said, hands in his pockets. "I did not."

Part of Sam screamed *Fuuuuck*, because her CD player was, without a doubt, sending her messages from some other universe.

Cathy held Sam's hands in hers. "I wouldn't have recognized you, honestly. I mean, you always had the brains, but now you're a real beauty."

"She's always been a beauty," Pearl piped up. "Inside and out."

"Such a doting grandmotherly response," Sam said with a smile.

"But no more black lipliner," Cathy said.

"Not at this time of the afternoon, at least," Sam said.

"You must be dating someone, right?" Cathy's eyes sparkled with hope.

"I'm not." Sam involuntarily looked at Damon, but he studied his shoes.

"How can that be? Damon, how can that be?" Cathy asked, as if he'd genuinely know the answer.

Damon rubbed the back of his neck. "I don't know, Mama."

"Anyway, honey, we're so happy to have you home." Cathy's expression was warm.

Sam knew that if she and Damon were together now, she'd likely be her mother-in-law. Sam had missed out on this kind of loving presence in her life in order to pursue her dream. Was it worth it?

"I've got vegan sliders on the table, and Humbe is making pork, if you're into that kind of thing."

Humbe wore a pair of massive gloves as he lifted the lid off the big green egg grill. A billow of smoke rose, along with a wave of pepper and paprika. Humbe closed the lid just as quickly, then turned, clocked Sam and called out, "Oi!"

"Hey, Mr. Rocha," Sam called back and made her way over.

Humbe removed his gloves, grabbed Sam's shoulders and gave her a kiss on both cheeks. "E aí, tudo certo?"

Sam's Portuguese was rusty, but she could never forget how to respond to Humbe's question of how she was doing. "Tudo bem," she said. *All good.* A white lie.

He clapped his hand on her shoulder. "You haven't forgotten your Portuguese. You always were the smart one."

Damon came next to them and eyed his dad warily. "You're not giving Sam a hard time, are you?"

"Why would I do that?" Humbe was very tall and very bald, and when he laughed his whole body shook. As he smiled, something else caught his attention, and he looked just past them. "Is that 'Oba, Lá Vem Ela'? Turn that up," he called out.

The volume of the samba music grew, and Sam chanced a glance at Damon. He groaned. She knew what was coming just as much as he did.

"Humbe, no dancing before dinner," Cathy said.

But it was too late. Once Humbe had the volume turned up, there was no stopping the rhythm in his feet. He extended his hand to Cathy.

"It's our song, meu bem," he said.

Cathy crossed her arms and pretended to be annoyed, but very clearly was not. She eventually moved to Humbe, took his hand and they began to dance.

Damon and Sam watched them in silence, until he broke it. "Sometimes I wonder how they ended up together, and how it still works."

"I don't know what you mean," Sam replied. Humbe and Cathy had met in the Peace Corps and, despite their culinary differences, worked well together. "She's a vegan baker, and he's a samba-loving carnivore. They're basically fated."

"Stop shit-talking your mother and me and get to dancing," Humbe said to Damon.

Damon huffed out a sigh. "You know he means I should dance with you, like old times."

"Old times," Sam said somewhat wistfully.

She'd learned to samba in Damon's backyard at a barbecue much like this one. She was pretty sure this song had played, too. The samba could be tricky—a lot of fast steps, hips and floating across the floor. But Humbe and Cathy were determined teachers, so they'd learned the moves quickly.

"May I have this dance?" Damon extended his open palm to her.

She should definitely *not* dance with him. But Humbe would be insistent, and maybe if they just did this one song, it would be over soon. So Sam clenched her jaw and took Damon's hand. His grip was strong and sure, and his other hand landed on the small of her back, but this time she didn't flinch.

He guided her across the lawn, and she watched his steps: two-two-two-four, two-two-two-four. The counting Humbe and Cathy had drilled into them came back, along with her hips circling in time with her steps. Once she remembered the footwork, Sam looked up, and Damon watched her. The tip of his tongue lingered at the corner of his mouth as he focused on her. And she knew this was all part of the samba—maintaining eye contact helped you stay in line with your partner. But then there were his fingers, which tightened and released around her hips as he spun her under his arm. Their hips met briefly as he pulled her back in, and his hot breath brushed across her neck as he brought her close.

Sam was breathless as he spun her out again. The end of the song approached, and Damon dipped her. He hovered above her and pressed his body tight with hers. Their lips were so close that his breath ghosted across her skin. They were locked in a moment, breathing with each other. She could just tilt her chin a touch up, and their lips would meet.

But then there was the squeal of the sliding glass door, followed by Marissa's high-pitched voice. "Guess who brought prosecco!"

Sam glanced over. Marissa watched them with an open mouth, but then seemed to think better of whatever was on her mind and held the bottle up high above her head with a smile.

When Sam looked back to Damon, he was still locked on her, like he hadn't noticed anyone else around them.

"Marissa's here," Sam cautiously said.

Damon frowned. He quickly straightened and brought Sam up with him. His hand held her just long enough so she could gather her footing. And once she did, Damon released her. "My dad must've invited her," he said.

Sam smoothed a hand down her dress and thought about that. Damon hadn't invited his own girlfriend to the barbecue? Still, he moved toward Marissa.

Pearl came next to Sam as Marissa kissed Damon on the cheek.

"So that's the girlfriend?" Pearl asked with all the subtlety of a shark in a paddling pool.

"Yeah." Sam tried not to sound too put out but she was. "She's a doctor and her hair smells the way heaven should."

"She's cute, but she's no you," Pearl said.

Sam finally exhaled at the realization that Pearl, at least, was in her corner.

"Not to change the subject, but you've got swamp pits, like I said you would."

Sam's attention shifted from Damon to her dress, as she looked down at the sweat stains blooming under her arms. But Pearl turned on her heel and headed straight for the table with the margarita machine.

Sam crossed her arms to hide the evidence, and watched as Marissa took her place next to Damon.

11

Back at Grandma Pearl's, Sam washed dishes. She'd changed into cotton shorts and a sweatshirt. Her sleeves were rolled up and she let the scalding water burn her hands as she scrubbed away at a pan. There was an ever-present fine layer of sand on the floor that Pearl brought in from her daily beach walks, and Sam's toes scrunched against the grainy feel of it. She thought going to the Rocha barbecue would be something to distract her, but now all she could do was relive the feel of Damon while he held her steady and they danced. There had only been her and him. The two of them reliving part of their past together. But then Marissa had shown up.

When she glanced out the window, there was a happy young couple holding hands and watching the sunset on the beach. The noise that rose from her throat wasn't a growl exactly, more of a harrumph. She tossed the wet sponge into the sink and pressed her palms into the counter. Her fingers twitched with nervous energy, like she could run a marathon if asked.

Within the span of a few days, she'd gone from thinking love would happen to her someday, to seeing a past where she was deeply in love. And now she was worried she'd passed up her one chance at happiness. Seeing two people just easily being with each other, the way Alt-Sam and Damon were, was turning her into Scrooge McAnti-Love, set to bah-humbug at anyone and anything that looked happy.

She was deeply in her feels, the way she'd been in high school whenever she'd turn on Dashboard Confessional.

It was then that Sam realized that she needed to talk to someone. Instead of wallowing over whether or not she'd made the right decisions in life, she needed a rational outsider. Not her grandma, who already had a broken wrist and didn't need a heart attack on top of it. Not Damon, for obvious reasons. So that really only left Rachel.

Rachel, who believed Sam was sipping cocktails while topless on a beach. Rachel, who had no idea that Sam was in her hometown and having some kind of out-of-body experience that was making her question her life choices.

But Rachel was, at her core, a rational person. Part of what made her a great pilot, really. Sam could call and Rachel would tell her what to do about this very bizarre situation.

The sun had just begun to dip low in the sky, and Grandma Pearl was busy watching a reality show about people who made moonshine, which gave Sam the opportunity to talk without Pearl overhearing. She went to her room, sat in her swivel desk chair and took a deep breath as she placed the FaceTime call. When Rachel answered, she wore her pilot uniform and, judging by the gelato in her hand, was in Rome.

"I'm surprised you picked up," Sam said, relieved. It would be one in the morning in Rome, and their international flights usually left by midnight. "Flight delay?"

"Please, please, please tell me exciting vacation stories while I wait for the crew to fix a passenger's screen. Thank the gods the airport lounge is open and still has food." Rachel took a bite of her pistachio gelato, then squinted at the phone. "Where are you? The lighting is tripping me out."

The lava lamp on Sam's desk was the only light she'd left on in the room. And because the thing was ancient, when she'd plugged it in, the pieces floated around like sad lumps; Sam was lit like a human blueberry in Willy Wonka's chocolate factory.

"That's the thing I didn't really tell you," Sam started. Then she panned her phone around her childhood bedroom and confessed that she wasn't on vacation at all.

"Sort of a weird thing to lie about," Rachel said. "But you *do* avoid talking about your family anytime I ask, so I'm not entirely shocked."

"There's more," Sam added. "I'm a little worried I might actually be experiencing a psychotic break or something."

"My family does that to me, too."

"No, it's not a joke—" Sam propped her phone against a stack of *Seventeen* magazines, then picked up her CD player. She told Rachel about the first time she'd put the headphones on, and the visions and Damon. Then showed that the batteries were removed, but the Walkman still somehow worked. And how each time she listened to a song she saw a new and different version of what her life could've been.

Rachel remained silent. Her face cycled through a series of emotions that were hard to identify but mostly bordered on concern.

"I know this sounds completely bizarre," Sam said.

"You're telling me you have a magic CD player that transports you to another life."

"Correct."

Rachel sat back and put the melted gelato down. "Like the wardrobe in Narnia."

"Uh-huh."

"Or, like *13 Going on 30*, when she goes into a closet or something, and then she's suddenly a thirty-year-old?"

"That's right." Sam crossed her arms and waited for the confirmation that she needed medical attention. "But I'm thirty-two going on sixteen."

"Did you take anything?" Rachel practically whispered the words, then looked around to make sure no one else was listening. To be fair, no one wanted a pilot on drugs, especially not the hallucinogenic kind. "Like old Tylenol? Or, I don't know what they do in Georgia, some peach-flavored shrooms?"

"I haven't, no." Sam nibbled her bottom lip and carefully weighed her options. She'd already done the hard part of telling the truth. Could she just take it all back? Say it was a weird joke?

After a good, long pause, Rachel finally asked, "What were the songs?"

Sam frowned. "Does that matter?"

"Well, sometimes songs put me in a real dark place. Like that Rihanna and Eminem song, 'Love the Way You Lie'? That song messes me up. And you're telling me this was a mixtape your high school boyfriend—"

"Not my boyfriend," Sam quickly corrected.

"Okay, fine, *not your boyfriend*. What did he pick out for you?"

"They're just songs we listened to in high school. Mostly emo songs that meant a lot to us at the time."

"Is it possible that the most important person in your high school life made you a CD, and the songs are hyper-nostalgic and you're having super-vivid memories?" Rachel's hopeful expression told Sam that what her friend needed was reassurance, because in that moment, Sam wasn't making any sense.

"Yeah, that could be…" Sam didn't say that she'd already considered this possibility, and then quickly abandoned the theory entirely.

"You're not buying it, huh?"

"These are not the memories I have from high school. They're totally different, like an alternate version. And they feel very real." Sam peeled a thigh off her leather chair and winced as her skin stuck to the material—sure to leave a stubborn mark. "And I'm just kind of freaking out, because what does this all mean?"

Rachel didn't answer. She blinked a lot, looked off and put the phone down. Sam stared at the ceiling of the airport lounge for a few tedious seconds. When she eventually picked the phone back up, Rachel asked, "I'm just wondering if maybe you should go to a doctor and get checked out?"

And there it was: the decision had been made that something was not quite right with Sam. This was a problem that couldn't be solved with a phone call. She needed to go be evaluated.

"You think I'm making it up?" Sam asked, maybe a little desperate to hear the opposite.

"I didn't say that." Rachel tucked a thick strand of hair behind her ear. "But, Sam, if I told you this exact same thing, what would you think?"

"I'd think you were…" Sam of course *wanted* to say that she'd believe her, but she wouldn't. Not even a little bit. "You're going to come visit me now, aren't you?"

"I can't just leave you in this aughts vault, hallucinating. What kind of friend would I be?" The overhead airport intercom blared, and Rachel put on her pilot's cap and stood from her seat. "We're being called back to the plane. Text me the address, okay? I won't call a priest until I'm there and can confirm the demons need to be removed."

Sam knew she'd do the exact same thing, but still…this was a part of her life no one had seen and it was about to be cracked open. Her shoulders sagged with the realization that she'd no longer be able to pretend this wasn't happening. "I just don't want to be here anymore."

The trip had been a nonstop whirlwind of blow after blow. And if it was up to Sam, she'd leave—but she couldn't, not until she finished this job for Pearl.

"Then do something about it." Rachel gave Sam a tough but

fair look. "The Sam I know doesn't just sit around. Stop trip‐
ping balls with your sad emo songs and get packing."

"Okay." And Sam was relieved to have someone telling her
what to do—even if it was what she'd already been up to.

"And don't touch that CD player anymore," Rachel added.
"Lock it up, or put it somewhere you can't reach, like the roof.
I know you never really ask for help, but I'm bringing some,
whether you like it or not."

Sam blew out a massive breath she didn't realize she'd been
holding. Being out of control was her least favorite thing, but
ever since arriving she hadn't been able to get her land legs
under her. At least Rachel could help dig her out of this mess
and get her back in the air, far away from Tybee.

12

"Grandma Pearl is worried about you," Damon said as he walked through the front door. Lemony, late-afternoon light poured in behind him as he carried in two motorcycle helmets and placed both on the entryway table.

"Is that so?" Sam called out, loud enough for her grandma to hear. "Pearl is worried about me?"

"Yes, I am!" Pearl called back.

Had her grandma overheard the conversation with Rachel the night before? Damon told Sam he was coming over in the form of a brief text—On my way over—but she didn't realize he'd been sent on a mission from Pearl.

"She spends too much time gossiping at your bar. And she worries about everything," Sam quipped back as she shut the door. "Yesterday she told me she thought the delivery guy might be having marriage problems because his hair looked rumpled, like he had to sleep on the sofa."

"Point taken, but it's my day off and she made me promise to get you out of the house to have a little fun." He picked up a deep purple helmet with a palm tree sticker on the side, and she wondered if he'd put that there, or Marissa. He held it out for her. "I'm not in the habit of disappointing Pearl. So what do you say, should we go for a ride?"

The helmet in his hand might as well have been an engagement ring, for all of the weight Sam was putting on it. Logically, she knew this was just a ride on a motorcycle. But was this an opportunity to finally say yes to Damon?

Some part of her was still afraid, though, because what if the universe was right, and she'd been wrong?

So in order to balance the scales, Sam blurted out a reason they couldn't be together. "Does Marissa know how often you're seeing me?"

Even she realized that wasn't quite the right thing to say, but then again, *did* she know?

Damon squinted. "What do you mean?"

"Well, you're here every day," Sam said. "I just don't want her to think—"

"Marissa knows we're old friends," Damon cut her off. "If that's what you need to hear."

An embarrassed flush crossed Sam's face. Old friends, of course that was what they were. Sam was just confusing her visions of them together with the present. But in the present, they were nothing but platonic to each other. "It's not what I need to hear. It's a small town. People talk. I don't want to be the source of any rumors is all."

"Come on, no more excuses, Sam-Sam." Damon reextended the helmet to her.

Sam blinked as she took the helmet. Damon put his black helmet on and signaled for her to follow him. And, despite her reservations, she did.

This wasn't Sam's first time on a motorcycle; she'd been on several Vespa bikes throughout her travels, sometimes as the driver and sometimes as the passenger. But watching Damon sling a leg over the seat, rev the engine and then nod for her to hop on was different. Could he feel her thumping heartbeat as he took her hand and wrapped it around his waist? It was humid, and through his thin cotton shirt a few beads of sweat trickled down. What would it be like to trail her hands across the length of him?

He revved the engine again and turned to her. "Hold on tight," he said.

Then he flipped his visor down, kicked the pedal up and the motorcycle shot forward. Sam tightened her grip around Damon. While the adrenaline had her body tense, she couldn't stop the grin that broke across her lips. She'd missed the unexpected fun Damon tended to bring to their friendship. When she hesitated, he pushed. If she saw red lights, all he seemed to see were green.

The bike hummed beneath her and their bodies grew flush as he took them through the main street, down past the lighthouse and along the sandy roads. When she'd lived here, they would cruise along the waterfront listening to music. But that had been in his ancient car, and they'd been kids. Now they were both grown, and she could feel the strength of him under her fingertips as the salty sea air mixed with his sweat. He was familiar, and yet she was getting to know him all over again. She was comfortable enough to trust him on this ride, but not to lay her cheek against his back.

When Damon pulled the bike into the parking lot of a beachside strip mall, Sam's mouth fell open. "Are we...?" Her smile overtook her words.

"This always used to cheer you up." He parked the bike, killed the engine and peeled off his helmet.

Sam gazed at the awning for Sandy's Kites and Pizza, a hole-in-the-wall they used to frequent on weekends. The sign had been repainted a blinding white, and a rainbow flag blew in the breeze. Maybe it had new owners? She wondered what else would be different.

"I get to choose first," she said.

"Fat chance," he replied. "Whoever's inside first gets to—"

But before he could finish the sentence, Sam took off at a sprint toward the entrance. Damon trailed at her heels, but she reached the door first. And while he could've accused her of cheating, he didn't, so she let out a courageous *whoop*.

The inside was so dim compared to the sunshine outside that Sam had to stand in the doorway and allow her eyes to adjust. There was the rental area at the front, with a large wall of hanging kites and a book with photos of more that they kept in the back. Then there was the pizza parlor toward the patio, where guests could order a pie and eat at a metal table in the sand. She hadn't remembered the arcade games against one wall, or the glittery disco ball above their heads.

"It feels…nicer or something?" she ventured.

"Less grungy, more modern." Damon pointed at a small table in the corner where a little girl in pigtails was ordering pizza off a touchscreen menu. "But they still serve beer. I'll get us drinks."

"And I will get our kites."

Sam picked an enormous green dragon kite with a lush fat tail, then she'd chosen an aggressively ugly cross-eyed octopus with eight long legs for Damon. She brought them out.

"I'm impressed you're not making me fly the one that looks like a goat-donkey," he said.

"You're enough of an ass without flying the kite version." She handed him the octopus.

His tongue poked out from the side of his mouth as he took the kite. "You almost make me want to take back the rosé I got you." He held the can out, and she deftly snagged it.

"What'd you get?" She popped open the lid.

"A bottle of my own beer." He held up the IPA with the signature Band Practice Brews label. "Don't judge me."

"You just make the jokes too easy sometimes." Sam unspooled the line of the kite, then carried it out into the sand

and waited for a strong breeze. The wind kicked up and she tossed the kite into the air, then ran ahead until it caught and soared up. Damon came next to her, his octopus a few feet from her kite. She carefully unspooled more line and let the dragon reach higher into the sky.

Closer to the water, Alligator Alice pumped her arms as she power-walked through the sand. She glanced up and gave a quick wave to Sam and Damon. Sam raised her glass of rosé in return.

"Alligator Alice never quits, does she?" Sam asked in a hushed tone.

"She'll outlive us all." Damon swerved his hands to adjust the kite as a breeze drifted through.

Sam slipped off her sandals and dug her toes into the sand. The sun burned hot and bright as it inched toward the water line, and scattered bonfires lit up the shore.

"How come we're the only adults doing this?" Sam eyed the younger kids flying kites nearby.

"We've always been the only cool ones," he said.

They locked eyes, and he gave her an easy smile. Eventually, he said, "So, you're really not seeing anyone, huh?"

She looked away, thinking of Marissa. "I'm not. But you are?"

"Casually, yeah," he said.

Her stomach tightened. Was she really jealous about this? Of course Damon was dating. He was in his thirties, owned his own business and was the walking definition of a glow-up. But still, she was indeed a bit jealous.

"The brewery keeps me pretty busy, though," he added.

"Exactly. I'm busy with work, too," she said. But was that just an excuse?

He changed the subject, thankfully. "What's the status with Pearl?"

Sam shook her head. "She thinks the best option is a retirement home. I just can't see her being happy in one of those. She's so independent."

"It's weird to see them get older, huh?"

"Yeah," Sam said. She couldn't shake one particular image of Pearl struggling to get up the three small stairs to their front door, and how frail she'd seemed. She was a mountain of a woman in a failing body. "I can't lose her," Sam said softly.

"She's still here," Damon tried to reassure her. "But I know what you mean. My mom had a breast cancer scare earlier this year."

"What? Oh, my God, Damon." If this had been high school, she would've been the first person he'd told about it; now she was likely the last.

"It's okay. She's okay. They caught it at stage one. She had a mastectomy and they got it all. But when that happened... I don't know. You never think about your parents' mortality until you have to. It's sort of impossible to wrap your head around. It scared me, though."

"I'm so sorry. I'm glad she's okay. I wish I'd known."

Damon gave her an uneasy look. "I thought about telling you, but we hadn't talked in years. Felt weird to reach out and tell you something like that after all this time."

"Can we just say it?" Sam asked.

He gave her a look, like he didn't know what she was talking about. So she filled in the blanks.

"I'm a shit friend," she said.

He chuckled. "I didn't say that."

"I know, because you're a good friend. But it's true. I'm a shit friend. And I'm sorry for not being there. Really, I am."

"Thanks." He licked his lips. "I did reach out, but you—"

"Changed my number and didn't tell you, yes, because—say it with me now—'Sam is a shit friend.'"

He wasn't going to say it, which just spoke to how much better of a person he was than her. But he gave a look like he wanted to move on. So she added, "You've been doing a lot for me the last few days. How about I try to make up for lost time by taking you out tomorrow?"

"I have work in the morning," he hedged.

"After work. I'll pick you up. It'll be a big surprise. Come on, we're old friends, right?" Why was she pushing this when he so clearly didn't want to? Maybe because she was wildly guilty about ditching him so long ago. And even though she knew that one day of her planning activities wouldn't fix things, the gesture could be a start.

"Okay, you can pick me up at the brewery when I finish up at two tomorrow." He offered a small smile, and that made a weight lift from her. "You know what song just popped into my head?"

Sam squinted and pressed her fingers into her temples, as if trying to mind read. "'MMMBop'?"

"Underrated anthem, but no. 'Ocean Avenue' by Yellowcard. Remember that summer we listened to it on a loop?"

"Yeah," Sam said with a knowing look. Unlike most emo songs, "Ocean Avenue" wasn't about a relationship. It was about a place, and a feeling and wanting to go back to a memory. "I told you the lyrics weren't romantic, but you wrongly said they were."

"Having nostalgia *is* romantic," Damon insisted. "It's the ability to never forget something you love."

He looked at her, and while he was talking about the lyrics, she also sensed that he might be talking about something else. About them, maybe.

Damon started to sing the song under his breath, breaking her thoughts. Sam playfully hip-checked him, and he lost his balance, which made his octopus flail. It jerked toward Sam's kite, and the lines tangled. The dragon dragged down the octopus and one of the long arms whipped Sam in the face. She shrieked as Damon tried to regain control, which is when a voice over the loudspeaker called out, "No drinking and flying!"

"That's a rule I should've known." Sam tipped her rosé can up and took a few long sips.

"You think he's talking to us, or those five-year-olds?" Damon pointed his beer bottle to a pair of twin girls slurping juice boxes while flying a small puffer-fish kite.

"It's anyone's guess," she said. "Just to be safe, we better head out."

The sun began to set, and the temperature was starting to drop. She'd need to get dinner going for Pearl. Sam reeled the kite back in and glanced over at Damon. He stared back, looking like he wanted to say something. But then thought better of it, and reeled his goofy octopus in, too.

As they drove home, soft light from the boutiques and homes along the road gave the night sky a warm glow. Maybe it was the rosé, but Sam wasn't nervous to be on the motorcycle this time. She wrapped herself tightly around Damon and let her head rest in between his shoulder blades. She was sleepy and happy nestled against him.

When Damon parked the bike, she unfurled herself, shook out her arms and handed over the helmet. She didn't want the night to end, but it was late and she knew he probably had to get back home…or to Marissa.

Her disappointment showed, because Damon leaned back in the motorcycle seat and considered her. "Do you want to talk about it?"

"It'll sound weird because you live here."

"I do." He held her helmet in his lap and his fingers tap-tap-tapped the top of it.

"I was just thinking that I feel sort of rooted here, in this moment, and this place… And with you," she said, surprising herself.

The words slipped out as easily as the wine had gone down, and now that she'd said them, she wasn't sure how to take them back. So she decided to plow forward and hope for the best.

"I've been going nonstop for the past few years, and I haven't been forced to come back to Tybee until now. Because of my mom, I just have a lot of mixed feelings when it comes to being here. But when I'm with you, I don't know... I feel a lot happier than I thought I would."

Sam shifted on her feet, suddenly aware she had no security blanket to grab and she'd just revealed way too much truth. She didn't want to feel this way. She didn't want to associate Tybee with comfort. Hadn't she worked hard enough to put it all behind her? But as she stood close to Damon, she couldn't help but acknowledge the fact that for the first time in a long time, she wanted to stay still.

Damon licked his bottom lip before he looked off toward the house.

"Do *you* want to talk about it?" Sam asked, mimicking his initial question.

Eventually, he looked back with an expression that was unmistakably torn. Like he was testing the words out in his head. "I feel good with you, too," he eventually said. "But I'll be honest, I'm sort of nervous about that. I know you'll leave in a few weeks. And then what? You'll probably just be gone again."

Any response she had caught in her throat. She'd spent so much time running from her feelings, but now that she was forced to stare them in the face, she wasn't sure what to do.

She quickly closed the gap between them and wrapped Damon in a hug. He didn't pull away, but also didn't initially hug her back, either. Eventually, he lightly wrapped her in his arms.

"I'm so sorry," Sam said into his shoulder. "I'm sorry that I am the way I am."

"I like you the way you are," he replied. "I just wish you'd come back sooner."

She didn't have a response to that. In hindsight, she wished she'd come back to see Damon, too. What would the harm have been, really? And if her alternate life was right, then maybe part of her would've flourished in Tybee. But she'd been young and selfish and didn't realize how addicting flying away from her problems could be, how freeing the sky was.

But by leaving, she hadn't given him any closure, and his damage was all her fault. She couldn't blame him for being disappointed with her. Sam's eyes welled, but she'd already done enough and didn't want to get his shirt wet. She took a deep breath in, then out, and pulled away, strategically wiping the tears with the back of her hand and averting her gaze. She turned and walked toward the house.

"Sam, wait," he started to say.

"See you tomorrow." She refused to look back, because she was scared that she'd come home too late to change their future together. Maybe what she'd seen in the alternate version of her life was exactly that: nostalgia for something she'd never get to have, and she'd never be able to forget, just like the "Ocean Avenue" song.

Damon didn't say anything back, but his engine revved as he peeled out of the driveaway.

She silently vowed to make the most of her time with him the next day. Because while she may not get another chance to truly be his, she could at least try to salvage a friendship, if that was still an option.

13

Sam worked well under pressure. Actually, she *thrived* when the heat was turned up, whether while flying or just trying to make it to a dinner on time. And luckily, she'd channeled that power-through energy into crafting a day with Damon that she hoped would say something along the lines of, *Sorry for being a bit of a fuck-up, but we can still have fun together, right?*

Right. She exhaled sharply. Either he would appreciate the fact that she'd stayed up well into the night finalizing details and adding thoughtful touches, or think she was pathetic. But she was parked out front of Band Practice Brews, sipping a latte and waiting for him to come out. So there was no turning back, really.

A little after two, the doors at the front opened, and Damon squinted against the light. Eventually, he found Sam and she waved a little too eagerly. She internally rolled her eyes as she unlocked the passenger door and tried to calm her breathing. She hadn't yet grown used to the way her heartbeat ticked up whenever she saw Damon. And as he walked to her car, in dark jeans and a long-sleeved shirt with a slight V-neck, she involuntarily licked her lips.

She had to stop doing that, because she and Damon were just *old friends*. While she desperately wanted his forgiveness so they could move forward, she also knew work was needed on her part. Which is why, when Damon opened the passenger-side door and settled into the seat, she handed him a brown paper bag.

"What's this?" he asked with a dubious expression as he peeled open the bag. He pulled out an apple, turkey jerky and a peanut butter sandwich wrapped in tinfoil. He looked at her like he'd just been given the saddest party favor bag.

"Well, let me explain." Sam turned to him. "We're going for a drive, and I wasn't sure if you'd eaten. So I made you lunch."

"But this is a brown bag lunch. Like, almost the exact lunch my mom used to give me in high school." As his words landed, she realized that maybe she could've just gotten him anything else. A bag of chips, a Happy Meal or something that didn't explicitly remind Damon of his mom.

"Cathy would never pack you something as vulgar as turkey jerky," she tried to joke, but was now worried she'd misstepped. She shifted the car into gear and drove out of the parking lot. "And besides, you need your wits about you for what I have planned."

"Which is?" Damon said as he took a bite of the apple. He handed Sam the sandwich, and she took a bite as she drove.

"Nice try, but I'm not going to spoil the surprise," she said through her chewing. Part of her didn't want to say where they were headed because Damon might try to jump out of the moving car, but the other part was just anxious about showing him this side of her. The route to their location was one she didn't need GPS for. She'd driven there in the early morning and late at night, through rain and fog and blinding sunshine. It was a drive she'd never done with Damon, or anyone else. But if someone was going to come with her, she realized that she wanted it to be him.

"I don't want you to feel like you need to do something special for me," Damon hedged. "You don't owe me anything."

Sam's grip on the wheel tightened. She didn't want their conversation to derail to drudging up past transgressions. This day was meant to be pure fun, like crowd surfing or scoring tickets to the 2005 Warped Tour, which, in Sam's opinion, had the best lineup—Fall Out Boy, My Chemical Romance and Relient K.

"I have another gift for you," Sam said to steer them back to happy thoughts.

"Is it a handwritten note reminding me to drink water?" he said, citing another Cathy-ism.

"If only I'd had that foresight, but no. It's better. I'm giving you control of what we listen to on the ride." She handed him a cable to connect his phone to the car. "I would never say you have better taste in music than me—we both know that would be a lie—but you're passionate about your playlists."

Damon cracked a side smile and opened his phone. After a few minutes of searching, he said, "For you, we're going to play the greatest hits of the woman you took all your style inspiration from." And then Avril Lavigne's "Sk8er Boi" began to blare through the speakers.

Sam had to bite her lip to stop from laughing. He was accurate about that. "You're such an ass," she said. But when she looked over, he smiled and the glint in his eye made her breath catch.

When they arrived in Savannah forty minutes later, Avril Lavigne's "What the Hell" was playing, and Sam was not entirely shocked about the fact that she still remembered each and every lyric.

"Speaking of what the hell," Damon said as they drove into the airport parking lot. "Where have you taken us, Sam-Sam?"

"You've never flown with me," she said. "This is where I went to flight school. Haven't flown one of these tiny Cessna planes in a minute, but they say it's like riding a bike."

Sam parked, unbuckled her seat belt and got out of the car. Damon frowned as he got out and shut the door. "When you say *tiny*, what are we talking about here?"

"Come on." Sam took his hand to lead him to the stairs and toward the flight school's airport tarmac. The way his palm fit just so against her own, and the feel of his rough skin… The fish in her stomach flipped again. She dropped his hand to remind herself that they were *just friends.* "I got on your motorcycle, now you get in my plane."

"I'm not sure that's a one-for-one comparison," Damon said, shaking out his own hand.

"You never got to see this, because we weren't hanging out as much when I was in flight school, and you were just starting to dabble in brewing your own beer. Our hours sort of conflicted."

Truthfully, she'd laser-focused herself on getting in as many flight hours as quickly as she could so she could leave Tybee faster. She and Damon still saw each other for Friday night movies, but they went from hanging out daily to only seeing each other once a week. Their relationship had shifted, and she'd chosen not to open up about flight school, because she began to pull back from Damon, knowing she'd need to find her own path without him.

"I've never brought anyone else here, actually," Sam acknowledged. "Not even Pearl."

Sam pushed through the glass doors to the flight school, where a reception desk and various placards dotted the walls. The office was set within an airplane hangar, certainly not the biggest one she'd ever seen, but when she'd first come here she'd stood in awe of the place.

Sam inhaled the scent of fuel and metal and the fresh air.

"I'm the only person you've brought here?" Damon asked.

Luckily, a booming voice called out to save her from answering. "Samantha Leto!"

Sam turned to see Captain Jonah Sires, her original teacher. The man who had mentored her to become the pilot she now was. "Captain," she said with a massive smile.

He opened his arms and she embraced him. He wore a black bomber jacket with the school's insignia. His once thinning hair was now completely gone, and his skin was weathered from all the time spent outside and in planes.

"When they told me you were coming, I almost didn't believe them," the captain said. "What do you want with one of our little guys when you've got a yacht of your own?"

"Was hoping to do a quick trip with my friend here." She nodded to Damon, who raised his hand in acknowledgment.

"Are we talking a discovery flight?" Captain Sires extended his hand to Damon, who shook it.

"Discovery flight?" Damon looked confused.

"No, captain," Sam answered. "Damon isn't interested in flight school. This is more of a joy ride."

"Ah, you want to show off, then? Some things never change." The captain gently elbowed her.

Sam smiled knowingly. She and Captain Sires had liked to egg each other on. Doing simple tricks in the air once she'd mastered the basics.

"Follow me," Captain Sires said, leading them farther into the hangar.

"Sam, this is small," Damon said under his breath as they approached the two-seater Cessna. "Smaller than your *tiny* led me to believe. It's more like miniature."

"Don't worry, this plane comes fully equipped with life vests. Worst-case scenario, we'll do a nosedive into the ocean and go for a swim." Sam gave him a wicked grin.

Like Damon said, the plane was small, smaller than she remembered. And when they were both seated next to each other, their shoulders pressed together from the lack of space. Sam helped Damon buckle in and gave him a pair of headphones to put over his head. "This will help us hear each other," she said as she put her own on.

"Testing, testing," she said.

He shook his head, and she leaned over to make sure the cords were connected. In doing so, though, her face was just in front of his. She could feel his hot breath across her cheek as she switched the power button on. She pulled back and heard his steady breaths coming in and out through the microphone. "Can you hear me now?" she asked again.

"Yeah," he said.

She stayed locked on him for a beat too long, nearly falling into the chocolate well of his eyes, then abruptly pulled back. She cleared her throat and refocused on the equipment. *Just friends.*

"We're cleared for takeoff," she said. "Let's kick the tires and light the fires."

"Could you *not* say *fire?*" Damon said, which made her laugh.

Damon had always been the thrill seeker growing up. And now here she was, scaring the hell out of him. She had to admit, something about that was kind of fun.

"Here we go," she said. As Sam brought the wheels off the runway, she chanced a glance at Damon, who bit his lip in either delight or horror.

Being in a smaller plane made the dynamics of the air more present, so they felt every bump and breeze. And with each bit of turbulence, Damon's arm pressed into her own, forcing them closer in the already tight space.

"I can't land us in Tybee, but I can fly over Band Practice Brews so you can say hello to Farrah," she said.

"Screw that," he said. "Show me something I don't see every day."

"You got it," Sam said. The flight to Tybee was twenty minutes, and she planned to circle around the island and then head back. She wasn't sure what she could show him that he hadn't already seen—he'd lived there his whole life—but she'd find something.

As they approached, the ocean came into view, along with the outline of the water where the sand met the waves. There were vast patches of untouched land, green and dotted with the occasional home. There was the top of Band Practice Brews with the neon guitar sign, and Pearl's house with the three Adirondack chairs. The world turned into her personal diorama.

But Damon could see this view in any plane, and she needed to show him something special. Something only she could. She searched the surface of the water, hoping to find her treasure. There was a disturbance just ahead of the nose of the plane, causing white seafoam to stir up and ripple.

"There." She pointed out to the horizon as she navigated them toward the movement.

"What am I looking for?" Damon asked.

She waited as the plane inched closer and the shape in the water became dark and more defined. And there it was: a right whale.

"Down there, do you see it?" She gestured for where Damon should look, and he did.

"Woah," he breathed out. "That's a whale, right?"

Sam laughed. "A right whale. They're endangered, but they swim through here to give birth."

"You always did remember everything from class."

Tybee wasn't a haven for whales, but the right whale was an endangered species they'd learned about as kids.

Sam was careful to keep the plane high enough so as not to disturb the mother whale. "Soon she'll have a baby with her," Sam said. For maybe the first time, she caught a glimpse of what Grandma Pearl saw when she looked out at the ocean—calm and serene and mesmerizing.

"It's beautiful up here," Damon said.

And Sam looked over at him, and while she was sure he was

talking about the landscape, he stared straight at her. "It is," she said, not breaking eye contact.

"I can see why you like flying so much."

She gave a soft smile. "Oh, yeah?"

"Yeah, it gets your heart pumping. You get a totally different perspective up here."

She swallowed in relief. She'd worried Damon wouldn't like this trip, but now it seemed like he was getting to see a part of her he hadn't before. And while her instincts were to hide in jokes, she found she didn't mind this more vulnerable option, either. "Ready to head back?"

He nodded, and she decided to please the adrenaline junkie in him by taking a sharp turn with the plane.

"Woo hoo!" she yelled.

"Sam!" he shouted, which made her laugh more.

"Don't worry, I know a bartender who can get you a beer when we land," she joked.

The engine buzzed beneath them, not unlike the feel of riding on his motorcycle. And they sat in the quiet purr for a stretch. "Thanks for showing me this," Damon said as the Savannah airport came into view. "I'm glad I got to share in your dream with you. You've figured out how to have everything you want."

Not everything. The thought popped into her head and she tried to ignore it. She had everything, didn't she? Just like Damon said, all of her wishes had come true.

"Prepare for landing," she said out of habit. And as Damon readjusted himself in the seat, she tried to focus on the descent instead of how much she liked being next to him.

14

"Look at my phone," Pearl said, shoving the phone toward Sam.

Sam was on her hands and knees, cleaning out the area under the kitchen sink—which was so loaded with unopened dish soap, various cleaners and packages of sponges that it was impossible to see the bottom. She sat back on her heels, tore off the cleaning gloves and grabbed the phone.

"What am I looking at?" Sam only saw the lock screen, with a photo of Sam and Pearl toasting champagne flutes on one of her trips to visit Sam in Paris.

"Something's wrong with my camera. I took photos of the sunrise. It's the wrong color."

"The wrong color?" Since Sam had been back, she'd fixed enough tech issues on Pearl's iPhone to qualify her for a spot on the Apple Genius team.

"Look." Pearl took the phone back, opened the screen and pulled up a photo of the neon orange sunrise splashed across the screen. "The sunrise this morning was pink, not orange."

Sam frowned. She missed the tiny Cessna with Damon. She'd

gone from being in flight to being on the ground, quite literally. "Grandma, I don't really know how to fix this."

"There must be some button." Pearl grimaced at the phone screen. An alert sounded. "Oh, my," she said.

"What now?" Sam said as she slipped the gloves back on.

"You remember Roberta Jones?"

Sam cleared her throat as she considered the name. "No."

"She was on my poker team. Anyway, she had a heart attack and died." Pearl shrugged, then walked off toward the fridge like she'd just reported the weather.

Pearl's friends were dying off one by one, which made Sam think about how long Pearl would have if she checked herself into a retirement home. She didn't want her grandma to just give up.

"Speaking of..." *death*, Sam thought, but instead said, "new life changes. I found a Realtor who specializes in downsize homes. You know, something smaller. A little bungalow might be nice. More manageable."

Pearl didn't say anything as she got a spoon, opened the lid of a yogurt and took a bite.

So Sam carried on trying to make the sell. "She said you'd get a great price for this place and could use that money to pay in cash for a smaller one."

"And are you going to help me look at these *more manageable* places?" Pearl waved the spoon in the air. "Fill out the paperwork? Apply for a loan? Cosign the mortgage when they see I don't have any income coming in?"

"Well, the Realtor—" Sam started again.

"I'm going to take a nap." Pearl held her hand up like a stop sign to end the conversation. And without even looking at Sam, she headed off to her bedroom, yogurt still in hand.

Sam pressed her palms into the floor and let her head fall between her arms. Pearl wasn't even willing to talk about alternative options. She couldn't force her grandma to do something, even if it would be better for her in the long run.

Yesterday she'd been flying high, quite literally, but now she
was grounded like a delayed flight and feeling helpless. She should
just keep cleaning out the kitchen, but she wanted to feel good
again. So she pulled her cell out of her back pocket and typed
to Damon.

Sam:

> Cleaning the kitchen today.
> Going to need a drink later.
> I'll swing by the bar?

She went to pocket the phone just as it pinged. She glanced at
the screen, but it wasn't Damon.

Rachel:

> Twenty minutes out. Bringing snacks.

Sam blew at a strand of hair that had escaped her ponytail.
Rachel was coming. She'd known this was happening, just not
so soon. Having her friend here would be good, though, because she still needed to sort out the CD player. Something she
couldn't talk to Damon or Pearl about.

Twenty minutes was a long time, actually. Long enough for
Sam to put the headphones on and listen to another song. After
all, how weird and embarrassing would it be if nothing happened? She hadn't touched the CD player in more than twenty-
four hours, and she had to make sure it still worked, in the sense
that it was a time machine to another reality.

When she found a comfy position on her bed and put the
player in her lap, she decided to text Rachel.

Sam:

> I'm doing something bad...

There. She'd admitted wrongdoing, and now she could do the bad thing.

The next song was queued up and waiting, so she put on the headphones. She hesitated, knowing that she *should* stop herself—but she couldn't, and her finger hit Play. Sam closed her eyes and the immediate drumbeat of Fall Out Boy's, "Dance, Dance" began.

A little smile crossed Sam's lips as she was sucked out of her reality and into a different one. Sam opened her eyes to Damon's family—Cathy, Humbe and Farrah—shouting for Damon and Alt-Sam to *smile, please!*

She peeled off the headphones and squinted to focus on Alt-Sam, who stood on the damp grass in a gunmetal black dress with poofy black tulle. Grandma Pearl stepped toward her and brushed something from her spaghetti straps while taking her aside.

It was jarring to see Pearl this young and strong. Her steps were sure. She wore contacts instead of bifocals. Even her hair was longer and thicker than it was now. This was the Pearl Sam saw whenever she thought of her grandma; the woman she knew didn't belong in a retirement home yet.

"I remember my prom night," Pearl said to Alt-Sam. "I took Owen O'Donnell's virginity. A night he'll never forget."

"Grandmahh," Alt-Sam whined.

But a small smile crossed Sam's lips. Prom night of 2009. She and Damon hadn't attended. They'd opted for a pizza and movie night, because prom would mean slow dances, and holding each other, and those were things that might make Sam reconsider kissing Damon. But in this version, they'd already kissed plenty. So Alt-Sam was going to prom with the guy of her dreams, just like every teen movie had promised her would happen. Sam should have been thrilled for her other self, but the pang in her stomach reminded her it was just one more experience she missed out on.

"I'm not saying you have to take Damon's virginity," Pearl clarified. "But I put some condoms in your clutch, just in case."

Alt-Sam quickly glanced at Damon, who was adjusting his long shiny black tie. "That's really, um, not necessary."

"I don't need to know. Just want to make sure I'm not a great-grandmother anytime soon." Pearl and Alt-Sam walked back toward the Rocha family. Though Pearl stiffened as a few piercing barks erupted from the house. Through the front window, a miniature pinscher—OG Rusty—growled at them.

Pearl discreetly growled back.

Damon approached Alt-Sam with a vibrant pink wrist corsage, and her teen self brightened.

"I picked out the corsage," Farrah said. She wore purple Soffe shorts that were rolled up a few times so they fell just below her butt.

"Really? Thanks, Farrah," Alt-Sam said, way too eager.

Damon held Alt-Sam's hand. "You look so beautiful," he said.

Alt-Sam deeply blushed through a smile. "And you are very handsome."

Farrah groaned. "Get a room."

"It's their prom night," Cathy said as she grabbed Farrah's shoulders in a gentle way. "Let them be happy."

And they were happy—Alt-Sam and Damon—as his thumb stroked the top of her hand, and she beamed at him through thick glittery eyeshadow.

"I have a surprise," Humbe said. Then, with a flourish, Humbe removed the tarp from the salmon-pink convertible Mustang parked in the driveway.

"Dad?" Damon asked, clearly stunned.

"It's a special night. Just drive safe." His dad threw the keys to Damon, but it was Alt-Sam who ended up catching them.

"Are you sure?" Damon asked again.

Humbe nodded and Damon gave Alt-Sam a smile so genuinely happy that she almost burst from the sight of it.

"This is so awesome, thank you, Mr. Rocha!" Alt-Sam gave Humbe a hug, then let out an excited squeal as she raced to the passenger's side, opened her door and slid in.

Humbe's car was the kind of precious that made everyone nervous to so much as breathe near the thing. He wiped it with baby diapers and an oil you could only buy from Italy. He loved that car more than he loved Damon, or so Damon claimed. So for his dad to lend it to them for the night was, well, monumental.

"Room for three?" Sam asked as she jumped over the door of the car and landed in the back. She had another minute and a half left on the song. She tried to categorize what she was seeing for her notes later: prom night, Humbe's car, Damon's happy family, Alt-Sam's bright eyes as she watched Damon in the driver's seat.

Damon put the key in, turned the car on and "Dance, Dance" blasted from the radio.

He flashed a wicked grin as he pulled out of the driveway with a stop and start. He waved apologetically to his dad. The Mustang was a stick shift, and despite Damon's lack of experience, the engine purred.

"I can't believe Humbe let you borrow the car." Alt-Sam touched the corsage absentmindedly.

"He must be in a really good mood or something." Damon's hands tightened on the wheel.

"Maybe he and Cathy…" Alt-Sam made an obscene hand gesture.

"Don't finish that sentence, please." Damon reached over for Alt-Sam's hand and she gave it to him.

"Speaking of…" Alt-Sam reached into her purse and pulled out a Trojan, flashing it at Damon. "Pearl gave me condoms."

"Really?" Damon laughed nervously. He revved the engine and Alt-Sam's grin widened.

"Damon!" Adult Sam squeaked out as he put his foot to the metal and the car kicked off like a racehorse leaving the gate.

Sam held on to the back of both of their headrests as the car sped down the residential street. A squirrel awkwardly darted out of the way as Alt-Sam let out a loud and satisfied "Wooooo!" and flung her arms over her head and up into the air.

Sam couldn't help but remember the day before, and the loud *whoop* she'd let out as she flew Damon through the sky. Now the steering wheel was in his hands, though.

"My dad may never let me drive his car again. We've got to make the most of it," Damon explained as he switched gears.

Damon's inner adrenaline junkie was coming out. The same way it had at the annual school fair, when he'd make them ride the Tilt-A-Whirl until they were borderline nauseated. But now that Sam flew for a living, she didn't crave the constant proximity to danger the way she sometimes had growing up. And to be honest, the speed and Damon's driving style made her queasy.

It didn't help that Damon kept looking over at Alt-Sam to gauge her reaction. Almost like he was doing all of this for her. Like he was trying to impress her.

"Damon." Alt-Sam's voice burst through her own thoughts and Sam blinked at the road ahead. Which is when she saw it—the stop sign that Damon was careening toward. A sedan started to move across the intersection. If Damon kept driving the way he was, he'd run right into the car.

Damon grinned at Alt-Sam, still unaware, and picked up speed.

"Damon! Stop!" Alt-Sam shouted.

There was twenty seconds left on the song. "Oh, God," was all Sam could say as she felt the car turn, and then saw the stop sign they were heading straight toward.

The final "Dance, Dance" lyrics raged from the radio. Sam wrapped her arms tightly around her body as she braced for impact.

15

Sam was back in her childhood bedroom. The song had ended, and so had the vision. But what happened to her and Damon in that car? Were they okay? Her fingers twitched as she looked down at the player. She'd planned to listen to a song and leave it at that. But there was no time to waste. She needed to know if they'd wrecked. She was about to hit Play when the doorbell ding-donged through the house.

Sam stood, looked out the window and spied Rachel's unmistakable perfect bob. *God dammit.*

The doorbell rang again and Sam knew she had to answer it. She couldn't just skip to the next song and leave Rachel waiting outside.

Sam hustled to the front door. She'd let Rachel in, explain the situation and then they could play the next song. Rachel would understand that.

But Rachel's smile immediately fell as Sam opened the front door. "What are you doing with that *thing*?" Her gaze landed at the CD player in Sam's hand.

Well, maybe she would *not* understand.

Rachel tossed her duffel bag into the hallway, then snatched the CD player from Sam. "We had an agreement."

"I had a bad day," Sam started to explain. "My grandma is sleeping, so keep your voice down." Rachel breezed past her, gave the room a quick once-over, then returned her focus to Sam.

"You have a bad day, you take a bath. You don't put on the headphones that are making you see things," Rachel said in a hushed tone. She held the player up and looked ready to smash it on the ground, which couldn't happen. Not until she knew the fate of Alt-Sam and Damon.

"Right," Sam said. "The thing is, in this last vision, it looks like maybe I died?" Sam waited for Rachel to react and, to her credit, she immediately did.

"I don't want to be dramatic," Rachel said.

"I know that." Sam shifted from one foot to the other, unsure of where this was headed.

"But you look like a person I'd cross the street to avoid," Rachel said. "I mean, you're in a sports bra and denim shorts and I think there's a tube of Dr. Pepper Lip Smacker stuck in your hair?"

Sam reached her hand up. She had put the lip balm into her ponytail to save for later. What was so wrong with that?

"So this is the bad thing you texted about?" Rachel held up the CD player but didn't wait for a response as she walked into the living room and plopped herself on the floral couch.

Sam sheepishly followed, suddenly feeling like a scolded teenager.

"And why are your hands moving like that?" Rachel gestured to Sam's hands, which fidgeted at her sides.

Sam tried to still them but found it hard. "I *need* that CD player back. Please."

Rachel pointedly sat on the player. "Here's what's going to happen. You are going to take a shower, wash your hair, blow-dry and put on actual clothes. I'm going to make you something to eat, and then I'm taking you to a bar where we are going to have a drink to calm down whatever the hell is going on here. Then and *only* then will we talk about this CD player."

"Rachel, I hear you, but I just need to listen to the next song." Sam approached her, but Rachel wiggled on the couch like a hen getting ready to roost.

"Shower. Hair. Clothes. Eat. Drink. Go do it," Rachel ordered.

Sam stared at Rachel, who stared back, but somehow harder. So Sam decided to do as she was told, because maybe if she looked reasonable, her friend would be, too.

But despite the blow-dried hair, high-waisted shorts and silk top, plus a bit of makeup for good measure, Rachel was not willing to discuss the CD player. In fact, she'd hidden the thing so Sam couldn't so much as try to grab for it.

"Eat," ordered Rachel as she pointed to a very sturdy turkey sandwich.

Sam ate.

When Rachel asked for a bar to put into their Lyft destination, Sam gave her the name of Band Practice Brews. Damon hadn't responded to her text, but she wanted to check and make sure he was still alive and the alt universe hadn't somehow seeped into this one.

As they walked through the entrance of the bar, there was Damon pouring out a pale ale from the tap. He looked up and, to Sam's relief, gave her a surprised smile.

She was so happy to see him standing there that she went behind the bar, wrapped him in a too-tight hug and held him.

"Woah, woah," he said as he hugged her back. "What was that for?"

"I'm just glad to see you." Sam pulled away, tucked hair behind her ear and looked up at him. Damon was okay. That was the only thing that mattered.

"Hi," Rachel said, breaking the moment. "I'm Rachel, Sam's best friend. And you are?"

"Damon," Sam and Damon said at the same time.

Rachel gave Sam a stern look that she deftly avoided by admiring the ceiling fan.

"I'm Sam's friend from high school," Damon added.

"Damon," Rachel said. "This is the guy you—"

"Yes," Sam quickly hissed.

Rachel's lips tightened. "Could we have two beers, please? I need something that pairs well with rage."

"Uh, sure thing." Damon wiped his hands on the towel slung over his shoulder.

Sam made her way back to Rachel, but Rachel squeezed her hand so tight Sam winced. "When I told you to bring us to a local bar, I didn't mean *his* bar."

Sam shook her hand free. "Then you should be more specific next time."

"You don't even drink beer," Rachel said, incredulous.

"I just needed to find the right kind."

Rachel glanced at Damon. "And you didn't tell me he was this hot."

Sam glanced at him, too. "Well, he is."

"Yes, he is." Rachel smacked her lips.

Damon slid two tall glasses across the bar top. One was the sour beer that Sam liked, and the other was a darker and richer color that smelled like honey. Rachel moved to take out her credit card. "What do we owe you?"

"Sam drinks on the house, and so do her friends."

"You might regret saying that," Rachel told Damon. "Okay, let's go. We need to talk," she said to Sam.

They sat in two Adirondack chairs on the back patio and watched seagulls run across the sand in search of discarded french fries. A flight of the bar's most popular beers was sent over a few minutes later, as well as a large pitcher of the sour beer for Sam.

"Are you mad at me?" Sam took a preemptive sip of her beer to ease the sting of the inevitable *yes*.

"Mad is not the emotion I'm feeling. Shocked? Yes." Rachel took a thoughtful exhale. "Well, actually, I take that back. I'm a little mad that you brought me to this bar where your ex-boyfriend works without any kind of warning."

"Not my—"

Rachel cut her off with a wave of her hand. "Yes, *not* your ex-boyfriend, so you keep saying. But then why were you all over him?"

Sam didn't have an answer for that. Well, she did, but Rachel wouldn't like it. "Do you want the truth?"

"My rental car smells like sour milk, but I still drove here to see you. Which is all to say that yes, I want you to tell me the truth."

Sam sat forward and decided to be honest, then. "When you came to my grandma's house, and I'd just finished listening to another song—don't roll your eyes, hear me out."

Rachel still rolled her eyes all the same.

"In the alternate version of my life—or whatever—Damon and I were going to the prom. He was driving us there, way too fast, and then…" Sam closed her eyes, remembering the sound of Alt-Sam screaming for Damon to stop. "I don't know. It seemed like we got in a car crash. I woke up before I could find out what happened."

Rachel carefully studied her. "That's why you looked like you'd been dragged through a swamp?"

"I wasn't that bad."

"Yeah, you were." Rachel bit her lip as she looked out. "Okay, so here's what I think. I think you are *not* losing it."

"Thank you."

"What you're saying *is* totally bonkers, but I'm going to just kind of go with this and believe you. Because the Sam I know doesn't make shit up. You hide things, apparently, but you don't just spin weird stories. I believe that when you listen to this CD, you are seeing things." Rachel leaned back into the chair and smoothed out her bob.

"Okay, so, now what?"

"I don't really know. I mean, the easiest solution would be to not listen to the CD, right?" She squinted at Sam.

But Sam couldn't *not* find out what happened to her and Damon on prom night—that just wasn't an option.

"Okay, I can tell you don't like that solution. But we've each had three beers, and I need to be sober to figure out alternate universes. So how about we finish up, call a Lyft home and figure out what to do in the morning. Does that sound fair?"

"Yes, okay." Sam gave her a weak smile. And then Rachel raised her glass, and Sam did, too, and they clinked them together in an understanding.

Then Damon stepped in front of them. Damon, with his thick hair and thicker legs, and those ridiculously gorgeous arms of his, sat in the empty chair next to Sam. "What are we cheersing to?"

"Alternate universes," Sam offered. Rachel raised an amused brow and took another sip from her beer.

The three of them sat there, searching for something to talk about. And Rachel found the perfect topic. "So, Damon, tell me, was Sam always so uptight?"

"I'm not uptight!" Sam was indignant. Since when did she sign up to be roasted?

"You have a weekly calendar and each hour is scheduled to the minute." Rachel then turned to Damon. "Do you know how hard that is to accomplish when you fly planes that are often delayed?"

"I write in pencil so I can move the items easily." Sam took a sip, then noticed Damon staring. "What?"

"Sam wasn't uptight in high school," Damon finally answered Rachel. "I mean, she was serious about tests and things like that, but the only thing we ever had planned were Friday pizza and movie nights."

"Mmm, pizza," Rachel said wistfully. "Pizza, though. I think we need some."

"Agreed," Sam said. The sandwich hadn't been enough for the amount of beer they'd already had.

"Let me go to the back and see if the kitchen is still open." Damon stood and took another sip of beer.

"No, I don't trust you to order pizza," Sam said and pushed herself up. "Your favorite topping is pineapple."

"Oh, Lord, no." Rachel shook her head. "Sam, please go make sure we get something edible."

Sam and Damon discovered that the kitchen was closed, but there was food to be had. They stood in the back, opening drawers and scavenging.

Damon opened a cabinet and pulled out a bulk bag of tortilla chips. He poured some onto a clean white plate. "I'm still thinking about that whale we saw."

Sam took a chip and chewed. "I just wanted to show you what I left Tybee for. I never meant to hurt you, and I'm sorry I didn't keep in touch."

He leaned across the chrome countertop and pointedly met her eyes. "We're allowed to make choices, and you made yours. That's not for me to judge."

Yes, she *had* made choices. All those years ago when she'd chosen not to kiss Damon, and then chose to leave Tybee. But now there was another universe where they had kissed, and ended up together, and they seemed sublimely happy.

She didn't want to lose Damon, not the way she'd lost him all those years ago. And maybe it was the three beers, the way his eyes sort of turned down and leveled her, or the way his biceps flexed with the pressure of the counter, but she moved toward him. She wanted to be close, hug him and let him know all was okay.

Only, when she went in for the hug, her face also awkwardly pressed against his cheek, her lips so close to his it could be a near-kiss. And there *was* a bit of a kiss as their lips briefly met. Damon quickly pulled back, and so did she.

"Oh, God." Sam's hand flew to her mouth to cover any evidence that she even had one. "I'm so sorry, that was an accident."

"You accidentally tried to kiss me?" Damon's brows furrowed.

"I was going to hug you, and then sort of fell on your mouth." Sam covered her own face with her hands.

"Don't worry about it," Damon eventually said. But when Sam looked up, his finger traced a line across his lips as he quickly turned away to scour for dip.

And Sam was glad he wasn't looking at her, because the truth was that she needed a moment to compose herself. Her lips still tingled from the warm feel of his mouth pressed against hers, and now that she knew what he tasted like, she wanted more of what she couldn't have.

16

Sam was quiet when they returned to the table. And so was Damon. He'd told her not to worry, but she had a hard time pretending like everything was fine and normal when it just wasn't.

She'd accidentally kissed Damon.

When their lips met, she'd wanted to deepen the kiss.

She could still taste the salt of him on her.

And Rachel must've noticed the shift, because as soon as they'd gotten into a Lyft, she decided to grill Sam about it.

"You kissed him?" Rachel said incredulously.

"Jesus, I said I fell onto his face." The seats of the Toyota Corolla were covered in a protective plastic that Sam squirmed against while buckling her seat belt.

Rachel leaned closer to Sam. "When you say you *fell on his face*, which part of you…?"

"Oh, my God, you and Pearl are truly disgusting." Sam looked out the window.

"Would you mind not taking the Lord's name in vain?" The Lyft driver, a pretty woman with a heart-shaped face and amazingly thick eyebrows, watched them in the rearview mirror, then pointed to the rosary hanging off it.

"Oh, sorry," Sam said.

"She doesn't want us taking the Lord's name in vain, but doesn't mind me asking if you sat on a guy's face?" Rachel said in a hushed tone.

"I'm all for women's pleasure!" the driver said with a smile. "But in my car, we follow the Ten Commandments, thank you very much."

Sam and Rachel eyed each other. After what was perhaps a too-long pause, Sam eventually said, "I didn't mean to kiss him, but I sort of tripped into him. It wasn't even a kiss, just a lip graze. So I don't think it counts. Right?"

Sam looked to Rachel for an answer, but her friend only slumped down in the seat. So she looked to the rearview mirror.

"Relationship advice will cost an extra tip and a five-star review," the Lyft driver said.

"He has a girlfriend, though, right?" Rachel asked.

"A casual something," Sam tried to say. Though, the mention of Marissa made Sam's stomach clench. She was a terrible person. The worst human being on the planet. She'd sort of kissed another woman's man. She was Julia Roberts in *My Best Friend's Wedding*, and she deserved to be always the bridesmaid, never the bride.

"Ohhh, girl," the driver said. "One of those Ten Commandments says, 'You shall not commit adultery.'"

"Yes, thank you for that." Sam avoided looking in the mirror and instead grabbed Rachel's hand. Rachel squeezed her palm, and Sam let her head rest on her best friend's shoulder as they drove down the dark road lit only by streetlamps and the starry sky.

"Don't think too much about this," Rachel said. "We'll talk more in the morning."

Sam didn't want to think any more about what had happened with her and Damon, because the whole situation was starting to feel too heavy. She let her eyes flutter shut and the blackness sink her into a deep sleep.

When Sam woke up, she was in her bed. The room was still dark, and the clock on her desk let her know that it was a little after three in the morning. She sat up and looked for Rachel but didn't see her anywhere. There was a bottle of water and two Advil pills on the desk, along with a note that read, "Eat me and drink me." Sam did both.

Her forehead was damp with sweat and she ran the back of her hand across it. She closed her eyes.

She was such a mess. Sam let out a sigh and stumbled into the hall. Her mom's bedroom door was cracked open, and when she pushed on it, Rachel was tucked into the queen bed, loudly snoring. Sam wouldn't wake her up.

The house was still, and Sam weighed what to do—go back to bed or get a snack—but just the thought of food made her stomach rumble. Sam wandered toward the kitchen. She opened the cupboard with the bread and bagels, but spied the tin of pralines tucked on the top shelf. She craved their salt and sweetness and instinctively reached for them. She pried open the lid, looked in and discovered where Rachel had hidden the CD player.

Sam stared at it, nestled amongst the candied pralines. She should *not* touch it. She should put the whole thing back into the cabinet, walk to her bedroom and go to sleep. She'd tell Rachel to find a new hiding spot in the morning, or they'd burn it, or…

Or she could just listen to the next song and see what happened to her and Damon. Just make sure they were okay. No one would need to know, not even Rachel. Sam would hit Play, see another vision and go to bed. This could be her little secret.

She quietly removed the CD player from the tin, shut the cupboard and tiptoed her way back to her room. She didn't bother turning the light on—not wanting to wake up Rachel. It would just be one song. She lay down on her bed in the dark, save for the purple lava lamp. She placed the headphones over her ears, opened and closed the CD player, and watched the screen light up. The next track was ready and Sam's finger hovered over the button.

If she died in the alternate universe, would she even have a vision? What if she'd lived, but not Damon?

There was no more guessing. No more wondering. She was ready to find out. Sam pressed Play, closed her eyes and tried to relax into the mattress.

A rough thrum of electric guitar and a strong drumbeat came in as The White Stripes's "Fell in Love With a Girl" began to play. The upbeat tune wasn't exactly matching her apprehension. It would be weird to have a song about the confusion between real love and lust playing at a funeral, right?

The now familiar *whoosh* transported her before she could think too much about that, and when Sam blinked her eyes open she was in her bedroom.

Oh, shit, was she not really having a vision? What did that mean? Her hands scrambled to take off the headphones. Warm, late-morning light poured in through the window and the clock read 11:30 a.m.—it'd been nighttime when she put the headphones on. What was happening?

Alt-Sam walked into the room with a towel clasped around her body. Her hair was wet and she detangled it with a paddle hairbrush. She favored her left side due to a large black medical boot on her opposite foot.

Adult Sam blinked. "Where's Damon?" There was a minute-thirty left on the song. She had to make sure he was okay.

Sam jumped off the bed and looked around the room for evidence of where Damon might be. She glanced at the desk—two tickets to the school carnival and an essay with a C+ at the top of the page.

"You got a C on this paper?" Sam tried to pick the paper up, but couldn't. "I loved French. I never got a C in my life."

But her line of thought was interrupted by a tapping at the window. Both Sams turned to see Damon gently rapping a knuckle against the glass. "Oh, thank God," Sam said. "Sorry, Lyft driver, wherever you are."

Alt-Sam grinned as she clenched the towel in one hand and unlocked the window with her other. Damon slid the window up and climbed in and over the desk, knocking off a cup of gel pens in the process.

"Be careful, Pearl will kill me if you break that lava lamp and it spills everywhere!" Alt-Sam said, almost giddy.

"Well, if she tells my parents I was here, my mom will kill me." But Damon, for his part, seemed energized by this fact, too.

Sam frowned. So they were sneaking around now? That seemed bad, even if it ignited something in their teen hormones.

"How's the foot?" Damon closed the window behind him.

"Boot-iful." Alt-Sam touched a finger to her temple. "But the double vision is still there."

"So, you're seeing two of me?" Damon tried to joke.

"Unfortunately, just one." Alt-Sam gave him a weak smile. "Usually hits first thing in the morning."

Damon reached for her hand and gently said, "Don't stress."

Alt-Sam pulled away and tugged at her wet hair. "If it doesn't go away, I can't go to flight school. They don't take people with serious vision issues."

"It'll go away," he insisted.

Alt-Sam softened as she reached up, grabbed Damon's face and kissed him. So effortless and natural, unlike the face falling Adult Sam had done.

"Ow," Damon said with a wince.

"Oh, no, still hurting?" Alt-Sam turned his head and drew a line along a Band-Aid across Damon's eyebrow.

"The stitches come out next week."

"Should I kiss it and make it all better?" she asked.

"I don't know," he said, licking his lips. "I had plans to do the kissing tonight." He lifted her up, put her on the bed and scratched his fingers down her thighs.

"Oh, okay!" Sam turned away and shielded her eyes. "I do not need to see this!"

Sam was relieved she and Damon were safe, but what did it mean if they were sneaking around? And Alt-Sam was having trouble with her vision? That was a serious problem. She'd have to analyze what was happening.

Her mind spun through the facts: *Sneaking around. Injured, but in love. Or lust? First ever C on an assignment.* The song was nearing the end, and Sam waited for the inevitable pull back to reality.

17

Sam was confused, honestly, about how she was supposed to interpret this latest vision. The playlist had been showing her how wonderful being with Damon was—and in some ways, Alt-Sam *still* seemed happy. But what about the car crash, her double vision and the C in a class she'd adored?

Her plan had been to listen to one song, but as the minutes passed by in the still quiet house, she realized that she could roll right into the next—no breaks, just Play. She wanted to make sure Sam's eyesight improved, and there was only one way to find out.

"Let's do this," Sam said to herself as "Read My Mind" by The Killers came through with its subtle synth opener. Damon and Sam had analyzed this song endlessly. It was both sad and upbeat, about longing for connection but also the desire for change. They'd agreed—one of the rare songs where their opinions matched—that this was an emotional and beautifully written piece of music, ultimately tapping into how hard being vulnerable and opening up to another person can be.

Sam didn't have a lot of time to rehash the lyrics, though, because when she landed, her eyes flew open at the intense bright light. She shielded her eyes with her hand as she realized that she was outside lying across two white plastic folding chairs.

Next to her was a guy with huge diamond earrings, a popped collar and bleached-blond hair tucked into a maroon cap with a tassel. His overly shiny aquamarine robe tipped her off to the fact that this was a high school graduation—*her* high school graduation. The ceremony hadn't started yet, but looked like it was about to. The high school a cappella group sang a version of "Read My Mind" on the outdoor stage, which was already filled with teachers in formal wear, and a podium waited for someone to step up and take the mic.

She'd be that someone. She hadn't loved high school but had used studying as a respite from the dark thoughts that threatened to consume her. And her valedictorian speech had been one she'd written as a kind of goodbye letter to Tybee. But she didn't see Alt-Sam seated onstage the way she'd been back then. She scanned the crowd for herself and Damon.

Sam snaked her way down the row of chairs—past soul patches, shell necklaces, enormous cargo shorts and carpenter jeans—and into the aisle. The space was a sea of teal, but as she searched, she spied a wave of red hair in the small crowd of people who hadn't taken a seat. Had she been the only redhead in high school? She couldn't quite remember as she stumbled toward the flame like a jittery moth.

As Sam approached, she immediately recognized her high school's college advisor, Mrs. Thrimble, deep in conversation with Alt-Sam. As valedictorian, Sam had been offered a full ride to several in-state schools. She could've accepted any of them. But the idea of pursuing a degree she had no interest in wasn't as appealing as the adults around her kept making it sound. Especially when all Sam wanted was to attend flight school, the one option she'd actually been excited for.

"You're one of the most curious and inquisitive students I've ever had the pleasure of helping," Mrs Thrimble told Alt-Sam.

"Thanks." Alt-Sam's cheeks burned pink under the attention. She pushed a pair of glasses up the bridge of her nose.

Glasses? Sam had always had perfect eyesight. But then, there had been the car accident, and the double vision. *Oh, no.*

"And you're smart. You could've been valedictorian if you'd really focused."

Could've been valedictorian?

Mrs. Thrimble continued, "While I understand that you don't want to go the traditional route of applying to colleges, I do hope you're taking my recommendation to look into some night classes at the community college?"

Just then, Damon's unmistakable spiky black hair came into view as he reached for Alt-Sam's hand and squeezed it. He gave her a warm smile, then acknowledged Mrs. Thrimble.

"Big day," he simply said.

"Yes, for me, too. I'm so proud of you both." She placed a hand on Alt-Sam's shoulder and squeezed. "Damon, are you getting the summer off before nursing school?"

"I might volunteer in the rehab center with my dad. Some of the nurses who took care of me after the car accident offered to show me the ropes."

He was becoming a nurse, like his dad? What about the brewery?

"That's excellent news," said Mrs. Thrimble. "I was just telling Sam she should get some classes in over the summer. See what interests her."

"I want to be a pilot." Alt-Sam tucked a thick chunk of hair behind her ear. "I just have to save up for this corrective surgery."

"Hopefully soon," Damon added, trying to sound encouraging.

"The woman who runs the flight school in Savannah told me that less than 5 percent of commercial pilots are female. So there's a real need for Sam." Mrs. Thrimble gave a small smile. "Hopefully, the surgery goes well."

The percentage of female pilots had increased, but only to 10 percent, so that statistic hadn't improved much over the last decade. The skies weren't friendly to women, but Sam had made it work for her.

"I should get to the stage, and you should both take your seats." Mrs. Thrimble glanced between them and then maneuvered away.

"Maybe Mrs. Thrimble is right. Night school could be rad." Damon turned to Alt-Sam, and she sort of shrugged him off.

"I know what I want. I don't need night school," Alt-Sam finally said.

Sam's fingers twitched. She guessed it was fine that Alt-Sam was taking a longer, more complicated route to becoming a pilot. But in this life, she wasn't valedictorian, *and* she didn't have an acceptance letter to flight school?

Damon wrapped an arm around her and she leaned her head on his shoulder. "Brandon Flowers is a genius," he said. "The way his lyrics so perfectly capture longing and love."

Alt-Sam playfully rolled her eyes. "You know it's about a breakup, right?"

"Sure, if you're a pessimist you might think that," Damon said. "But I happen to be an optimist. The relationship he's singing about turns around. I mean, the way he asks the question at the very end tells us he wants to give it another chance."

Alt-Sam shook her head. "He wants to be understood, but isn't," she insisted.

"Whatever you say." Damon gave her a kiss on the cheek. "I'm going to check on my parents. Save me a seat?"

Alt-Sam offered a small smile as he walked off, but once he was out of sight, that faded. Her gaze landed on her hands, which shook.

What the fuck? Sam wasn't sure why she was so mad, but this didn't seem right. What had been one of the most encouraging and life-changing moments for her now seemed completely mucked up.

Sam took a step toward her younger self, hoping to still her shaking hand but, as she did, the image in front of her dissolved like sand. The *whoosh* she'd felt coming in returned as she blinked back to the room.

She yanked the headphones off. Something had been very wrong with what she'd seen. How long was it going to take Alt-Sam to reach her pilot goals? Was losing focus and not being valedictorian all worth getting to be in a relationship with Damon?

Her Lisa Frank notebook was on the desk. She walked over and opened to the page where she'd been keeping a running list of songs. She added the latest tracks to see if they made any sense of the puzzle.

SAM AND DAMON'S MAGICAL PLAYLIST

Track One: "Bring Me to Life" by Evanescence. Otherworldly song about being understood by another human. Tybee High parking lot. Questionable amounts of eyeliner. Alt-Sam kisses Damon. Missing earring is found.

Track Two: "I Believe in a Thing Called Love" by The Darkness. A bop about being head over heels for someone. Alt-Sam and Damon are officially dating. Myles continues to disappoint. Marissa didn't have an awkward phase in high school. JanSport backpacks are timeless.

Track Three: "Supermassive Black Hole" by Muse. Inarguably the best song and movie scene pairing ever.

Damon and Alt-Sam make out during *Twilight* and get kicked out. One too many hickies.

Track Four: "Want You Bad" by The Offspring. A banger about a bad boy wanting to corrupt a good girl. Myles gets owned by Alt-Sam. Damon skips detention. Alt-Sam skips her extracurricular. I miss Dunkaroos.

Track Five: "Dance, Dance" by Fall Out Boy. A song about a guy meeting someone he likes at a school dance, and the angst of trying to desperately impress them. Damon tries to impress Alt-Sam and they get into A GODDAMN CAR CRASH. Soffe shorts. Condoms from Pearl. Looks like I never get to go to prom.

Track Six: "Fell In Love With a Girl" by The White Stripes. Can I ever hear this song again and not think about Alt-Sam and Damon sneaking around (??) and probably having sex (??). Alt-Sam's vision problems continue AND she's getting a C on an essay?

Track Seven: "Read My Mind" by The Killers, which is all about uncertainty. Makes sense, since in Alt-Sam's high school graduation, I'm not valedictorian and waiting on a surgery to get into flight school.

Sam tapped her gel pen against the paper. What did any of this mean? As she reread her notes, a little stone formed in her gut that refused to budge. She was having a hard time understanding how Alt-Sam could be so different from whom she'd been.

Or maybe her perfectionist self was being judgmental of Alt-Sam. After all, Alt-Sam *was* going to go to flight school, but by a different route. So what, she wasn't valedictorian? She was having reckless fun, which was something Sam had never done in high school.

Sam placed her head in her hands and closed her eyes. She was tired of overthinking everything. Maybe she just really needed to stop doing this—she should be asleep instead of trying to make sense of something that was impossible to understand. She tucked the CD player into a shelf of her desk, along with the notebook, and tried to let her mind go blank.

18

Rachel sat across from Sam at the kitchen table. She'd poured them both bowls of bran cereal—the only kind Pearl had—and they chewed in silence until Rachel finally said, "You're terrible at keeping secrets."

Sam stopped chewing. Rachel sat back in her chair, crossed her arms and looked triumphant. "Ask me how I know," Rachel added.

Sam swallowed the bite. "Fine, how do you know?"

"You start ruffling your hair and it turns into this kind of fuzzy chicken feather nest on your head. Your hair looks worse than I've ever seen it."

Sam reached a hand up to her hair, which was, admittedly, a bit ruffled.

"So let me ask." Rachel sat forward for this. "Is something bothering you?"

Sam resisted the urge to run her hands through her hair again. There were many things bothering her.

She'd kissed Damon.

She'd listened to more songs on the CD player.

She was a horrible person, in general.

"Well, I'm a homewrecker, for starters," Sam said with a sigh.

Rachel went to say something, then stopped herself, apparently thinking better of it. "I think drunkenly tripping into someone does not a homewrecker make."

"Why did I even get close to him at all?"

"Well, the beers probably didn't help but...do you have feelings for the guy?"

Sam fingered a piece of splintered wood at the edge of the table. "I don't know."

"I think you *do* know."

Sam sipped her coffee and brought the cup up far enough to hide her eyes.

"What else is wrong?" Rachel asked. Then she gasped. "Oh, shit, you found the CD player, didn't you?"

"What?" Sam didn't sound convincing, though. "No, I—"

"You found it, and you listened to another song." She shook her head. "I shouldn't have hidden it where there was sugar—that was my mistake, but I didn't have much time. And those massive headphones don't fit many places easily."

"Yes, okay?" Sam slammed a defeated fist down on the table. "I found the CD player and saw fucked-up visions and now it's messing with my head even more. And all I want is to listen to *another* song. Is it bad for me? Maybe. But if you saw a different version of your life, wouldn't you want to know how it all ends?"

Rachel blinked. Many times. "What happened in the visions?"

"Teenage hormones on blast and then my high school graduation and..." Sam didn't really want to believe that she wasn't valedictorian in her alternate life—something she was genuinely so proud of—but that was what she'd seen. "I don't know. I wasn't valedictorian. And maybe not going to flight school."

The dismayed expression on Rachel's face was impossible to miss. "Not valedictorian? No flight school?"

"Yeah," Sam said.

"So you and I never meet in your alternate life? That's so…"
Rachel bit the tip of a nail. "That's not right."

"I know. It's not."

Rachel drummed her fingers on the table and looked off.
She sighed deeply. "Well, you have to listen to another song."

Sam wasn't sure she'd heard correctly. "I do?"

"I'm heading back to Atlanta this afternoon for my next
flight. They're predicting a tropical storm, and I need to get
out of here before it hits. And I also need to know if you're my
best friend in this other life, or if I've found a different copilot."

"You better not have." The thought of that was genuinely
upsetting.

"Well, you never know, maybe the person I fly with doesn't
hog all the baked goods. Maybe *she* shares." Rachel raised a
brow, like a challenge.

"Fine. I'm getting the CD player." Sam pushed herself up
from the table, and Rachel closely followed.

Having someone else in the room as Sam put on her headphones was…different. Maybe a little unsettling, because what
if the Walkman only worked when she was alone? Sam wanted
to have a vision just to show Rachel that she wasn't lying. But
she also wondered if Rachel would see an alternate world if
she listened to a song.

"Do you want to try it?" Sam asked.

Rachel's mouth opened, then closed. "Do *you* want me to try it?"

Sam thought about the possibility that Rachel could listen
to a song, and nothing would happen. Which might confirm
that Sam needed to go seek help but, ultimately, wouldn't that
be better to know?

"I think you should, just to see." Sam held the player out to
Rachel, who hesitated before eventually taking it.

Rachel placed the player on her knees and adjusted the headphones to cover her ears. Then her finger tapped the play but-

ton. Then the back button. But the screen remained blank. "It's not working," she said.

Rachel took the headphones off, and Sam grabbed the player, more than a little concerned it had somehow broken. But when Sam had the player in her lap, it lit up. "Guess I fixed it," she said.

Sam handed the player back to Rachel and, as she did, the screen went black again.

"Oh, no." Rachel stilled. "Make that a *hell no*."

Rachel passed the CD player to Sam like a game of Hot Potato, and the screen once again lit up when Sam opened and closed the top.

Rachel stood and tripped over the purple blow-up chair Sam had found and resurrected. "Okay, that's freaky. It doesn't work for me, but works for you."

Sam looked up at her friend, whose expression had shifted to terrified. "They say we learn something new every day."

Rachel let out a massive breath. "So we're learning that evil forces are among us?"

Sam ran her fingertips over the player. She was no longer afraid, but she needed to understand why. "I think it's trying to tell me something."

Rachel sat in the blow-up chair, which squeaked as it met the fabric of her jeans. "Well, put on those headphones and figure out the mystery fast, because the sooner you do the sooner we can toss it into the ocean."

Sam sat on the floor and put the headphones on. Rachel scooted the blow-up chair over and grabbed her hand. "I'm going to be right here. I'll make sure nothing bad happens, okay?"

"Okay." Sam smiled to reassure her, but her stomach twisted into one enormous knot. Still, Sam closed her eyes, squeezed Rachel's hand and waited for the music to start as she hit the play button.

19

The comfort of holding Rachel's hand evaporated as The Fray's "Over My Head" started. Damon had loved this song about wanting so desperately to be understood. It was almost a ballad in the vocals, but undeniably an anthem in the power of the chorus.

When Sam opened her eyes, she was on someone's lawn and her bare thighs rubbed against long blades of grass. She took the headphones off, and almost immediately heard Damon's voice behind her.

"Keep your eyes closed."

He walked up the driveway and led a blindfolded Alt-Sam behind him and toward a slightly rundown beach shack.

As they reached the front, he pulled out a set of keys and unlocked the door. Sam pushed herself up from the lawn and closely followed behind them.

"Okay, ready?" Damon asked.

"I guess," Alt-Sam said nervously.

Damon undid the bandanna and her younger self blinked against the light. She took a pair of glasses out of her pocket and placed them on.

"Where are we?" Alt-Sam asked.

Good question.

"I know you want to get out of Pearl's place." Damon smiled. "So I got us one of our own."

"Our own place?" Alt-Sam looked skeptical. "How?"

They were moving in together? And Damon had rented them a house without so much as asking Alt-Sam if that's what she wanted? Well, that was certainly…bold, she supposed.

"Farrah knows a guy and he's giving us a deal," Damon explained. "I know it's rough around the edges, but I can paint the outside, and the yard is big enough for a garden. It'll be our own place. A project. And we won't live here forever, just while I go to school and you save up money. You can figure out what you want to do, ya know?"

"Flight school," Sam reminded herself. "She's going to flight school."

Alt-Sam smiled. "Okay."

"Okay?" Damon grabbed her shoulders and Alt-Sam nodded back. Then he kissed her, lifted her up by grabbing her ass and she wrapped her legs around his waist as he walked backward into the house.

Sam walked through the front door to find Damon peeling off Alt-Sam's shirt, while Alt-Sam got busy working on his belt buckle. "Now would be a good time to make a to-do list. A two-year plan. You want to focus. Flight school, leaving Tybee. The dream!"

But her shouts were not heard, as they never were, and Alt-Sam and Damon were nearly naked. When her teen self began to shimmy out of her jeans, a neatly folded piece of paper fell out of her pocket. Damon bent to pick it up.

"What's this?" he asked, a curious look on his face as he began to unfold it.

"Weren't you about to show me the bedroom?" Alt-Sam asked.

Damon grinned, then tossed the paper toward the door. "As you wish," he said and picked Alt-Sam up again.

Alt-Sam buried her face in his neck, but her eyes stayed on the paper near the door. As they disappeared into the bedroom, Adult Sam tried to grab the paper, but it stayed face-up on the floor as her hand passed through it. The song neared the end climax, just forty seconds left. The lyrics about the singer being over his head rang out like a plea.

Sam squatted next to the paper and saw the Planned Parenthood stamp at the top. She scanned the document. They were test results. A pregnancy test.

Alt-Sam was pregnant.

"No." Sam clawed at her neck. She couldn't be pregnant. Pregnant at eighteen, just like her mom had been. She had to stop this, whatever it was. She couldn't end up like Bonnie. She couldn't! She started toward the bedroom door, but as she did, her body was yanked abruptly back with a *whoosh*. Then there was blackness and the unmistakable release of air as she sagged against the carpeted floor.

"Sam." Rachel's voice was tense. "Are you okay? You look like you're about to be sick."

And she *was* going to be sick. She managed to launch herself up just in time to grab the garbage bin tucked under her desk. She retched and retched and continued to vomit until her throat burned.

There was Rachel's steady palm on her back, rubbing in slow and light circles. Sam's shoulders sank as she carefully sat in her desk chair. She let her head fall against the closed Lisa Frank notebook as she wiped her mouth.

Sam didn't like what she saw in the alternate version of her life. No flight school. Pregnant. Moving in with Damon. But maybe the alternate her *was* happy. She seemed mostly happy, didn't she? Was it a bad thing to want a house and to start a family with Damon?

No, Sam knew in her bones that those things were totally fine to want and to have. But then, if Alt-Sam *was* happy living with Damon, would that mean that Sam had made a mistake all those years ago? Would she have a family with Damon, and eventually be a pilot if she'd kissed him?

"What did you see?" Rachel gently asked.

Sam couldn't talk to Rachel about this because she wasn't even sure if she understood what she was feeling in that moment. "I'm sorry. I think the beer from last night finally caught up to me."

Rachel eyed her, dubious of her excuse.

"I don't know if I can talk about this one, not yet anyway." Sam rubbed her head.

Rachel nodded. "It was…a bit scary to watch, to be honest. You were totally still for a long time. And then you took in this big gasp of air. I tried to wake you, but you couldn't even hear me. I took off the headphones and everything."

Rachel waited for a response. But Sam hadn't known that was what happened to her, either, and she was almost in as much shock. No one could snap her out of the alternate life when she was in it? That was unsettling.

"Let me get you some water." Rachel moved to the door.

Being left alone gave Sam time to pore over the vision. She couldn't imagine juggling flight school and being a new mom. Would she just go to school once the baby was old enough?

Her stomach churned from the unknown. She needed a break from the CD player, and Damon, while she processed all of her new feelings. So she tucked the player into a drawer, determined not to touch it again.

20

"When's Damon coming over?" Pearl licked a blob of sugar from her lips.

The Leto women sat at the kitchen table with mugs of hot coffee and two enormous cinnamon rolls Sam had picked up from the farmers' market. She'd stopped there after Rachel left, in need of some comfort. Cinnamon rolls for lunch were perfectly reasonable.

"I'm not seeing him again." Sam watched as Alligator Alice power-walked down the beach.

"What happened?" Pearl asked, taking an enormous bite of cinnamon roll.

Sam wasn't going to tell Pearl everything, but she could give her a crumb. "I accidentally kissed him. It was a mistake."

Pearl sat back in her chair, and absentmindedly scratched a spot on her cast.

"Go ahead," Sam said. "Just say whatever it is you're thinking."

"It sounds like you've got feelings for him. Not that I can blame you. The man has the thighs of a rodeo cowboy."

"Grandma." Sam wished Pearl could keep it in her pants sometimes.

"I slept with a cowboy once on a trip to Dallas." Pearl looked off, as if remembering. "It's true what they say. Everything's bigger in Texas."

Sam was learning way too much about her grandma's sex life. As if coming to Tybee had not only caused some magic portal to open, but also allowed Pearl to finally reveal exactly how grand of a life she'd once led.

"So, do you have feelings for him?" Pearl tried again.

That question made Sam tired. Of course she had feelings for Damon, but how could she know if what she felt was genuine, or just a projection of the possible life she'd never been able to lead?

"Of course I do," Sam said. "Like you said, he has the thighs of a rodeo cowboy."

Pearl gave her a look like the joke had been funnier when she said it—which was true.

"I can't have feelings for Damon. We're way too different."

"Yeah, but ever since you've come home you seem more relaxed. Whenever I usually see you, you're so…"

"So what?"

Pearl sat back in the chair and cleared her throat, as if preparing for a long speech. "You've changed a lot in the last few years. Not necessarily for worse, or anything, but when I see you with Damon, you're all lit up again, the way you used to be when you were around him."

Sam was done fighting against the memory of who she was and the suggestion that she was somehow a different person entirely. She wasn't different at all—she was still Sam—she'd just left Tybee.

"I don't want to talk about Damon anymore," Sam insisted.

"Suit yourself." Pearl found a dribble of icing on her plate and scooped it up with her finger.

"Let's make a to-do list." Sam pulled her phone out and opened the Notes app. She wasn't different. She'd always been motivated and organized, and she could prove it. "Which room should I clean next? We've got yours—"

"That's a no," Pearl cut her off. "I need to be here for that, but Jessie and I are trying a new lemon rotisserie chicken at the Handy Market."

"And that's an all-day endeavor?" Sam asked.

"Krissy Conway choked to death on a chicken bone, you know. It takes time to eat a chicken safely." Pearl sipped her coffee.

"Mmm," Sam eventually said. "There's the living room, linen closet—"

"Save those for last," Pearl said.

Sam blew out a breath through her lips. "Mom's room, then."

Pearl started to say something, then stopped herself. "Bonnie stayed away for all those years. It was silly of me to reach out. It's for the best she never came back."

Sam reached for Pearl's hand and intertwined their fingers. They both knew that Bonnie's room was one of those places they had a hard time acknowledging. Sam had always assumed her mom would find her way back. Maybe Pearl had, too. Neither of them talked about it much.

But cleaning out the room would be good. Healthy. Help Sam and Pearl move on. Or at least that was what she told herself as she stood from the table, cleared the plates and headed down the hall to open her mom's bedroom door.

Rachel had stripped off the sheets before she left and folded them neatly at the end of the queen-size bed. But other than that small change, Bonnie's room remained untouched. The textured walls were sponge-painted red, and a giant metal celestial moon hung on the wall. The furniture was a heavy matching light wood, with a giant TV armoire against one wall. A clear beaded curtain led to the en suite bathroom, and the curtains against the picture window matched the bed skirt—a museum of nineties interior design so well preserved it could be submitted to the Smithsonian.

Sam had spent so much time in this room as a kid—crawling into bed with her mom when she'd had a nightmare, then crawling into her mom's empty bed when Bonnie left. Sam used to walk into the closet, close the door and bring the old clothes to her nose, just to remember what her mom smelled like.

Sam opened the top drawer of the armoire, which still had some neatly folded cotton T-shirts, like Bonnie had never left. While there was a faint scent of the lemony citrus perfume her mom liked to wear, it was almost completely gone, some phantom memory Sam had.

She would treat this as a job—something with steps to follow—rather than wiping away any trace of her mom. Starting with removing all of the items from the drawers. So she carefully took out each flannel, tie-dyed and acid-washed item before tossing them into an open trash bag. She'd emptied out the drawers and filled up two garbage bags with clothes, scrunchies, knee-high socks and vests. She was great at her new job, as it turned out.

But when she opened the third and last drawer and lifted out a moth-eaten quilt, she discovered a small pile of neatly folded cards. They were the handmade kind Sam had given her mom every Mother's Day. The first was from when Sam was just two years old, the date on the card—written in Grandma Pearl's handwriting—was 1993, and a series of squiggly lines covered the white paper, which had been cut into a heart. The last card, the one on the very top, was from 2005, the year her mom had left. On the front, Sam had drawn a portrait of Bonnie, and even captured the square-tipped French manicure her mom had loved getting. She opened the card and read the message.

Dear Mama,
Happy Mother's Day! You're the best mama ever, and I'm so lucky to be your daughter. I love you. Thank you for being here with me.
Love, Sam

Sam licked her bottom lip as her eyes welled with tears. It was pointless to cry over this card, and she wasn't even totally sure why she was so upset. But she was. Her mom had left these here, along with Sam. The tears rolled down her face and smattered her shirt until her top clung to her chest.

She didn't know how long she sat there, looking at the card and crying, but eventually the tears dried up; she had no more left. She'd planned to bring the bags to the front door so she could load them into the car and donate them, but she suddenly felt very tired, like her head was floating in jelly. If she didn't lie down soon, she'd fall down. So Sam crawled onto the bed, brought the card to her chest, curled up on the bare mattress and closed her eyes.

When Sam woke up, the sound of the overhead ceiling fan churning in a slow and steady loop greeted her. The room was pitch-black, save for a small seashell-shaped night-light. A blanket had been carefully draped over her, and she figured that Pearl had managed to cover her up while she slept. The digital clock on her mother's dresser blinked back that it was a little after 10 p.m., which meant Sam had slept all day. It was nighttime in Tybee, but early morning in Paris.

She missed her bed with the fluffy comforter she'd bought from a French flea market, and the gray morning light that streamed through her one enormous window. She missed the copper teakettle she used to make slow-drip coffee, and the smell of fresh baguettes from the bistro at the bottom of her building.

Instead of waking up rested in Paris, Sam was hungry and groggy in Tybee. She stretched her legs and arms until her fingers and toes reached the ends of the mattress. When she stood up, she was wobbly from all of the sleep. Still, she managed to make her way out of the room and into the hall. She paused at Pearl's bedroom door, peeked through the crack and heard the unmistakable sound of her rainstorm white noise machine.

Sam switched on the overhead light in the kitchen and rummaged through the fridge. She pulled out a pitcher of sweet tea and the leftover rotisserie chicken Grandma Pearl must've brought home. She sat at the table and ate cold chicken and drank down two tall glasses of tea, focused on nothing but feeding herself.

When she was done, she wiped her greasy fingers on the front of the newspaper Pearl had left out, smearing the headline about an approaching tropical storm. She listened as the waves from the ocean sloshed onto the shore.

This was the first day she hadn't seen Damon. They hadn't even spoken to each other. Sam unplugged her phone from the charger, but there were no new messages from him, just a text from Rachel to let Sam know she'd made it home to her wife, and that the turkey sandwich from a new kiosk in Terminal A was worth the trip. Sam gave the text a thumbs-up.

Isolating herself from Damon was likely for the best. This way there would be no more distractions, just packing and leaving. She could get back to the life where she was a respected pilot, where she didn't have to think about high school. Pearl would be taken care of, and Sam would find ways for them to see each other without having to step foot in Tybee again.

Sam put the remaining chicken and pitcher of tea back in the fridge, flipped the light off and walked back to her room. The glow from the lava lamp spilled into the hallway, like a beacon. She was ready to get back into bed.

When she pushed her bedroom door open, it wasn't just the lava lamp that glowed, though. There was an eerie light from her desk drawer, too. When she opened the drawer, her eyes met the silver of the CD player. She took a step back.

So now it was just running by itself?

Sam shouldn't touch it. But then again, the thing glowed up and begged her. Her hand didn't wait for Sam to decide, apparently, because she reached right for it.

21

Sam immediately recognized the rapid strumming of the electric guitar, followed by the steady drumbeat, as "Maps" by the Yeah Yeah Yeahs began. The lead singer's emo bangs had inspired Sam to make the mistake of cutting her own. Plus, Sam had loved this song written by Karen O about her then boyfriend, Angus Andrew. She'd figured out before Damon that "Maps" was an acronym for My Angus Please Stay, and that the lyrics pleaded with Angus not to leave.

Sam took in a deep breath and closed her eyes as Karen O's sweet voice sang to her. Like a *whoosh* of air leaving her lungs, her whole body lightened. The unmistakable give of powdery sand made Sam's eyes shoot open as she clocked that she was on the beach. She pushed herself up to standing and glanced around at the long stretch of tumbling waves.

The light was soft and warm, the way it changed as the sun dipped closer to the horizon. A strong sea breeze blew hair into her mouth and she coughed. She tugged the headphones off and threw them, along with the player, into the sand.

She caught a glimpse of a figure marching near the shore,

and when she took a closer look, she recognized Alligator Alice pumping her arms in a red-and-white-striped Adidas tracksuit.

"Hey, you sure you're okay?" Damon's voice came from behind Sam.

She turned as Damon stepped off the nearby boardwalk with Alt-Sam at his side. Damon was in dark blue nursing scrubs with a low ponytail and slightly longer hair. Not a terrible look for him, but a *choice.*

Alt-Sam wore a rather questionable snake-print halter dress. Her long red hair was swept up into a bun, with two tendrils styled around her face, framing the matching red-stained lip.

"Remember what the doctor said? After a miscarriage, they recommend you rest for at least a week," Damon tried again.

A miscarriage?

Alt-Sam's expression darkened as she glanced away from Damon. "I remember."

Sam's heart sank. She hadn't wanted Alt-Sam to be a teen mom, but a miscarriage was…awful, she imagined. She'd known women who'd been through the same thing—Rachel's wife had tried to conceive with IVF for the past year, and they'd had one miscarriage that was so traumatic they'd put their fertility journey on hold. How was her eighteen-year-old self handling all this?

Not well, judging by the tension between them.

"Okay," Damon eventually said. "We can go home. Just say the word."

Alt-Sam kicked a spot in the sand and glowered. Damon looked like he was about to hug her, but that was when Farrah's voice broke through.

"Time to party!" Farrah tucked a loose strand of hair into her newsboy cap as she bounded onto the beach. Her airbrushed tee read, "Farrah," in a swarm of puffy clouds, and the gold belly chain hit just above the start of her gaucho pants.

Farrah opened her small shoulder bag and took out a flask.

"Happy first day of nursing school, little bro!" She handed Damon the flask. He glanced at Alt-Sam before taking it.

"Sorry, but I couldn't fit a full bottle in this small-ass purse." Farrah shrugged.

"Is this one of your moonshine brews?" he playfully asked.

Farrah pulled out another flask and shook it at Alt-Sam. "*This* is a delicious pale ale that I've been perfecting. How about you, Sam-Sam?"

Alt-Sam shrugged, slightly brightening under Farrah's gaze. "Yeah, let's celebrate."

Damon seemed to finally exhale at the change, like he'd been holding his breath to see what she'd do before he decided how to proceed. He opened the flask and sipped.

"What do you think?" Farrah looked at him expectantly.

"Not bad." He took another sip. "Are you still entering the local brews competition?"

"Well, I *thought* we'd be entering together. But now that you're deep in nesting mode, I'm not sure."

Hmm. That was interesting. So Farrah was striking out on her own, and Damon wasn't involved in the brewery at all?

"I keep telling him to work with you." Alt-Sam sipped from the flask and crossed her arms. "He faints at the sight of blood."

Damon shot her a hurt look, but Alt-Sam tipped the flask up and downed the rest of it.

"You know I never liked school. I'm not smart, like you," Damon said. "And we need the money, remember?"

Alt-Sam dug her toes into the sand. "I can save for the surgery by myself."

"Wow, you both are clearly in the middle of *something*." Farrah playfully rolled her eyes at them. "When you're done with whatever this is, come over. I've got real bottles we can drink. Congrats, Damon."

Farrah gave Damon a kiss on the cheek, and he watched her leave. When she was out of sight, he turned to Alt-Sam.

Alt-Sam spoke before he could. "I don't want to fight."

"Then let's not," Damon gently said. He wrapped Alt-Sam in his arms. "I'm sorry, Sam-Sam. I know you don't want to talk about it, but I'm sad, too."

"You're right. I don't want to talk about that." Alt-Sam didn't meet his eyes. "And I'm sorry I've been…moody, lately. I've just been dealing with a lot."

"I know," he gently said.

"I have something for you." Alt-Sam reached into the top of her halter and pulled two tickets out from her bra.

Classy.

"Ta-da!" Alt-Sam said with a smile.

Damon took the tickets. "You got—you got us Blink-182 tickets?"

Alt-Sam's smile widened. "Had to get them from a guy off Craigslist. I knew you wanted to see them. A first-day gift—and, not to get you even more stoked, but I heard they're bringing on The All-American Rejects, Asher Roth and Fall Out Boy, too."

A small frown creased Damon's face. "Can we afford this?"

Alt-Sam scratched a spot on her leg. "I dipped into my flight school fund. I think we need some fun."

"Sam," Damon started to say.

"By the time I get the surgery and recover from that, I'll have saved up enough again." Alt-Sam waved off his concern. "Don't worry, I thought this through."

"But the concert's tonight in Atlanta…"

"Oh, right, that." Alt-Sam put her hands on her hips and dramatically tapped her foot. Then she pulled out a BlackBerry cell phone covered in stickers and charms. "It's the weirdest thing, but I gassed up the car, got a bunch of terrible junk food for the drive—including those awful beef jerky sticks you love—and if we leave now we should make it in time."

Damon gave her a close-lipped smile, like he was fighting back a grin so wide it would hurt his face. "I love you," he said.

"But you're gonna love me even more when you hear 'What's My Age Again?' live." Alt-Sam smiled.

"I might black out if they play 'All the Small Things.'" Damon smiled back.

"Don't worry. My boyfriend's a nurse. He'll help." Alt-Sam wrapped her hand behind Damon's head and pulled him down for a kiss. They were in love. They loved each other.

Sam had never been in love before, but in this version of her life, she was. Was being in love worth more than what she had in the real world? As their lips were about to meet, Sam blinked and found herself back in her room.

What she'd just seen were two people going through difficult times, but getting through them together. It wasn't the happiest she'd ever seen them, but they were dealing with real-life issues. And they had each other. That was what couples did, she supposed.

Sam went to her desk, opened her notebook and wrote down the new track in the playlist.

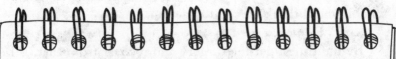

SAM AND DAMON'S MAGICAL PLAYLIST

Track One: "Bring Me to Life" by Evanescence. Otherworldly song about being understood by another human. Tybee High parking lot. Questionable amounts of eyeliner. Alt-Sam kisses Damon. Missing earring is found.

Track Two: "I Believe in a Thing Called Love" by The Darkness. A bop about being head over heels for some-

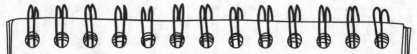

one. Alt-Sam and Damon are officially dating. Myles continues to disappoint. Marissa didn't have an awkward phase in high school. JanSport backpacks are timeless.

Track Three: "Supermassive Black Hole" by Muse. Inarguably the best song and movie scene pairing ever. Damon and Alt-Sam make out during *Twilight* and get kicked out. One too many hickies.

Track Four: "Want You Bad" by The Offspring. A banger about a bad boy wanting to corrupt a good girl. Myles gets owned by Alt-Sam. Damon skips detention. Alt-Sam skips her extracurricular. I miss Dunkaroos.

Track Five: "Dance, Dance" by Fall Out Boy. A song about a guy meeting someone he likes at a school dance, and the angst of trying to desperately impress them. Damon tries to impress Alt-Sam and they get into A GODDAMN CAR CRASH. Soffe shorts. Condoms from Pearl. Looks like I never get to go to prom.

Track Six: "Fell In Love With a Girl" by The White Stripes. Can I ever hear this song again and not think about Alt-Sam and Damon sneaking around (??) and probably having sex (??). Alt-Sam's vision problems continue AND she's getting a C on an essay?

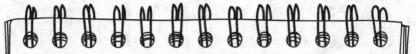

Track Seven: "Read My Mind" by The Killers, which is all about uncertainty. Makes sense, since in Alt-Sam's high school graduation, I'm not valedictorian and waiting on a surgery to get into flight school.

Track Eight: "Over My Head" by The Fray. Written about a fight, where one person was totally out of their depth. Alt-Sam is pregnant and moving in with Damon. Maybe they're not ready to be parents?

Track Nine: "Maps" by the Yeah Yeah Yeahs. Damon's starting nursing school and not a brewery. Wanting someone to stay is the theme of the song, and maybe Damon wants Alt-Sam to know he'll stay by her side and through the miscarriage?

Sam absentmindedly doodled in the notebook as she waded through the songs. Damon had been a rock for Sam when her mom left, and he was being a rock for Alt-Sam through miscarriage and life-changing surgery. If anything, all signs pointed to the fact that Damon was *the* guy no matter what happened.

And maybe that realization should've comforted her, but all she felt was unsettled by what she'd seen.

22

There was always a calm before the storm. The calm was when the waves slowed to a lapping, the breeze dulled and the sky cleared of all clouds. If you didn't know that somewhere in the ocean violence was brewing, it would be a perfect beach day. But there was also a kind of eeriness to the lull. Because the animals around Tybee sensed the shift more than the people themselves. Even the caw of the gulls became muffled, almost like they were preemptively going into hiding.

While hurricanes occasionally happened in Tybee, they usually turned long before it was ever a concern for Grandma Pearl. But this one—Tropical Storm Courtney, which had just been upgraded to Hurricane Courtney—appeared to be heading straight for them.

"It'll turn," Pearl chided as Sam took the planks of plywood out from the storage space in the garage. The wood was specifically cut and fitted to be pressed against each window and nailed tightly to the frame to prevent strong winds from knocking something through the glass.

"Maybe the storm will pass," Sam agreed. "But if it doesn't, we'll have the hurricane panels up just in case."

On top of being necessary, the storm prep was also provid-
ing a welcome excuse to avoid the CD player. The thought
of seeing another vision wasn't as appealing after the last one.

"Aren't those a little heavy?" Pearl waved her cast in the general direction of the planks Sam had carefully brought out and
stacked neatly in the driveway.

"You and Mom used to carry them, didn't you?" Sam huffed
as she lugged a panel out. The panels *were* heavy, but who else
was there to handle them? Each panel was the same height as
her, maybe a touch taller. She was just barely able to grip each
side, and the stretch of it already had her arms aching. She didn't
hesitate to put the plank down on top of the pile.

"We did," Pearl conceded. "But there were two of us, and
your mom and I are short, so our centers of gravity are closer
to the ground. You, on the other hand…"

Sam placed her hands defiantly on her hips but, as she did,
a rather loud and fat bumblebee flew in front of her face. She
squealed and frantically waved her hands to swat it away, tripping over the pile of wood in the process.

"Mmm-hmm," Pearl said. "Exactly."

Sam frowned as Pearl turned on her heel and walked back
inside. Pearl wasn't wrong—this was a two-person job, but Sam
only had herself. So she would just have to do.

What she couldn't help but wonder, though, was why whoever built this house decided that a huge bay window would
be appropriate? Couldn't it be one of those homes with several
small windows versus one big one? Because the massive one
required an equally huge piece of wood that was both taller
and substantially wider than Sam. She managed to nail up one
corner but got splinters in both of her hands. So she had to use
pot holders to hoist up the other side; gloves were apparently
not something the Leto women owned.

When she'd finished the bay window, Sam decided to lie in
the overgrown blades of grass and close her eyes. The stagnant
air and the heat from the unobstructed sun made her drowsy.

She could nap. That way, when the hurricane *did* come, she'd die in her sleep. She let her body go limp, wove her fingers into the grass and took luxuriously long and deep breaths. This was how people who did hot yoga must feel; so physically depleted that they mistook delirium for euphoria. Because Sam was, at least for the moment, unencumbered.

That is, until her moment of peace was interrupted by the low rumble of a motorcycle. Motorcycles made Sam think of Damon. But Damon wasn't the only person on Tybee who owned one. Plenty of people did. So she kept her eyes closed and tried to refocus.

Grass.

Sun.

Not Damon.

The engine grew louder, like the motorcycle was cruising down her street. Still, that could be anyone. It was when the engine stopped in front of her house that she realized what was happening and attempted to become one with the lawn, because she knew in her bones that Damon had just arrived.

She tried her best *not* to breathe so as to avoid being detected, but her tactic didn't appear to work, as Damon's heavy boots clomped across the driveway.

"Sam." His tone was concerned.

She opened one eye and there was Damon, blocking the sun in a way that also surrounded him in a halo of light, like some hot biker angel.

"Damon." She tried to sound casual, like this had been her plan all along.

"I see you're lying on the ground."

"You see correctly," she replied. She could do this deflection thing all day. And besides, she didn't owe him an explanation or anything, really.

"I asked him to come help. So sue me," Pearl shouted from the porch. Sam tried to express how angry she was through her eyes, but Grandma Pearl stood down to no one. "I'm going to take a nap, which is all I'm good for these days. You two have fun."

Pearl waved to Damon just as he raked a hand through his hair, like he was in a goddamn shampoo commercial. Like he didn't realize the move made Sam suck in a deep breath.

"Pearl said you were trying to use a hammer." Damon put his hands on his hips. "She sounded pretty worried about it."

"I've used a hammer before." Sam finally sat up. Damon extended his hand and she took it. When she stood, they were face-to-face and way too close. She could smell the burn of the road on him, nearly feel the scratch of his shadow of a beard across her cheek. She took a step back and unhooked the hammer from the belt loop of her jean shorts. Then she waved it at him, like that was a normal thing someone did with a hammer.

"Yes, you're very skilled." Damon peeled off his leather jacket, which revealed his short-sleeved fitted shirt and the defined line of his triceps. He draped the jacket over the back of his bike. "Let me help you prep for the storm. We both know this is a two-person job."

She did know that, but she really wished her grandma had called anyone else to be there with her.

"Okay," Sam said, resigned. "You'll be my other person."

They didn't have to talk about their non-kiss. She could just accept the help, get the house safe and then Damon would leave. Simple and clean. Sam pointed toward the stack of boards. He grabbed one end and she the other. As they maneuvered the board to the side of the house, she couldn't help but remember the way Damon had looked at Alt-Sam in her most recent vision—so caring, like she could do no wrong. Meanwhile, this Damon couldn't even meet her eyes.

"How was your day?" Sam decided that if they were going to be stuck together, small talk was a safe lane. She gestured for Damon to lift one side of the panel, as she grabbed the other.

"We were doing storm prep, mostly, but I did have a middle-aged tourist tell me I look like Colin Farrell, which was nice," Damon said.

"That *is* nice." Sam and Damon lifted the panel up until it covered the window perfectly. "Was that before or after they grabbed your ass?"

"Oh, definitely foreplay to the ass grab," he grunted out. "You've gotta buy me dinner before you get a handful."

Sam couldn't help notice the bulge of Damon's biceps as he held the plank in place. The little line of muscle that spanned the length of him. The way his shoulders popped and revealed their own strength. "Noted," she said and glanced away.

"Where are the nails?" Damon asked.

Sam snapped out of her gaze and reached into her pocket with her free hand. She passed a long nail over to Damon and he pinched it from her grasp. The small graze of his fingertips sent a little jolt through her, and she quickly shoved her hand back into her pocket for another nail.

She propped the wood on her knee, positioned the hammer over the top of the nail and *thwack, thwack, thwacked* it into place. When the nail was flush with the wood, she passed the hammer to Damon.

"Hey, you weren't kidding. Maybe you *have* used a hammer before."

"A gal has to have her tricks." She winked at him and he gave her a small smile back.

"The rain is coming." He hammered away at his own nail, then opened his palm for another, which she placed into his hand without having to touch him.

"You can still smell it, huh?"

"What can I say, it's a gift." He placed the nail slightly away from the last one and hammered again.

Damon rubbed his arm across his forehead to remove a thin sheen of sweat. With the rain came thick and dense air as the sun was swallowed up by gray clouds. "Not to be rude, but Pearl promised a cold beverage in exchange for my services."

"Oh." Sam wiped her palms against her shorts and made for the front door. "Lemonade? It's not homemade, but it *is* filled with sugar and other terrible things."

"I love terrible things," Damon said as he casually rolled up his shirtsleeves so that his biceps were fully exposed.

And frankly, Sam was surprised. His arms were the kind of chiseled that didn't just happen from helping people lift wooden panels up to a window. No, Damon clearly put some effort into himself, and Sam felt compelled to acknowledge those efforts.

"You have muscles, Damon." Her hands rested on her hips as she admired him. "When the hell did that happen?"

He dramatically stretched his arms over his head and leaned from one side to the other, just showing off. "I'm not a piece of meat, Sam. Please don't harass me in the workplace."

"You're right. Of course you're right." She turned to go into the house but looked back, maybe lingering for a beat too long.

"My lemonade, with ice, please!" He mimicked her hands on hips pose and she swore he flexed his arms just to tease her.

When Sam walked into the house, Pearl was perched at a window that hadn't been sealed yet. She watched Damon with a blissed-out expression.

"It's okay, Grandma." Sam placed her hands on Pearl's shoulders and squeezed. "The calm before the storm stirs something up in all of us, doesn't it?"

"Close this window last," Pearl suggested. Sam stifled a laugh as she went into the kitchen to grab two glasses of icy lemonade.

There were twelve windows to cover, and while each window became easier the more they fell into a routine, the work was tiring. Sam's arms ached from the strain of holding the wood in place, and then swinging the hammer. She'd tied her hair up into a messy ponytail, and Damon's arms gleamed with sweat.

As they picked up the last piece of wood paneling, a fat rain drop landed on her forearm, then another on her nose. "You sniffed out the rain, all right."

"I felt them, too." Damon squinted as he glanced up at the

gray-black rain cloud above them. "We just need to get this last one up and we're done."

"Right." Sam hoisted the panel higher and lined it up with the window. She handed Damon a nail and the hammer, and he got to work nailing down his side.

The rain started to come down harder, less of a dribble and more of a steady pour. Sam's shirt clung to her, and the wisps of her hair tangled in soaked strands around her face. Damon handed the hammer back. She grabbed a nail with her wet fingers and lined it up with the wood. She nailed it in fine, but decided to give it one last swing for good measure. Maybe the sudden downpour made her sloppy, but as the hammer swung toward the nail, she knew even before it made contact that her aim was off.

The hammer landed on her thumb, and she instinctively sucked the tip of it into her mouth to try to stop the overwhelming pain. "Shit!" she exclaimed. When Sam looked up, there was Damon—hovering with concern.

"Let me see." He took her finger and rotated it. Rain ran down his hands and onto hers in cool rivers. He stroked his thumb across the top of hers. "Can you bend it?"

She bent the finger but felt a surge of pain.

"It's not broken," he said. "At least there's that."

And then, as unexpected as the biceps, he brought her finger to his mouth and placed a soft kiss over the throbbing red part of it. He held her hand in his, his mouth on her skin, and neither of them moved.

Sam blinked rain out of her eyes and looked at him. He stared back and a kind of heat flashed through her. When he swallowed, his Adam's apple bobbed, and she heard him suck in a breath.

"Damon," she said so low she wasn't even sure he'd heard her.

"Sam," he replied.

He held her fingers inches from his lips, the lips that had just brushed against her skin.

"What is this?" Her voice was cautious, not wanting to break the spell of them.

"I don't know." He took her hand and placed it on his chest. His heart thudded wildly and she flexed her fingers against him.

He rested his forehead against hers and his free hand traced up her rain-soaked arm, then back down again. Sam wanted nothing more than to keep going; she really did. But she couldn't do that to Damon or Marissa—not again anyway. She wasn't going to be the other woman, no matter how badly she wanted him.

"You have a girlfriend." Sam removed her hand from his chest.

"I don't," he quickly said.

Sam blinked away the rain. "What are you talking about?"

"We were never serious. And she ended things."

Sam felt guilty for a moment—was it because of the barbecue? Or the accidental kiss? She stepped away from him. "I'm sorry, Damon. Maybe you could try to get her back? Marissa is a catch—she's a doctor and her hair looks like something out of a Disney movie." Ironically, Sam was making the hard sell for the woman who wasn't her.

"She's not you," he said. "I couldn't... I *haven't* stopped thinking about you since you left. And then you came back, and..."

He cut himself off. The rain was cool and Sam couldn't help but lean toward the heat of Damon as his fingertips ran up her neck and into the back of her hair. He pulled and her face tilted up toward him. His eyes searched hers for some kind of sign that he could continue. And she really, really wanted him to.

She closed her eyes and was about to lift on her tiptoes to make her intentions clear, but then he spoke.

"Sam?"

Her eyes slowly opened. Judging by the look on his face, she wondered if he was having second thoughts. "Yes?" she tentatively asked.

"Why didn't you kiss me?" he asked. "All those years ago, why didn't you want to?"

23

Rain continued to drip into Sam's eyes and she tried to blink an answer into existence. Why hadn't she kissed Damon when he'd asked her?

She'd been scared. Terrified that kissing him would seal her fate and she'd be stuck in Tybee. She'd liked Damon then, of course she had, and she knew that if she acknowledged those feelings in any real way, she'd never leave him. And she needed to leave. She couldn't stay, not even for him.

But maybe Sam had been wrong not to kiss him. Despite how she'd broken his heart once, here he was again, standing with her in the rain, and cradling her neck just so. Maybe this was the universe giving her a second chance. Maybe she'd seen the life she could've led so that when she had the opportunity, she wouldn't fuck it up again. He had a question, and he deserved an answer.

"I wanted to kiss you," she said. "I always wanted to kiss you."

"But you didn't." His thumb stroked a line across her cheekbone. "Why?"

"I have thought about that moment over and over for years.

You know, one of those *what if* questions. It was complicated, because I cared about you too much back then. I was afraid that it wouldn't just be a kiss. It would be forever."

"You were scared of forever with me?" The rain was so heavy it created a kind of thundering white noise that Sam could barely hear her own thoughts over.

"I was scared of becoming my mom." Her voice was louder now. "I'm so sorry, Damon. I just couldn't be her. It wasn't about you. It was never about you."

"And what now?" Damon asked.

Sam swallowed. She lived in Paris. He lived in Tybee. Worlds away. But here he was, in front of her, and she knew this was her moment. "What I want is you."

He waited a beat, maybe processing. And she was so still, wondering if she'd said too much, or not enough, but hoping that he believed her.

"I still want you," he said.

And with his admission, she fisted her fingers through his hair, pulled him in and finally kissed Damon Rocha. Their lips crashed against each other, and then her tongue met his, and his hands pulled her in so close that they became one moving, breathing being together. Her hands trailed along his back, and he pulled her shirt up and off over her head. He moved her so she was pressed against the siding of the house, his body covering hers like he owned her.

He grabbed one of her legs, then the other, and she wrapped herself around him. She would never say no to kissing Damon again. She couldn't. Not when she knew he tasted like the salty sea air. Not when he moaned into her mouth as she pulled his shirt up and over his head.

"I need you," she said and pushed into him.

He winced in pleasure, or pain, she wasn't sure, but said, "Your grandma is inside."

"She's asleep. We can be quiet."

"Not with what I have planned for you."

The wind had started to kick up, and the palm fronds frantically blew around them.

"Look, we either go to my bedroom, or we try out here and potentially become two fatalities of the storm."

Damon gripped her tightly and proceeded to make for the screened-in porch door.

The realization that her childhood best friend was carrying her to her old bedroom in the middle of a hurricane was surreal. All perfectly fine, she hoped. And, to be honest, she really didn't care if it wasn't, because what she wanted more than anything was all of Damon.

He lightly pushed open the door of her bedroom and managed to kick it closed behind them. Damon led them to her bed and as he dropped her on top of it, he stopped to look at her. "You are so goddamn beautiful."

"Even on top of a dolphin-print duvet?"

He smiled. "*Especially* on top of a dolphin-print duvet."

"You are wild, Damon Rocha." Sam sat up and pulled him in for another kiss.

He slicked a hand through his wet hair, but a thick strand fell in front of his eyes. He kept his gaze trained on her as he kicked off his boots. She came to the edge of the bed and reached for his belt buckle, undoing it with a click.

"Are you sure?" he asked as she reached for the button on his jeans.

"I think I've been waiting for this moment since I left." She began to push his jeans down his hips. "I can't wait any longer."

He closed the space between them, kicking his pants off as he grabbed her face and slowly kissed her. He was soft, but the stubble was rough, and the combination of the friction and sweetness sent a gasp through her. He reached his hand around to unclasp her bra, fumbled, and she finished the clasp for him. She slid her bra off and he sucked in a breath as she leaned back on the bed.

He licked his lips and traced down the middle of her with his index finger. He carefully pulled her shorts and underwear down, and she was suddenly self-conscious to have Damon just staring at her. Or, rather, highly aware that Damon was drinking her in, in a way no one had before.

"When you blush, your whole body turns pink," he said.

"Fair skin, I guess." Sam bit her lip and added, "Wanna find out what color I turn when I…"

She didn't have to finish the thought. Damon climbed onto the bed and sucked the bud of her nipple into his mouth. The sensation was so unexpected that she gasped and pulled back, but he held her steady with a palm on her back and brought her toward him again.

She couldn't have predicted what Damon would feel like; how strong his arms would be as he lifted her up and sat her on his lap. How his back would flex as she scratched a trail across his shoulder blades. And how her legs would wrap around his waist so effortlessly.

His hands were eager and firm, and the cold rain droplets that fell from his wet hair and onto her skin made her shiver. He licked one droplet off as it traveled down her neck.

If this moment were a song on Damon's playlist, it would start with a steady drumbeat and fingers gently strumming a guitar. "I'm ready," she said.

"Not yet," he said. He got on his knees and carefully lowered her onto the pillow. Her legs stayed parted for him as he made his way down her torso with his tongue. He nipped at the sensitive skin of her inner thigh, then blew a soft breath across her. Her knees tightened around his ears and he laughed. But then his tongue. Oh, God, his tongue. It flicked at her and teased her and lapped and circled and devoured.

He savored her, and as she dug her nails into his hair and let out a deep moan, she knew that she was taking him in, too. Her body tightened as he brought her to the edge she was so desperate to reach. "I'm…" she started to say.

And then a thick finger slid in and circled around as he sucked her bud into his mouth. She couldn't help but show him how much she loved everything he was doing. She shuddered over and over again as pleasure rolled through her. Damon tightened his grip as he continued to make her come.

She could cry from how good her whole body felt. She'd had many partners, none of them meaningful, and now she was being shown what it was to be worshipped by someone who truly saw every part and accepted those pieces.

And the realization of that was…scary. Because what did any of this mean? And where would it go? But before she could ask, Damon had picked her up and rolled her on top of him. She helped him push down his boxers, and the way their bodies fit erased any questions she had.

Sam slid off him and he sat up on his elbows, watching as she pulled a condom out of her travel bag. She tore the wrapper open with her teeth and rolled it onto him. And then she was back on top and took him in her hand to guide him to her entrance. She sank down and closed her eyes from the pressure and the bliss of being filled by him.

Damon, Damon, Damon.

She couldn't tell if she spoke his name aloud, or just to herself as a silent mantra as she moved with him. He sat up and pulled her closer against him until he tensed beneath her.

And then they sat there, tangled and holding on and not saying a word. Sam rested her head against his shoulder and heard the steady pulse of his heart as it slowed. He scratched along the length of her back, and she knew she could fall asleep there in his arms, surrounded by him, and not ever leave the spot where they were.

And they didn't leave, not until there was a tentative knock at Sam's door. Damon clumsily pulled the sheets around Sam, then tugged his boxers on just before Pearl turned the knob.

"Damon," Pearl said, averting her eyes. "Your mom called. She's been trying your cell and couldn't reach you."

They weren't in high school, but this situation sure made Sam feel like she was. Was this how Alt-Sam and Damon felt when they'd been sneaking around in her room?

"Oh, okay," Damon said. He gave Pearl a forced smile, then seemed to think better of it and awkwardly cleared his throat.

"Grandma," Sam said. "We'll be right out."

"You two woke me up from my nap. Just saying." Then she closed the door.

Sam grabbed a pillow and buried her face in it as Damon chuckled. Which then made Sam hit him with the pillow.

He gave her a soft smile, and despite her embarrassment, she smiled back, too. Damon raked a hand through his hair as he pulled his pants back on. "You pulled my shirt off outside, which means Hurricane Courtney owns it now, along with my leather jacket. Can I borrow something to wear?"

Sam pulled the top sheet around her chest and dragged it along to the closet. She pulled the lightbulb cord, fingered her way through the hangers and stopped on an old concert T-shirt they'd picked up at a Good Charlotte show. She held the shirt out to him.

He grabbed it and eyed the tag, then tried, and nearly failed, to pull the slim shirt on. It clung to his skin just as tightly as the rain had, and landed an inch above his belly button.

"Crop tops are in right now." Sam pulled on a new pair of underwear, shorts and a Tybee High marching band sweatshirt.

"Should we talk about…" he started to say. "I mean, was that okay?"

Sam snorted. What they'd done had been more than okay. Life shattering. If this was what Alt-Sam had felt with Damon all along, she now understood why her alternate self hadn't given him up. Sam walked to Damon and stroked her thumb across the line of his chin. "That was *everything.*"

Relief crossed Damon's face as he pulled her in tight and wrapped his big arms around her. He breathed in the scent of her, then said, "For me, too."

He held her there. Her body turned the kind of warm and gooey that made her want to slide under the covers and cuddle. If she were in Paris, she'd go get them lattes and croissants and they'd spend the rest of the day in bed. She was about to tell him as much, but his expression was shadowed.

"You okay?" she asked.

He couldn't hide the crease between his eyes. He took a step back from her, and the space he'd left grew cold. Sam crossed her arms to keep warm. This was why she never got into relationships—she didn't speak the language. She had no idea what was going through his head, but she'd clearly done something wrong.

"Silence is always a good sign," she said, her voice anxiously kicking up.

Damon cracked his neck, then his knuckles, and finally said, "My mind is all over the place right now. Just thinking about where we go from here."

Sam's face burned, because she didn't know the answer. They weren't dating, but they'd slept together. They were a couple in an alternate life, so maybe they could be in this one, too. Wasn't that what she wanted? Weren't these visions telling her she *should* want that?

But then, would she still be able to fly all over the world if she had someone waiting at home? Would Damon resent her being gone so much? This wasn't a straightforward situation, and she didn't want to promise him forever if she couldn't stick the landing.

Another gentle knock at her door interrupted them. "Damon, your mom says it's urgent." Pearl came back into the room. She held her cell out, where there was a text chain with Cathy. "She's texting weird emojis. Is that an evil eye? Or just a very big eye?"

Damon took the phone and exhaled sharply.

While he frowned, Grandma Pearl smirked. "Cute crop top. Those are in now."

He bit his lower lip as he looked at Sam. "We'll talk soon."

He handed the phone back to Pearl, then made for the door, and Sam followed him out.

"Is it safe to ride in the storm?" she asked. Though she knew she wouldn't be able to convince him to stay.

He scratched a spot on his forehead. "I have to go."

He kissed her briefly. And while Sam knew he had to leave—he had his family to help—she also wondered if maybe he was giving her a taste of her own medicine. Fleeing abruptly. The emotions were so raw and real that even she was a little scared. But she wasn't sure how much of that she could show if she wanted to prove that she trusted Damon.

He gripped her fingertips and looked like he wanted to say something. Eventually, he did. "Bye, Sam-Sam." Then he headed for the door, and she held on until the tips of their fingers broke apart.

As she watched him leave, the comfort of him did, too. And in his absence, a little knot formed in her stomach. She wanted to figure this out with Damon. She did. But also, what if they couldn't? What if they'd had their chance once upon a time, but now their lives were far too different and complicated to find a way back?

24

"Sam!" Pearl's accusatory voice hit her.

Sam looked up from the refrigerator. She was removing ingredients that would sour if the power went out in the storm—boneless chicken breast, yogurt, heavy whipping cream. She wasn't a great cook, but she'd picked up a few tips from her Parisian neighbors. She might as well *try* to make them dinner with what they had.

Not that Sam was even hungry. But she had to do something to stop her thoughts from spinning about Damon.

"Yes?" Sam asked back.

Pearl was on the couch, but she'd partially turned to glare at Sam. "I told you not to mess with my fridge. If you keep the door shut, the cold will stay in and keep everything safe."

"Just let me help," Sam said, but started putting the ingredients back into the fridge. She knew Pearl well enough to understand she wouldn't win this fight.

Pearl winced as she shuffled over to the kitchen. Her grandma's wrist was broken, but the injury seemed to have affected her whole body. She was slower. More pained. The full eighty years actually showing. Though maybe the injury wasn't to blame. Maybe she'd been this way for some time, and Sam was now around to actually notice all the physical changes.

"So, how was it?" Pearl asked.

"The fridge?" Sam played as if she didn't know Pearl's implication.

"Like I said, you woke me from my nap." Pearl yawned, as if to prove the point. "I think you can cut the horse shit."

"Grandma…" Sam hid her eyes behind her hands.

"It is *fine* that you have sex, Sam. *More* than fine. But next time, maybe turn on some music so you don't wake your grandmother up?" Pearl cocked her head, waiting for acknowledgment.

Sam was about to try her best to evaporate into the tile floor when a loud knock sounded at the door.

"Oh, perfect timing." Pearl patted Sam's back. "Go on, get that for your poor grandma."

The wind had kicked up significantly, and the storm pummeled the house with rain. "Who did you invite over?" Sam asked as she flung the door open.

It was Jessie, in a neon orange rain slicker, carrying a slow cooker and a plastic grocery bag. Of course she'd come—the Thelma to Pearl's Louise. Jessie shook her shoulders out as the door closed behind her.

"Hurricane parties are the best!" Jessie exclaimed as she set the slow cooker down on the kitchen counter.

Sam forced herself to smile, some of the pilot customer service mentality kicking in. Hurricane parties *were* the best. A time when there was nothing to do while you waited out a storm, so you invited friends and family over. There was usually food, drinking and games. But Sam's emotions were still tied up in the what-if of Damon, so getting excited for a party was proving hard.

Still, she was a little curious. "What's in the slow cooker?" Sam asked.

Jessie brightened. "Hurricane punch."

The punch, as it turned out, was mostly rum with a lot of fresh citrus juice from Jessie's trees. "I make a big bowl every time there's a hurricane, just in case the wind takes the damn orange trees."

Jessie ladled a big cup of punch and handed it to Sam. When Sam took a sip, her mouth burned from the syrupy sweet taste of rum, oranges and…something sharp. She winced as she swallowed.

"That's the hot sauce," Jessie said knowingly. "I'm experimenting with a few dashes in the punch. What do you think?"

"She's always doing this," Pearl said, putting her own cup down. "Ruining a perfectly good drink with some absurd ingredient."

Once the mixture made its way down, Sam discovered she was both instantly buzzed and suffering from heartburn. Still, she took another sip. "I don't know why I like this," Sam said. "But I really do."

She liked it because it was taking her mind off Damon and how much they still had to talk about.

"Drink up," Pearl instructed. "And then you're going to tell us about what's going on with you and Damon."

"Sounds like draaa-MUH." Jessie took a sip of punch, then stuck her tongue out dramatically. "Oh, Mylanta, that's awful." She reached into the grocery bag and pulled out a twelve-pack of mango White Claw. "Good thing I brought backup."

Two White Claw drinks later, Sam found herself on the couch sandwiched between two overeager octogenarians.

"Your grandma has thrown some truly wild hurricane parties." Jessie crossed one leg over the other, sitting primly and in stark contrast to the sentence she'd just uttered. "Remember the time that Wild Boar Willie brought a keg?"

"Who is Wild Boar Willie?" Sam laughed.

"We call him that because he asked us to," Pearl explained. "We never questioned it."

"That, and the fact that he has these two canine teeth that are super pointy." Jessie mimed the teeth. "Kind of like a boar's tusks. But he wasn't a bore in bed—if you know what I mean."

Pearl leaned back into the couch and sipped her White Claw. "Speaking of…should we talk about the Damon in the room?"

"You kids overthink everything." Jessie popped a tortilla chip into her mouth. She spoke through the bite. "He's hot. You're hot. Be hot together."

"Say *hot* one more time," Pearl said.

"Hot." Jessie and Pearl stared across Sam at each other, then burst out laughing.

The whole thing made Sam miss Rachel and having her best friend to be silly with. "You're both drunk," Sam said. But then again, she felt buzzed, too.

"Do you like him or *like* him?" Jessie asked.

"Forget *him*," Pearl said, "what do *you* want, Sam? Be selfish. Think about what you want your life to look like."

Sam swallowed hard. The can of White Claw rested against her upper thigh, and drops of condensation ran down her skin. Before coming back to Tybee, all she wanted was to keep flying. But now that she'd seen the past she could've had, her wants were muddled. Maybe she *did* want to be in a relationship. Maybe she *did* want to have a place to call home. Maybe she *didn't* want to say goodbye to Damon.

But she wasn't willing to give up everything she'd worked for just to be with him. That wasn't what she wanted. She couldn't outrun the past, not while she was here. It hit her every day, from all sides. But she also couldn't just hop on a plane and vanish into the clouds.

There was a banging so loud that all three women shrieked. Sam's legs shot up toward her chest and she curled in on herself. The banging sounded again and Pearl held up her cast like a weapon. "That's coming from the door," she said.

"Damon?" Jessie ventured a guess.

"Maybe," Sam said. She checked her phone, but there were no new messages from him. Still, Pearl gave her a gentle shove to signal that she should get off the couch and go answer it.

Sam, not for the first time, wished she were wearing anything else, but settled for smoothing out her hair as she walked to the front door. Damon's return meant they could hash out some of the details she was sticking on, but she tried to temper her feelings as she unlocked and opened the door.

Her smile fell, though, as the umbrella lifted and she saw her mother standing there.

25

Sam's mom was at the house, standing on the welcome mat, wearing capris and a clingy top, and blinking back at Sam.

"Bonnie?" Sam said, almost like an accusation. She hadn't called Bonnie *mom* to her face in a long time. The switch had happened somewhere around the late teens mark, when Sam's hope that her mom would return vanished like sand in the high tide.

"Bonnie?" Pearl echoed, even louder.

Pearl was by Sam's side what seemed almost instantly, and the three Leto women were all in the same place for the first time in years.

A wild gust of wind came and turned Bonnie's umbrella inside out. Which is exactly when the power in the house blinked off. Sam saw the spark from the generator first, then the lights behind her dimmed. Sam and Pearl looked at each other and then at Bonnie, who seemed a few seconds from blowing over herself.

"Well, don't just stand there like a possum in the road, come in." Pearl stepped aside and Bonnie brushed past both of them.

Because the windows were boarded up, there was no light in the room. Sam had had the good sense—pre–White Claw drinks—to bring out flashlights. She picked up a heavy blue one from the coffee table and flipped it on.

Her face lit up, like she was telling a spooky story around the campfire. Only this horror tale was about a neglectful mother who returned at the worst possible moment. Then Sam shined it at Bonnie, who held her hand up to shield the light from hitting her eyes directly.

"Why are you here?" Sam asked with an unintentionally forceful tone.

"Your grandma called a few weeks ago to let me know she was selling the house," Bonnie said.

"Well, I didn't think you'd just show up without so much as a warning," Pearl said.

"Mom also mentioned you were back in town," Bonnie said carefully. "And I wanted to see for myself. We have some things we'd probably like to say to each other."

"Not to interrupt," Jessie said as she lit the wick of a candle. "But do you want some hurricane punch? It's got a nice kick to it."

"I don't drink anymore," Bonnie said.

Sam was in shock. How else to explain why she didn't let fly the hundred questions she'd had percolating for her mother since the day Bonnie walked out of her life?

Why did you leave?

What did I do wrong?

Did you ever even love me?

Instead, the only thing that came out of Sam's mouth was, "I'll have some punch." Because, really, if ever there was a time to drink, it was now.

Jessie wasted no time opening the slow cooker and ladling out a cup.

"Sam," her mom said. "You're so grown-up."

"I'm thirty-two," Sam said. "The last time you saw me was

when I was a teenager, so…yeah. I grew up. On my own." Sam hadn't known she'd be this angry but well, she was.

Jessie handed Sam a cup and her timing couldn't have been better. Sam hadn't had more of the hurricane punch yet, but her insides had taken a punch to the gut. She gulped without looking and held back the cough that threatened to spill out.

And Jessie, ever the purveyor of Southern hospitality, opened her arms to Bonnie for a hug. "Welcome home," Jessie said. Bonnie hugged her back, but kept her eyes trained on Sam.

Sam held her gaze. This wasn't Bonnie's home, not anymore, and she didn't exactly want her mother to think she was welcome there.

"I know this must be really strange, Sam," Bonnie said as she pulled out of the hug. "It's been years, like you said. I would've seen you sooner…" Bonnie chanced a look at Pearl, whose face had hardened. "When you're ready, I'd love to talk to you about what happened. Get to know you, if you'll let me."

"You never bothered to get to know me before. What changed?" Sam crossed her arms to protect herself.

"Sam," Pearl warned, stepping between them as if anticipating a fight.

But Bonnie put a gentle hand on Pearl's shoulder. "I deserve that." She lifted her soaked top, and then touched a hand to her hair, which was flattened in a wet mop.

"Bonnie, why don't you go clean up a bit?" Pearl offered.

"By all means, try to wash the guilt off." Sam gestured toward the bathroom.

"Sam," Pearl chastised.

"What?" Sam bitterly laughed. "We can't make jokes now that Bonnie's back?"

Bonnie didn't respond to the jab, though. She turned around and searched the space, almost like she didn't even remember where the bathroom was. And maybe she didn't; eighteen years was a long time to be gone, even if she had grown up in this house. Eventually, Bonnie walked down the hall and toward the bathroom.

Pearl grabbed Sam's hand, which was when she realized that her fists were clenched into two angry little balls at her sides.

"I'm sorry, honey," Pearl said. "I didn't think she'd come at all."

"I understand," Sam said, even though she didn't. Bonnie never wanted the house, or Tybee, or her old high school T-shirts—or Sam. She'd abandoned those things and fled, so shouldn't she do them all the favor of never coming back?

"She can't stay here," Sam added.

"Well, we can't just send her out in the storm." Pearl chewed her lip. "But maybe we can tie her to the fence outside for a bit and let her think about what she's done."

Sam glanced at Pearl, not taking the easy route of smirking back. Pearl seemed to take the hint, as she added, "As soon as the storm clears, we can talk about options. But, Sam, she's my daughter and your mama. If she came all this way, I'm guessing it's for more than some old junk."

Sam swallowed. She wasn't so sure that Grandma Pearl was right—her mom was selfish. There was a distinct possibility that she'd come solely because she'd realized that her favorite tank top hadn't made it with her in the mad dash to leave town.

The bathroom door opened, and Sam and Pearl stared down the hallway at Bonnie. Bonnie froze under their scrutiny, then shook her head as she walked toward them. "The walls in this house have always been paper thin. My therapist said that if y'all want me to leave, I should respect that." Then she moved toward Sam. "And I understand why you'd want that, but I do hope you'll give me a chance to talk to you. Even if it's just for a few minutes. I need to say a few things."

The power was out. And a hurricane was coming. And Sam was exhausted from nailing boards to the windows and then, well, getting nailed herself.

"You can stay," Pearl said. "This is still my house. I haven't sold it yet. So I make the rules."

"Thank you, Mama," Bonnie said.

There was something bizarre about her mom calling Grandma Pearl "Mama," like she was a little girl again. The sentiment made Bonnie seem more vulnerable than Sam had imagined possible, like she still needed her mother. Bonnie had left Tybee when she was in her thirties, but now the skin on her hands had crinkles and there were deep laugh lines around her mouth.

Who had given her those? She'd clearly been living a good life without them in it.

"I don't plan to stay long," Bonnie added.

"Some things don't change, then," Sam said. But she couldn't help notice Bonnie wince at the words.

"Am *I* supposed to leave or...?" Jessie's voice startled all three of them.

"Jesus, Jessie, you nearly made me pee myself." Pearl clutched a hand to her chest.

"Well, I'm not the one who made things awkward by getting into a family squabble. You just don't do that in front of guests." Jessie crossed her arms and pointedly looked at Pearl.

Eventually, Pearl said, "Jessie is right. This is a hurricane party, and we're not about to have a bad time. Can we agree to have whatever conversations need to be had in the morning?"

Bonnie clasped her hands in front of her, and Jessie took another swig of her White Claw.

But Sam wasn't in the mood to be one big happy family. This whole day was, apparently, cursed. First, with the uncertainty around Damon, and now her mom unexpectedly showing up like an air pocket midflight. She wasn't about to sit in the living room and pretend that Bonnie's being here was okay—it absolutely wasn't. But like Pearl said, this was her house and her hurricane party, and if they wanted to act like everything was normal, that was on them. Sam didn't have to play along, though.

"You ladies have fun." Sam grabbed a bag of open pretzels off the counter and another White Claw. "I'm going to bed."

"Sure you are," Pearl knowingly said. "See you in the morning."

"Good night," Bonnie said, and Sam shot daggers her way.

As she headed down the hall, Pearl asked, "Jess, did you bring Scrabble?"

"Winner gets an extra White Claw," Jessie said.

"Then you better prepare to be—" Pearl searched for the right word "—*annihilated*. That's eleven letters, in case you were wondering."

"Challenge *acknowledged*," Jessie said. "That's twelve letters, and the *W* is worth four points."

Sam wondered if Bonnie would follow her—after all, her mom seemed insistent on talking—but she didn't. Of course she didn't. Sam stopped at the hall closet to grab another flashlight. She flipped it on, walked to her room and closed the door behind her. She picked up her phone and sent a text to Damon.

Sam:

Hey, just want to make sure you're ok?

Loud gusts of wind blew outside the window, and she had the urge to open it and feel the intense rush of air and rain whipping around the room.

When she was in middle school, she'd once opened the front door in the middle of a hurricane and the thing had nearly torn off the hinges. She'd profusely apologized as Pearl dragged her back inside and managed to slam the door shut. But secretly, there'd been a thrill to nearly being taken along with the storm. Sam had hardly been able to catch her breath as the wind slammed into her. There was a kind of release to not having any control.

The lack of control she had in her situation with Damon

was altogether different, however. And now Bonnie was here, throwing yet another hook into the sea of Sam's messy life. She didn't want to give Bonnie a minute of her time, but she couldn't run—there was the hurricane, for one, and she wasn't about to leave Pearl alone with someone like Bonnie. Who knew what her mom was after; maybe she thought she could cash in on Pearl's house, or grab jewelry she hadn't stolen the first time around. Her mom couldn't be trusted, and Sam knew that much. She'd have to keep a close eye on Bonnie.

Sam glanced at her phone, but there was no text back from Damon. If this were high school, Sam would bring her CD player under the covers and tune out the apprehension about Damon, and the voices of her mom and grandma until morning came. But this wasn't high school, and her CD player, as it turned out, was more than what it used to be.

If ever there was a moment when Sam needed an evacuation slide, it was now. But there was no emergency exit. She was trapped in the house with Bonnie and the memories of all that pain.

She knew what would make her feel better. What had always brought her an escape when she had to deal with Bonnie. And on impulse, she reached for it.

26

There was a long electric guitar intro, but Sam knew the opening to "The Curse of Curves" by Cute Is What We Aim For from just about anywhere. She'd had more than a crush on the dreamy lead singer, with his shoulder-length hair and square jaw as he sang about being a charming guy who wanted to sleep with a girl he thought was hot.

Lust. A song about pure and unadulterated lust. Something she and Damon had in the present as well. So this would likely be another glimpse of how right they were for each other, which was exactly the kind of reassurance Sam needed.

Sam closed her eyes and there was the usual *whoosh* as she traveled from the real world to the alternate one. When she was able to catch her breath, there was cold metal beneath her, and she shivered as an equally icy blast of AC shot down from a vent above. It was the smell, though—sugary artificial vanilla—that immediately told her everything she needed to know.

Mermaid's Ice Cream had been Sam's after-school job starting at the age of fourteen. Drizzling hot fudge over banana splits to earn spending money and, later, help pay for school expenses.

The Scenes of Tybee calendar on the wall marked the month of July of 2010, the summer before Sam started flight school. When Sam took the headphones off, "The Curse of Curves" hummed out from the speakers in the store.

The click of a lock made Sam turn, and she watched as Alt-Sam pushed her glasses up the bridge of her nose and flipped the Open sign to Closed. She went behind the counter and readjusted her skinny scarf before she grabbed a wet rag and began the process of wiping the counters. Then she took a spray bottle and spritzed the glass display window.

Well, she supposed not all of her visions could be momentous. But "The Curse of Curves" was such a specific song. And where was Damon?

Her thoughts were interrupted when a random guy came out of the back storeroom. His face was obscured by enormous containers of ice cream, and Sam stood to try to get a good look at him. As she did, he set the two bins down on the floor and stretched out his arms.

Myles. The rude jock who was now friends with Damon in the real world. What the hell was he doing there? Sam had never worked with him.

"Hey, boss, you ready to let the dogs out?" He gave Alt-Sam a kind of amused smirk that Sam didn't much like the look of. He tugged on the collar of his Hollister shirt as he waited for a response, then added, "That's a quote from *The Hangover*."

"I'm not your boss," Alt-Sam replied while she wiped down the glass with a paper towel. "And that movie was lame."

"It was not lame. A movie about a vampire and a dog is lame." Myles reached into the cooler to remove a mostly empty tub of ice cream.

"If you're talking about the *Twilight* movies, there's no dog. Jacob is a shapeshifter who can become a wolf. There's a difference."

"You heard yourself, right?" Myles hefted in the new tub.

"If you're not my boss, then why do you take 60 percent of the tips?"

"That's my fee for training and, in general, putting up with you."

Clever girl, Sam thought. But also, where was Damon? Why was she being shown this vision if he wasn't even here?

"Because you're my boss." He gave the same cocky smirk she remembered from the bar. "I really need the money before going to Emory."

Alt-Sam shrugged as she crumpled up the paper towel and deftly tossed it into the trash can. "I hate hauling those ice cream bins. So keep up the grunt work."

So Myles the asshat had gotten into Emory University, and Sam was training him? Well, that was certainly different.

Alt-Sam blew out a long breath as she counted out her tips. Myles watched and licked his lips. If Sam didn't know any better, she'd say his eyes were appraising Alt-Sam.

Then Myles grabbed a can of whipped cream from the back counter, shook the bottle and sprayed it into his open mouth. Alt-Sam turned and gawked. "What the hell, Myles?"

"It's good," he said through a full mouth of whipped cream. "Give it a try."

"I'm not guzzling whipped cream like some frat boy," Alt-Sam said. "And we're going to have to throw that out." But she turned to Myles, all the same, and watched him.

"Might as well enjoy it, then." Myles shrugged and sprayed more into his mouth. Then, without warning, he sprayed some of the whipped cream at Alt-Sam.

Alt-Sam held her hands up in defense and let out a surprised holler. Myles laughed. Then Alt-Sam quickly grabbed a cup of sprinkles and launched them at Myles like rainbow confetti.

"Oh, is that how we're playing it, then?" Myles pointed the whipped cream at her, and she grabbed a cup of shredded coconut. They held their weapons, waiting for one of them to move first.

Myles bit his bottom lip, and Alt-Sam couldn't hide the tight smile that crossed hers.

"You aren't, like, *friends* with this jerk, right?" Sam asked.

As she waited for the answer that would never come, there was a tap on the front door. They all turned, and there was Damon with an uneasy expression.

Alt-Sam looked surprised, but quickly recovered and grinned back. She glanced at Myles, whose expression turned stoic as he eyed the door.

Alt-Sam came around the counter, unlocked the door and Damon greeted her with a kiss.

"Did you get off your shift early?" Alt-Sam asked.

"I'm going to work a double next week so I can take tonight off." Damon's hands went to her hips and he pulled her in tight to him. "Tomorrow's your big surgery. I want to be with you."

"Sure." Alt-Sam glanced back to Myles, who looked away and started to sweep up the sprinkles on the floor. "I just have to close."

Myles straightened and gave a casual glance their way, and Damon clocked him, too.

"Hey, Sam's boyfriend," Myles said, maybe a little cocky.

"Damon," Damon said.

"Right." Myles didn't look at Damon, though. His eyes were on Alt-Sam. "How about I close tonight? You can rest up before the surgery."

"You sure?" Alt-Sam asked. "It'll just be another ten minutes or so."

"Go. I've gotta finish this whipped cream anyways." Myles took the can as if to prove his point and sprayed some into his mouth. "Sure you don't want me to feed you some?"

Oh, Sam thought as she looked between Myles and where Alt-Sam and Damon stood.

"She's okay, man." Damon grabbed for Alt-Sam's hand, and she let him take it. There was some kind of intense male energy—like two dogs eyeing the same bone—but Sam didn't love the idea that Alt-Sam was the bone. And besides, it wasn't like Damon had anything to worry about. Her alternate self would never go for this meathead when she had a filet at home.

Still, Myles stared at her, and Damon most definitely clocked that as his grip on Alt-Sam tightened. The whole thing was, honestly, too much, and Sam was relieved to hear the last sounds of the guitar and cymbals from the song playing from her headphones as she was yanked out of the memory.

27

"Ugh." Sam slid her headphones off.

And while her own music had turned off, Pearl and Jessie scream-sang the words to "Silver Springs" by Fleetwood Mac from the living room. The iconic song about losing the love of your life felt a little too on the nose to Sam and Damon's situation, to be honest. She held a hand to her forehead. Maybe it was the hurricane punch, or the lack of any kind of proper pitch to the women's voices, but the noise was unpleasant.

Was Bonnie singing along with them? Dancing on the couch like nothing had changed? Casting a spell over Pearl to make her believe that all was well and she didn't have to hold any kind of grudge?

A loud crack sounded outside the window, like a branch falling from a tree. The singing in the living room stopped and Pearl called out, "You okay, Sam?"

"Yeah, probably just a palm frond." Sam's eyes darted to the window, wishing she could catch a look outside. They'd find out in the morning where the branch had fallen, and if there was any damage.

"I'll go check on her," Bonnie said.

Sam was about to repeat that she was fine, but Pearl chimed in. "Leave her be. She needs her space."

"She's had nearly twenty years of space, Mama," Bonnie replied.

"Whose fault is that?" Pearl's tone was firm now.

"Partially yours," Bonnie fired back. "Do you want me to remind you of the conversation we had?"

"Letos, please." Jessie tried to be the mediator.

And this was how it always was. Pearl and Bonnie fighting over Sam. Nothing had changed.

Sam blinked hard. She didn't want to be part of this fight as a teenager, let alone now as an adult. Hearing her mom and grandma bicker triggered some kind of ancient response, and Sam pulled her knees into her chest. This was why she'd moved so far away from home, so she'd never have to think about being in this room and hearing the chaos outside it.

Her gaze landed on the CD player. Her old friend. Her creature comfort. The energy of the last vision must have been some kind of blip; watching Damon and Myles in a tug-of-war over her was not all that fun. She needed a palate cleanser before bed. She'd listen to another song and by the time it was over, maybe the fight outside her room would be, too. And maybe the next thing she saw would be Alt-Sam in flight school…

She shook out her shoulders and readjusted the headphones. She was ready to hear the next song that would show her the future she could've had. So she reached for the play button and hit it.

When Avril Lavigne's "My Happy Ending" started, Sam flinched. The song was about the opposite of a happy ending—more like the end to a relationship that was supposed to be perfect. What was she about to be tossed into?

Her eyes slowly opened, and she found herself in a booth at a bar.

She turned around and it didn't take long to spot the pony-

tail of long red hair seated at the booth next to hers. And there,
next to Alt-Sam, was Damon, wearing distressed skinny jeans
and a black vest over a white tee. Alt-Sam fit snugly into the
crook of Damon's arm, but still wore glasses.

Why would Alt-Sam have glasses if the surgery happened?

"It's nice to see you two cozied up, but can we talk about the
eyesight thing?" Sam asked. "How are we doing there?"

Alt-Sam and Damon *were* cuddled up, but they weren't talking. The way Damon rubbed the same spot on her neck over
and over again, like he was trying to work something out, made
them seem...off...

"Ah shit." Sam slumped onto the top of the booth. "Please
be wrong, please be wrong." She waited for one of them to
speak and, eventually, they did.

"Are we okay?" Alt-Sam asked.

Damon looked down at her, slipped his arm off from around
her shoulder. "I don't know. You tell me."

Alt-Sam sat up stiffly. "I think you're feeling weird about
being at the opening of your sister's bar."

Alt-Sam reached for the bowl of popcorn in the center of the
round table. Next to the bowl was a Grand Opening placard,
with the words, "Sister Brews" surrounded by celestial stars
and a crescent moon. The logo was witchy and feminine, and
so different from the Band Practice Brews Damon and Farrah
had opened together.

Alt-Sam continued, "You both talked about doing this. It
was basically *your* idea—"

"That's not why I'm mad," he cut her off.

"Okay, so you *are* mad," Alt-Sam said.

"You just seem so distant lately. And whenever I ask what's
wrong, you say nothing. But I know you, Sam-Sam. Tell me
what's going on," Damon pleaded.

Alt-Sam chewed a handful of kernels, either ignoring or not
hearing Damon.

"Sam, look at me." He lifted her chin up.

"Nothing is wrong. I'm just feeling a bit down." Alt-Sam scratched at the surface of the wooden table and didn't meet Damon's eyes.

"Talk to me." He grabbed her hand, but she pulled away.

And then, like the vulture he was, Myles planted his hands firmly on their table. He wore shutter sunglasses and a trucker hat. "Hey there, boss." His words were slurred.

"Hey," Damon replied for Alt-Sam.

Alt-Sam eyed Damon, maybe annoyed. "I told you not to call me that," she said, definitely annoyed.

"This is a party," Myles continued, oblivious. "You should be having fun. I mean, did you see the giant piñata in the shape of an old lady?"

"That's supposed to be a witch," Damon said.

Alt-Sam allowed a small smile to cross her face. "You are literally too stupid to insult."

"Wait a minute. Did you just quote *The Hangover*?" Myles raised his beer to her in acknowledgment, then he finally looked at Damon. "Later, dude."

"That guy is an asshole," Damon said.

"Maybe we should go home." Alt-Sam grabbed her absolutely enormous black purse from the seat and moved to leave, but Damon blocked her with his arm.

"It's Farrah's opening night. We can't go yet. And you didn't tell me what's going on with you," Damon added.

Alt-Sam tried to leave the booth again. This time, Damon let her, but he followed closely behind.

"Come on," he tried again.

Alt-Sam stopped in a small archway, away from the crowd of people and private enough for the two of them to tuck into.

Sam blew out a big breath that rattled her lips. There was a lot to delve into, but she didn't have the context. She felt like she was trying to navigate a flight without a map. "Maybe just kiss and make up? Isn't that what couples do?" she offered. But, she had no experience being part of a couple, so what the hell did she know?

Alt–Sam scratched at a spot on her forehead, then shook out her hands. "I'm going to be honest, okay?"

"Okay," Damon said as he leaned against the wall.

Eventually, she said, "I feel...stuck."

"Stuck?" Damon asked.

Alt–Sam sighed. "I don't really want to talk about this here. Can we just go home?"

"Is this about the surgery?" Damon instinctively wrapped her in a hug. "The doctor said she could try again, in time." Alt–Sam eventually hugged him back, but her eyes looked off, lost in thought.

Oh, God. The surgery hadn't worked?

"Statistically, if it didn't work the first time, it won't work the next time, either." Alt–Sam pulled back from Damon, then hunched into herself, as if self-conscious about saying the words out loud. "I was supposed to be in flight school by now. I mean, what am I even doing? I'm working at an ice cream shop. I can't afford to go to school. Like...am I just supposed to be serving people sundaes for the rest of my life?"

"This is all my fault," Damon said. "If I hadn't gotten us into that accident..."

Alt–Sam shook her head and wiped a tear that rolled down her cheek. "I'm not trying to make you feel bad. I'm just sad."

"My sister said you could bartend here, remember?" Damon rubbed a spot on her arm, but Alt–Sam's eyes fluttered in irritation.

"Okay, so instead of ice cream it's somehow better if I'm serving beer? That's not what I want, Damon."

Alt–Sam pushed out of the corner and made for the front door. Damon was, once again, chasing after her.

"Well, what *do* you want?" he asked as they left the bar and poured out onto the sidewalk. It was dark and an overhead light shone on them like they were in an interrogation room. A Jeep drove by and "My Happy Ending" blared from the speakers at an annoyingly loud volume.

"I can't do this anymore," Alt-Sam said, her voice so low and sad it was almost hard to hear her.

Damon pulled back and studied her. "Can't do…"

Alt-Sam's face shifted into a kind of pained grimace. She seemed to weigh her words carefully, but eventually said, "I can't be here. I feel like I'm disappearing. It's like what happened to my mom."

Damon frowned.

"I love you, Damon, but I can't keep acting like everything is okay. I'm not okay. Something is very wrong. I'm broken. I don't deserve you. You deserve someone who will be happy here."

Even in the dark, Alt-Sam's eyes clearly glistened with the threat of tears.

"But we love each other." His voice was so tender, and the statement so pure, that Sam's breath caught.

"I know. I know that." Alt-Sam rubbed her temple.

"We'll figure this out." Damon's fingers wove through Alt-Sam's loose strands of hair, and she pressed her cheek into his palm. "And you're not broken, but you've been through a lot. Can you go to therapy, like you promised?"

Sam's chest was so heavy with confusion that it was almost as if she was sinking into the ground. Only, she did slip into the nothingness as she was sucked out of the vision to Avril Lavigne's resigned words ringing through the headphones.

Sam's eyes flew open and she was surrounded by the duvet, and the darkness of the room and the light coming from the flashlight at her side.

There was a strikingly loud boom of thunder and Sam jumped. Even through the headphones, she heard the whip of wind slam against the side of her grandma's house. The whole place shook from the next crack of thunder. She'd been through worse hurricanes, but it'd been so long that the sensations and sounds all felt new. She tucked her legs into her chest and let out a deep breath.

What the hell had she just seen with Damon and Alt-Sam? Her younger self was trying to end their relationship, but that didn't make sense. Why would she be shown something like that? How was the vision any better than where she and Damon were now?

Unless it was just a bump in their road together. There were thirteen total songs on the CD, which meant there were only two more left. She wouldn't know how Alt-Sam and Damon turned things around unless she listened to the next song. She opened her notebook, took her pen and wrote down the new tracks.

SAM AND DAMON'S MAGICAL PLAYLIST

Track One: "Bring Me to Life" by Evanescence. Otherworldly song about being understood by another human. Tybee High parking lot. Questionable amounts of eyeliner. Alt-Sam kisses Damon. Missing earring is found.

Track Two: "I Believe in a Thing Called Love" by The Darkness. A bop about being head over heels for someone. Alt-Sam and Damon are officially dating. Myles continues to disappoint. Marissa didn't have an awkward phase in high school. JanSport backpacks are timeless.

Track Three: "Supermassive Black Hole" by Muse. Inarguably the best song and movie scene pairing ever.

Damon and Alt-Sam make out during *Twilight* and get kicked out. One too many hickies.

Track Four: "Want You Bad" by The Offspring. A banger about a bad boy wanting to corrupt a good girl. Myles gets owned by Alt-Sam. Damon skips detention. Alt-Sam skips her extracurricular. I miss Dunkaroos.

Track Five: "Dance, Dance" by Fall Out Boy. A song about a guy meeting someone he likes at a school dance, and the angst of trying to desperately impress them. Damon tries to impress Alt-Sam and they get into A GODDAMN CAR CRASH. Soffe shorts. Condoms from Pearl. Looks like I never get to go to prom.

Track Six: "Fell In Love With a Girl" by The White Stripes. Can I ever hear this song again and not think about Alt-Sam and Damon sneaking around (??) and probably having sex (??). Alt-Sam's vision problems continue AND she's getting a C on an essay?

Track Seven: "Read My Mind" by The Killers, which is all about uncertainty. Makes sense, since in Alt-Sam's high school graduation, I'm not valedictorian and waiting on a surgery to get into flight school.

Track Eight: "Over My Head" by The Fray. Written about a fight, where one person was totally out of their depth. Alt-Sam is pregnant and moving in with Damon. Maybe they're not ready to be parents?

Track Nine: "Maps" by the Yeah Yeah Yeahs. Damon's starting nursing school and not a brewery. Wanting someone to stay is the theme of the song, and maybe Damon wants Alt-Sam to know he'll stay by her side and through the miscarriage?

Track Ten: "The Curse of Curves" by Cute Is What We Aim For. Myles at the ice cream shop being a little too friendly with Alt-Sam, much like the song suggests. Eye surgery set for the next day. Damon and Myles acting like weirdos.

Track Eleven: "My Happy Ending" by Avril Lavigne. Saw anything but a happy scene. Alt-Sam and Damon at Farrah's bar's opening night, big fight. Eye surgery didn't work. Damon asked Alt-Sam to see a therapist.

Sam shook out her hand, so unused to writing that even those few lines made her fingers cramp. She couldn't see a pattern. Or rather, she didn't understand why the last few songs had sad memories when the other universe was meant to show that she and Damon were fated. She understood no one was perfect, and even the best couples had rough periods.

"But what am I missing?" Sam asked to the room.

She took her phone out and tapped the screen, but there were no new messages.

What she was missing—in this life at least—was a reply from Damon. And the realization of that hit her like the loud booms of thunder just outside her grandma's home.

28

Sam wasn't angry, exactly, but also…a little mad, yes. She'd texted Damon a simple question to check in. And all he had to do was send a response—any response, really. Something like, *I'm fine and I know we had sex, so I want to acknowledge you as a human being*, for example. She'd even take a "k" at this point.

But no, he hadn't sent anything. So she was left to think that he'd either been swept away in the storm or was just plain avoiding her. Either option wasn't great and left her feeling like no matter what she tried to grasp, everything was slipping through her fingers: Damon, Alt-Damon and keeping Bonnie out of her life.

She just wanted to be carefree Pilot Sam again. But for the moment, the only place she had was her room, and the only thing in it of any use was her phone and her CD player. The phone, however, was a reminder that Damon wasn't answering her. And the CD player, well…the thing had started to turn her moments of voyeurism into confusion.

Still, the CD player *would* go back to happier visions. After all, there were just two songs left. And if she'd learned anything from aughts teen movies, the leads always got together in the end. Alt-Sam and Damon were endgame, and their love story wasn't over—she just had to keep listening.

Sam cautiously returned to her bed, where the player waited for her. Two more songs would really just be a few minutes of her life. She could listen and see her very own happily-ever-after. Maybe even glean some insight from the visions to apply to her present-day no-text-back predicament. Crazier things had happened, like the magical playlist itself. She put the headphones on, settled into place and hit Play.

The plucking of strings was familiar, and within a few seconds she recognized "I Write Sins Not Tragedies" by Panic! at the Disco, which was a song about cheating. This was totally something she and Damon had listened to—everyone had. But if she was hearing a song about betrayal, then that might mean her happily-ever-after wasn't about to hit her. She lifted her hand to yank the headphones off, but she plunged down and found herself unable to move until she landed on a chair.

Cold AC blasted and Sam quickly blinked her eyes open to the creamy white walls of the ice cream shop. She grabbed the sides of the bistro table and peeled off her headphones just as the band sang the catchy chorus over the shop's speakers.

She had two minutes and fifty-five seconds left, and what she knew about the ice cream shop was that Alt-Sam worked there, along with...

Her gaze caught on Myles, lifting a tub of fresh ice cream into the glass case. Alt-Sam came out from the back and took her apron off to reveal skintight jeans with holes at the knees and a button-down plaid shirt.

Sam pushed up from the table and crossed her arms. She suddenly never wanted a cup of cookie dough with gummy bears again. Which was very sad indeed. But as if reading her mind, Alt-Sam grabbed an ice cream scoop, reached just past Myles and scooped herself a cup of cookie dough. He shoved his hands into the pockets of his khaki shorts and watched her as she worked, but Alt-Sam didn't seem to notice. She then went to the toppings and loaded up with way more than a standard serving of gummy bears. She set the cup down on the counter, then hoisted herself up and started to eat.

"I just wiped that down and now you're putting your ass all over it," Myles said, though he didn't sound annoyed at all.

"Don't worry," Alt-Sam said through a bite. "My ass does a better job of wiping these counters than you do."

Myles raised an eyebrow. "The boss makes jokes," he said.

"You gonna have any?" Alt-Sam asked as she shoved another spoonful into her mouth.

"That depends." Myles put his palms on the counter and leaned forward. "Are you gonna take it out of my tips?"

"Totally." Alt-Sam smiled as she chewed.

Myles rolled his eyes, then sighed as he grabbed the ice cream scoop and loaded up a cone with three scoops of chocolate fudge.

"You'll get sick if you eat all that."

"I'm not like your skinny jeans boyfriend. I play soccer. I need the carbs. More of a Jacob than an Edward, to speak your language." Myles took a large bite, as if to prove his point, but then he held his palm to his head and groaned. "Brain freeze."

"At least my boyfriend listens to me," Alt-Sam said. "Unlike someone in this room."

"Is that why you like him so much?" Myles asked, then took a smaller bite. "Because he does whatever you say?"

Alt-Sam frowned. "He doesn't do whatever I say. It's not like that."

"I saw you two fighting at the brewery," Myles said. "Sounded serious. You know, we're way too young to be in sad relationships."

Alt-Sam quickly raised her brows, then looked into her cup. "My relationship is none of your business."

"I just can't imagine only being with one person for the rest of my life." He let the words hang there, maybe hoping she'd respond, but she didn't. Myles licked his spoon and moved closer to Alt-Sam. "Is he the only guy you've ever *been with* been with?"

"Could we please stop talking about this?" Alt-Sam put the now-empty cup down on the counter and, as she did, Myles boxed her in with his hands.

"I've had a thing for you since forever." Myles's nose skimmed over the top of her head and he seemed to inhale the scent of her.

"Uhhh, girl," Sam said to her younger self. But Alt-Sam wasn't pushing Myles away. In fact, her eyes fluttered closed and she licked her lips.

"I can tell you've been down lately, but I can make you feel good, you know," Myles said. "Are you going to tell me to stop?"

"Yes," Sam said, waiting for Alt-Sam to say the same.

Her younger self made no sound at all.

Sam planted her hands on her hips and started to tap her foot. "Sam, come on. This is ridiculous."

"We should stop," Alt-Sam said.

"Exactly." Sam blew out a relieved breath. But then, Alt-Sam's little pinkie inched closer to where Myles's hand was, and she touched his skin.

Myles looked down at her, and she looked up at him, trapped in each other's gaze. Sam moved to stop them herself, but when she tried to pull them apart, nothing happened.

"Sam!" she yelled as loud as she could. "Do *not* do this. Okay? I know you're hurting. You've been through so much. Way more than I went through. But don't just hook up with this doofus. He's not going to fix you. He's a total asshole. Remember how he bullied you and Damon? Yes, being young is for making mistakes and trying things out, but not with him."

Alt-Sam didn't hear her, though, and Myles seemed to take her silence as a kind of agreement that he could kiss her, because he started to tilt his mouth toward hers.

And just like that, Sam opened her mouth and screamed "No!" with the force of a hurricane storm wind. "Both of you, stop!" Sam couldn't stop them, though. There was no way for Alt-Sam to hear or feel her. Still, Sam took a step forward and, as she did, was pulled backward as the song on her headphones ended.

Sam came back to the room and found she was thrashing, but her arms were being held down.

"Sam! Sam, wake up!" Grandma Pearl and Bonnie shouted at her.

Her eyes focused and she saw both women standing over her with panicked expressions, which made her stop kicking her legs.

"Okay," Grandma Pearl let out a relieved breath. "She's okay."

Sam realized that she was wet, and there was wind— hurricane strength wind—whipping through the bedroom. She looked up, and the crown of a massive palm tree had pierced through her bedroom window.

Sam shot up and the CD player fell to the floor, but she was too busy gaping at the *tree* in her room.

"Come on." Bonnie grabbed Sam's hand. It was the first time she'd touched her mom in over a decade, and Sam found that she felt nothing. Or maybe it was the shock of the tree in her room. "We have to get out of here and into the hallway."

The hallway became a windowless hurricane fortress when all the doors were closed. This was the spot where they hid out during particularly intense storms, and a place where Sam and Damon used to play Flashlight Tag.

Sam swung her legs around, got out of the bed and followed them out.

"We thought you were dead!" Pearl said. "There was a big bolt of lightning, and we heard a boom and then the house shook." Her grandma's voice cracked, and Bonnie, to her credit, gave her an empathetic look.

Bonnie closed the door behind them, and they were in complete darkness.

After a click, a flashlight turned on and shined up directly at Jessie's face. Pearl huffed out, "Jessie, can you ever *not* scare the shit out of me?"

Jessie gave a delighted grin. "It's just too easy. I can't help myself."

Bonnie flipped on another flashlight and took the opportunity to pull Sam aside. "When we went to check on you, it was like you were in some kind of a trance. I was shaking you, and you didn't respond. Are you feeling all right?"

Sam's heart rate ticked up, and she swallowed down a lump in her throat. The CD player was still in her room. Every part of her wanted to stand up and retrieve it, but now that her mom was on high alert, she couldn't without provoking suspicion. "That's weird," Sam said. "I must've been in a really deep sleep."

Bonnie eyed her, then grabbed her elbow and leaned in. "Is there something going on, Sam? Something you want to tell me? Like my therapist says, I can be a safe space."

"I think you lost all rights to knowing what's going on with me when you left." Sam shook her arm free from Bonnie's grasp.

"I'm worried about you," Bonnie said.

"Well, you don't have to be. I was just exhausted." Sam sat down on the floor and leaned back and into the wall for support.

"What are you two bickering about?" Pearl asked.

"Nothing," Sam said. "Bonnie just doesn't realize how potent Jessie's hurricane punch is."

"It'll take the paint off your car," Jessie said with the kind of authority of someone who'd actually tested it out.

Sam's jaw clenched as she curled her legs into her chest. "I'm fine," she said.

Bonnie smoothed the front of her button-down shirt, and the veins in her hands popped against her gently crinkled skin. In Sam's mind, her mom had been permanently stuck at thirty three. So seeing her with two prominent frown lines, crow's feet around her eyes and a silvery hue to her blond hair was like meeting a completely new person.

Her pencil-thin eyebrows that she'd plucked obsessively hadn't ever filled out, though, so there was that.

Bonnie sat close to Sam. "I know you're mad," she said. "I completely understand. But I do hope—"

"Bonnie," Sam started to say. She grabbed a couch cushion they'd dragged into the hallway and laid her head on top of it. "Can we just talk in the morning, like Pearl asked? I'm exhausted, if you didn't notice."

Bonnie opened her mouth as if to say something, but then seemed to think better of it. "All right."

Sam closed her eyes and pretended to fall asleep. Eventually, Pearl and Jessie's argument over Scrabble died down. The wind outside kicked up. And her mother's breaths continued to come in evenly next to her.

When the threat of actual sleep came this time, Sam let it take her.

29

Sam woke with the kind of stiffness that only comes from sleeping in an awkward position—something she'd experienced many times when having to stay overnight in airport terminals due to flight delays. As Sam sat up, she was alone and the storm had passed. It was bright and sunny outside, and she realized she had slept through the entire morning. Sam massaged a spot on her neck as she walked through the hall and toward her bedroom.

Waking up and immediately thinking of the CD player was silly. Almost as silly as the fact that she wanted to check her phone to see if Damon had texted her back. She was not a teenager, and her thoughts shouldn't be fueled purely by the guy she had a crush on, but well, they were.

She turned the knob on her bedroom door and there, staring her down, was the palm tree. *This* was what she should be worried about—a hole in her grandma's house—but instead her eyes roamed the space to try to find the CD player.

"Hey!" Grandma Pearl called out. Sam looked up and out of the space that used to be her window to find Pearl, Jessie and Bonnie in the driveway. "Get out of there, it's not safe!"

"I'm just looking for my phone," Sam called back. She tucked her hair behind her ears and glanced around the room again.

"We took a few things out already." Bonnie was as close to the window as was safe, and held up Sam's phone in her hand. "I got your phone."

But did you get the CD player? Sam wanted to ask, though she had the good sense not to. "Okay, I'll be right out, then," she said.

Sam waited for Bonnie to leave so she could keep scouring the room, but Bonnie seemed to also be waiting for Sam to leave. Which irritated Sam in a way only her mother could. She'd forgotten this feeling of being closely watched and monitored by her mom, which had occasionally happened throughout her childhood when Bonnie mustered up the strength to act like a parent.

Sam cleared her throat and turned around to leave the bedroom. She'd have to come back for the CD player, because at the moment she was between a Bonnie and a hard place.

When Sam came out through the front door, the sky was dotted with salt-and-pepper clouds that hinted at the storm from the night before. She rubbed her temple as the humidity filled her sinuses with thick air. Squinting out to the street to assess the damage, there was Alligator Alice, power-walking down the sidewalk and stepping over fallen palm fronds as if there hadn't just been a massive hurricane.

Sam shielded her eyes against the glare of the sun as she approached her mom. Bonnie handed her the cell phone, and when Sam tapped the screen she discovered it was dead. Because of course it was.

"So, the palm tree," Sam said, resigned to her tech-free fate. "Who do we call for something like this?"

"Insurance first," Grandma Pearl said. "After your mama cuts the thing in half and we haul it out of the window."

Bonnie nodded toward the garage, which was open with a chainsaw lying in wait on the concrete slab of the floor.

Then, as if by Southern lumberjack magic, Damon emerged

from the garage, talking on his cell phone. His dark hair wasn't styled, but fell around his face in waves, and his shadow of a beard had thickened overnight. He must've sensed Sam's eyes on him, because he turned and met her gaze. He quickly glanced away, though, and the sinking feeling of all not being well returned.

She didn't need to recharge her phone to know he hadn't responded to her message, or, if he had, there would be nothing good to see.

"I called Damon to ask if he could help with the cleanup," Grandma Pearl said, reading her thoughts. "He thinks Farrah might be able to bring her pickup truck over to cart away the pieces."

"It was nice of him," Bonnie added. "Didn't know you two still kept in touch."

"We didn't," Sam surprised herself by answering. "But now we do."

"Oh, they definitely keep in *touch*," Pearl said with a side smile. Jessie elbowed her.

Bonnie frowned as she looked between Sam and Damon, likely piecing the not-so-subtle clues together.

"Hey," Damon said as he walked toward them. Finally, he locked in on Sam. Despite the fact that she knew they had unfinished business, her stomach did the silly fish flip trick again. He hesitated, then wrapped Sam in a hug and brought her into his chest. She closed her eyes as she leaned into the steady solidness of him.

"So, Bonnie's back, huh?" he said into her ear.

"She came last night," Sam answered. "Along with the tree in my room."

Damon looked from the tree, to Sam, to Bonnie and scratched his head, maybe feeling as overwhelmed as Sam did.

For her part, Sam didn't exactly want to be in this situation, either, and she was starting to get anxious about the possessed CD player. "I might grab a few things from my room before the tree trimming starts," she said. She didn't know if she wanted to listen to a song anytime soon, but she did want to have the option. And she felt weirdly protective over the thing.

"Is it safe to go back in?" he asked.

"I'm sure it's fine." Sam brushed his comment off. But as soon as the words were out of her mouth, an overweight water rat scuttled across the trunk of the fallen palm, rushing for Sam's bedroom window.

"Stop!" Sam shouted at the rat, who turned just long enough to sneer and continue its route into the house.

"Never seen one that big," Damon said.

"I have," Pearl said, and a dark look crossed her face. "They don't call Panama City the Redneck Riviera for nothing."

"Okay, well, we'll get an exterminator," Sam offered.

"Honey, you need more than an exterminator to fix the hole in your house. Especially if you let Pearl get her way with selling this place." Jessie gave Sam a *there-there* pat on the shoulder. "Pearl, you can bunk with me for the week. And Bonnie can use the couch."

"And Sam…" Pearl looked over to Damon, which made Damon shift from one foot to the other.

"You can stay at my place, Sam-Sam." He met her gaze.

"What a smart man you've grown into, Damon." Pearl elbowed Sam. "And what a generous offer, which we will of course take you up on."

"You do not need to do this," Sam said. She knew he was only agreeing to help because Pearl had asked. But there were other easier options, like Jessie's floor, or the middle of the road. "I've obviously intruded on your space enough already."

"A Rat Queen just moved into your bedroom," Damon said. "I'm taking pity on you."

Well, Sam couldn't think of anything to say to that, really.

"Before you go, can we talk?" Bonnie's frown lines increased, as if already bracing for the *no*. "Is now a good time? It will only take a minute."

Sam knew enough about life that when anyone said it would *only take a minute* that meant a solid ten. And it was *not* a good time for whatever nonsense Bonnie had planned. "No, no, thank you," Sam said, then gave her a hard look.

"Do you want to go?" Damon asked in a low tone, likely sensing her angry vibration.

"Yes." Sam fisted the side of her shirt and gritted her teeth. Damon headed toward his motorcycle, and she did, too.

"Sam," Bonnie called out. When Sam glanced back, she knew she was breaking a piece of her mom's heart, but hadn't this woman done the same thing to Sam, and worse?

"Let her go," she heard Grandma Pearl say. "She'll come back in her own time."

Damon handed Sam a helmet and then settled his own on. He scratched at the back of his neck and then looked over to her. Their eyes met, and she saw a flash of something that was distinctly apprehension. He quickly glanced away.

"I promise to be a better house guest than the Rat Queen," Sam said as she settled in behind Damon.

"For all you know the Rat Queen is very tidy and thoughtful. Maybe she's making your bed right now." Damon flipped the kickstand up.

Sam gagged and Damon laughed. "I love that for her. I hope she stays," she said.

"Ready?" he asked.

She'd done this once before with him—hopped on the back of his bike, held on to him fiercely and taken a ride. But now...

"Sam?" he tried again.

She wrapped her arms around him, and his body momentarily tensed. "Is this okay?" she asked.

"Yes," he said. Though his voice was low and deep and coming from a place inside him she'd only heard a day ago.

He revved the engine, which was when she saw Bonnie across the lawn, watching them with tight lips. Bonnie's words once again rang in her ears. *Don't end up stuck in this place.*

But she was stuck in this place, at least for now, and Sam couldn't help but feel safe pressed up tight to Damon.

So maybe Sam was a disappointment, but she also no longer cared what Bonnie thought. Still, she hated the fact that her mom had a smug look on her face, like she'd always known this would happen, and was finally proven right.

30

Damon's house was situated on a large plot of land just off the bike path. He pulled up to the seashell-covered driveway and parked in front.

Sam had often wondered what kind of place Damon lived in. Her Parisian studio apartment was in the perfect spot to hop around to different countries for traveling. So what kind of a home would Damon pick for himself? She'd imagined something edgy, modern and sharp—the way Damon's style had always been. But as her flip-flops crunched along the broken shells and they walked toward the wooden porch, she could see that he'd chosen a classic A-frame. The house had to be at least seventy years old and elevated on hurricane-friendly stilts. While the shape was one that had existed in Tybee since her grandma was a kid, the outside was painted a rich and deep midnight blue.

Perhaps more importantly, the trees had been placed far enough away that there were no palms breaking into the house. As they took the steps in awkward silence, she asked, "How long have you lived here?"

Damon unlocked the front door and held it open for her. "Almost five years now," he said as she walked inside.

She glanced around. There was a dark olive L-shaped couch with striped accent pillows. Behind the couch was a wall covered in framed albums from some of Damon's favorite bands—My Chemical Romance, Tegan and Sara, Simple Plan, Paramore, Taking Back Sunday, Yellowcard and Good Charlotte. The walls were a warm evergreen, and the floors were a sleek polished concrete. From the outside, she'd assumed a traditional interior, but Damon had modernized the furniture and floors so it perfectly reflected his indie sensibilities.

Sam liked walking into his space and feeling surrounded by evidence of who he was now, but she'd never admit that to him. Not when she had the opportunity to tease him first. "So, when you decided to get a bachelor pad, did you just kind of google things that you should put in your home, or...?" Sam tried to hide her smile.

Damon bit his lip, then said, "I rewatched all of the episodes of MTV *Cribs* and picked and chose from there."

She inspected every inch of the place. After all, she knew who Damon had been in high school, but who was he now? Apparently, he was a guy who played enough Ms. Pac-Man to have the arcade game in one corner of his living room. Along with a truly meticulous and well-appointed built-in bar cabinet, which had slots for wine, racks of Band Practice Brews bottles, cocktail shakers, beer steins, martini glasses and top-shelf liquor. Damon rested his palms on the concrete slab of the kitchen island behind him. She tried not to notice his triceps, but they were definitely there.

Sam sat on the couch, far away from his muscles. "All you're missing is a stuffed deer head."

"Pretty sure I saw a lava lamp and inflatable chair in your room yesterday," he said. "Just saying."

The mention of Damon being in her room sent a rush of blood to her cheeks. She was sure he noticed her blushing wildly and looked down at her hands to try to hide the bloom there.

"Not sure it's fair to compare my teenage design choices with your own adult ones, but if it helps you sleep at night…"

Sam noticed a guitar hanging on another wall. "Remember when we tried to teach ourselves to play guitar the summer before senior year? I really wanted to learn, but you were so bad your dad threatened to ground you if we didn't stop."

"I remember." His eyes roamed the length of her. "That's the same guitar we tried to learn on."

"The same…?" Her words caught as she realized he'd kept the guitar from their childhood. Even though he didn't play, and even though she hadn't been around to try herself. There the guitar hung in the center of his wall, like a reminder of that time.

Damon broke through her thoughts. "How about we go on the deck? I can't have you finding more things in the house to make fun of me for."

"Challenge accepted." Sam followed Damon out of the back sliding glass doors and onto an expansive deck.

Unlike Pearl's place, Damon's was surrounded by lush and overgrown plants. He had a large back lot, but hadn't done much other than adding a firepit, grill and some rattan chairs.

Damon came to stand next to her. Sam listened to the singing of happy insects as a leftover gentle breeze from the hurricane blew through her hair. Maybe it was the sun's burning yellow rays shifting to a warm marigold or the fact that she was with Damon—a man who'd known her when she was deeply broken and stayed her friend just the same—but she leaned her head on his shoulder. He wrapped an arm around her, and they watched fireflies sparkle between the trees.

Those quiet minutes weren't something Sam had experienced in a long time; being so comfortable with another person that you could just sit in the silence with them.

Eventually, Damon broke it, though. "Do you want to talk about Bonnie showing up?"

Sam lifted her head from the nook of his arm. "She sure knows how to make an entrance. It's like she waited for the hurricane to hit just to add some extra drama."

"You didn't know she was coming?" He pressed his palms into the railing.

"No one did." Sam shook her head, still trying to wrap her head around *why* Bonnie had come back at all. "Pearl had apparently left her a voicemail saying we were cleaning the house out. I guess Bonnie didn't want to part with her collection of scrunchies."

"Scrunchies are back in now, to be fair," he said.

To her surprise, Sam started to laugh. A lot. Too much. She laughed so hard that tears streamed down her face. And then she was crying, actually crying, and Damon wrapped her up in his arms. She accidentally elbowed his ribs when she tried to hug him back, and she was apologizing and he was telling her to stop, but she was sniffling and embarrassed, and he managed to scoop her up and carry her inside.

Damon put Sam on the couch, poured her a glass of water and handed it to her. He sat next to her. She took a big sip and eventually stopped crying and wiped under her eyes with the back of her hand.

"I didn't get a lot of sleep," she tried to explain.

He gave her the gentlest look imaginable. "Let's get you to bed, then."

Sam nodded. Damon disappeared into a room, and when he came back, he said, "I've got a T-shirt and boxers for you in the bathroom, and a toothbrush. Your breath is terrible," he joked.

She blew a breath into her palm and sniffed. Yeah, he was right. "Mind if I borrow your phone charger, too?"

"Sure thing. I'll charge the rental fee for the cable to your room."

Sam cracked a smile. She was starting to feel too comfortable with Damon and she needed clarity, even if it killed the mood. "What are we going to do about us?"

"Let's talk tomorrow. Your mom randomly showed up at your door. And there's a rat the size of an overweight dog living in your room. You need sleep. Then in the morning, after you've rested, we can talk." Damon bent down and left a soft kiss on her forehead. "You need a break. Let me take care of you tonight, okay?"

Sam closed her eyes. She was exhausted. Since coming home, she always seemed to be exhausted. Damon was right; she needed sleep. But she also needed him.

"Will you stay with me?" she asked, her voice so low she barely heard it. But Damon did.

"Yeah." He shoved his hands into his pockets. "I'll be here."

She brushed her teeth, took a quick shower, slipped into his T-shirt and boxers, then came out, and Damon was there, just as he said he'd be. He pulled back the covers of his bed, and she crawled under the comforter. He lay next to her. She grabbed his hand and wrapped it around her waist so he was spooning her. His chin rested above her head on the pillow. His chest rose and fell behind her, and the rhythm of him made her close her eyes.

Sam woke up alone, but the note on the pillow next to her relayed that breakfast would be waiting. She hadn't slept so well in weeks and allowed herself a long and indulgent stretch under the covers. Eventually, her stomach made a disgruntled noise, and because hangry Sam wasn't a pleasant one, she threw off the covers and got up.

She'd expected to look in the bathroom mirror and discover a sea witch, but it was kind of amazing what lots of sleep could do. Her eyes were bright, the puffy bags were nearly gone, her skin had cleared and her hair had a natural beachy wave from how she'd fallen asleep on it while damp. If she didn't know any better, she'd say she looked well rested. Like her trip to

Tybee had accidentally turned into the kind of vacation Rachel wanted for her.

Sam opened the bedroom door and peered out. Damon was at the kitchen stove and, judging by the smell in the room, working on bacon. She'd just woken up in Damon's house, and now he was making her breakfast. This would almost feel like they were a couple, if she hadn't had to ask him to cuddle her.

"I don't suppose you make coffee, too?" Sam ran a hand through her hair.

Damon turned. "My Keurig can." He pointed to the sleek machine in the corner of the kitchen, took out a pod and popped it in. The machine whirred to life and he grabbed a branded Band Practice Brews mug from the cabinet. "How'd you sleep?"

Sam sidled onto the bar stool at the kitchen counter and propped her elbows up. "How did *you* sleep? I hope you didn't mind me using you as a human body pillow," she joked.

"I didn't mind." Damon picked up the coffee cup and put it in front of Sam. His eyes locked on to hers and she couldn't look away, not even if she tried. Eventually, he grabbed a carton of milk and she poured in a few glugs, then sipped.

Damon brought over two plates loaded with bacon, eggs and toast, then sat on the bar stool next to her. He took a deep breath, then turned to face her. She did the same, and their knees touched, but he didn't move away so neither did she.

"Should we talk about what happened the other day?" he eventually said.

"We should." Though Sam had no idea where to start.

"I know we joke around a lot, but that was a big deal," Damon added.

The *that* was sex, Sam knew, and the fact that they'd leaped from childhood friends to adults who had sex *was* a big deal. In that what they'd done hadn't been meaningless. Not a one-night fling they could occasionally remember and just as easily forget. They weren't nothing to each other, and now they were closer in a way they'd never been.

"Right," she acknowledged. Still, Sam knew through her bones that their situation wasn't clear. If it had been, they wouldn't be shuffling around the subject like two kids at a middle school dance. "But you live here, and I'm in Paris. And we both have these super busy jobs."

"Yeah, we do," Damon quickly said. He waited for her to say more, but she couldn't say the words *I'm afraid this won't work.* Eventually, he said them for her. "So maybe we'll just kind of treat this as it is, then. You're here now, and we have time to be together. But when you leave…"

We will be over, Sam finished the thought in her head. All of that made sense, logically. She'd basically made the argument herself. So why did she feel so disappointed?

His free hand tucked a strand of hair behind her ear, and she leaned her cheek against his open palm. He bent toward her, and she tilted her chin up. Damon closed his eyes, and she closed hers, and their lips met for a kiss that rolled through like a silky wave. His fingers squeezed hers as he pulled her in close. And then he stood and lifted her off the chair, and she wrapped her legs around his waist.

He brought her to his bedroom. All they had was the time she would spend in Tybee, nothing more. They had to make every minute count. And as the too-bright morning light streamed in through the curtains to reveal the painful truth of the present, their bodies crashed and rocked together as smoothly as they had the day before.

31

Later that morning, Damon drove Sam back to Grandma Pearl's. Just yesterday, she'd made this ride with him, but now she wrapped her arms tighter because she knew there was a clock ticking down the minutes on their time together.

As they stopped at a red light, Damon lifted one hand off the handle and put it on top of her own clasped hands, as if he wanted to savor what they had, too.

When they pulled up to the house, Grandma Pearl and Jessie were out on the front lawn, sitting in metal chairs with big sunglasses on and a beer for each of them.

Damon killed the engine and flipped the kickstand out. As she got off the bike, she peeled off the helmet and squinted at the two women. "Little early for beer, isn't it?" Sam called out.

Pearl startled, as if she hadn't even heard the motorcycle and was only now registering that Sam was even there. "The power is still out. If we don't drink the beer now, it'll get lukewarm."

Sam laughed at that.

Damon lifted the face shield of his helmet, then said, "You sure it's okay if I head to the brewery? I want to make sure the generator's still working."

She knew that if she asked, Damon would stay. And while she wouldn't mind having him around to deal with the fallout, she also knew he'd come running back if she really needed him.

"Go," she said. "I'll be fine."

"Keep me posted."

He still wore his helmet, but she angled herself to kiss his lips, then flipped the face shield back down; as simple as breathing.

Damon put the kickstand back up, revved the engine of the bike and then took off down the street. Sam watched, and when the sound of his motorcycle faded, she turned to find Pearl and Jessie smiling widely at her.

"Enjoyed the ride, did you?" Grandma Pearl asked with a knowing smirk.

Sam tried to hide her own smile. "I did," she eventually said. Jessie let out a wolf whistle.

A man in a hazmat suit carrying an animal crate came out the front door and onto the lawn. Which was when Sam noticed the rather large white van parked on the street just ahead of them. "Rodent Rick!" was emblazoned over a massive cartoon smiling rat.

"Tell it to me straight, Rick. Did you catch her?" Pearl slid her sunglasses down her face, and Rick lifted the hat part of his hazmat suit.

"Oh, I got her." He held the cage up. "And you're lucky you called when you did, because this mama is about to give birth to a whole litter of pups."

"Pups?" Pearl gripped the plastic armrests of her chair. "Thank God for you, Rodent Rick."

Sam tried to hold back the bile rising in her throat. "Yes," she finally said. "Thank you, Rodent Rick."

"You cool if I keep this little lady?" He patted the side of the cage. "I lost my gal Rosie the Rat recently, and it'd be nice to have some kids around."

"By all means." Pearl waved her hand in some kind of blessing. They all watched as Rick lovingly carried the rat cage toward his van, like the odd proud new father he was.

"I think *I* need a beer now," Sam said.

Jessie reached into the cooler next to her, popped the top and handed one to Sam. Sam sipped the beer and glanced around the lawn for signs of life from her mom, but saw nothing. "Where's Bonnie?"

"She's at my place taking a shower," Jessie said.

Sam's gaze drifted over to Jessie's single-story cottage next door, almost identical in style to their own, but with a hot orange door painted to match Jessie's nails. Somewhere in that house was the person she'd dreamt about seeing for years, and now she was just a short walk away.

"She didn't sleep well," Pearl added. "Why don't you go over and make sure she's all right?"

Sam wasn't sure if the women were giving her an opportunity to be alone with Bonnie, or just politely telling her to leave, but Sam decided that she might as well take them up on the offer, either way. She didn't owe Bonnie anything, but she did owe it to herself to try to get the closure she needed.

"Speaking of my place…" Jessie told Pearl as Sam walked away. "I think you Letos will be bunking with me until the roof gets mended."

"But you hate my sound machine, and it's the only way I can sleep through your snores," Pearl said.

"Well, the insurance isn't covering the cost of a hotel, so I'll just have to invest in earplugs," Jessie said.

"Or get those nose strips I keep telling you about," Pearl chided. "I saw them again on the Home Shopping Network."

Sam bit the corner of her lip as the voices of Pearl and Jessie faded. She hadn't been in Jessie's house in years but wasn't surprised to find that it still smelled like the watercolor paints she liked to use. Jessie was an artist who not only specialized in nudes, but also painting scenes from Tybee—the rolling waves, the lighthouse, the row of colorful beach cottages that were protected from development. Jessie's art hung in simple wooden frames throughout the home, and Sam stopped to stare at a new painting: a woman with bright purple hair in an Adirondack chair, flanked by two empty Adirondack chairs. She recognized this to be Pearl, and a little ache in her chest rose at the idea that her grandma would be remembered as alone on the beach and surrounded by the ghosts of the women who'd left.

Bonnie stood next to Sam and looked at the painting. "I miss sitting out there with both of you," she eventually said.

Sam turned to Bonnie. She could say something mean like, *You have a funny way of showing it*, but held back. Fighting wouldn't solve anything. It wouldn't answer the questions Sam had for Bonnie. And, ultimately, what was done was done.

"I'm ready to talk, if you are," Sam said instead.

They walked along the wet sand of the beach, and the smell of seaweed and suntan lotion surrounded them. The beach wasn't soothing to Sam the way it was for Pearl, but in some ways this scenario *did* feel safe—they could walk without having to look at each other so Sam could say exactly what she wanted to.

"Are you sure you're feeling okay?" Bonnie asked. "You were so out of it the other night. It was weird. I'd never seen you like that before. You've always been such a light sleeper."

This little reminder that at one point, her mom had been a *mom* and noticed things about her was a little unnerving, especially as Sam had squarely filed Bonnie away in the land of people who didn't deserve nice things.

Sam deftly changed the subject. "What I want to talk about is why you really left."

Okay, maybe *not* so smooth of a transition.

Bonnie pulled at the ends of her sleeves. "I know it's hard to imagine, or even to forgive me, but I was suffering from depression. I didn't know what else to do except leave. Pearl, you know, she's from a different generation of women. When I told her something was wrong, she told me that I needed to get a hobby. When I said it didn't help, she told me I was being selfish. And it's not her fault—that's how she was raised. They didn't talk about mental health back then. She just didn't think what I was going through was real. She made me feel worse, like I was crazy for having any feeling that wasn't gratitude."

Bonnie must be crazy for leaving this, Pearl would say when they sat on the beach. *You're crazy!* Pearl would scream at Bonnie during their epic fights. Sam had always cringed at Pearl's use of the word, but she didn't know what to believe.

"If I didn't leave when I did, I'm not sure I'd be here today. I felt so stuck and broken, like I was drowning. Do you understand what I'm saying?"

Bonnie searched Sam's eyes for understanding, and Sam *did* understand what she was saying. Or at least, her visions of Alt-Sam saying a similar thing to Damon helped her to. After the miscarriage and failed eye surgery, Alt-Sam said she'd felt stuck and broken and needed to leave. Had Bonnie felt the same? Alt-Sam hadn't had a baby, but her mom had. Alt-Sam arguably had more choices than Bonnie had at the same age. So part of Sam could understand that her mom had felt *stuck*, even if Sam had been the thing keeping her that way.

"Why didn't you bring me with you?" she asked.

Bonnie kicked a spot of sand as they walked. "I didn't think I'd be gone for very long. I could barely take care of myself at that point. I'd been self-medicating with drinking, and I knew I wouldn't be able to take care of you. I waited as long as I could. And then you were fourteen, and you seemed so grown-up. Looking back, I know you were just a kid. You needed me. But then, your grandma convinced me that maybe you didn't."

"What do you mean?" Sam started, but then stopped herself. She didn't want to seem insensitive, but she also didn't totally buy what Bonnie was pushing. "Grandma convinced you that I didn't need a mother?"

"That's not what I meant to say," Bonnie said. "Grandma Pearl wanted what was best for you. And she told me your life was better without me in it."

"She wouldn't say that." Sam scowled to herself. How many nights had Sam spent sobbing into Pearl's shoulder, asking *why* her mom had left and *when* she would be back. There was no way her grandma would keep them apart, not when she knew how broken Sam was over the loss.

"I was there, honey." Bonnie gritted her teeth. "My memory isn't always perfect, but I do remember your grandmother telling me not to come back once I decided to leave. That's a hard one to forget." Bonnie looked out to the ocean and the gulls cautiously circling over the water as if gauging whether or not the storm would return. "But all you need to do is ask her about it."

Sam took a deep inhale and studied her mom. Why would Bonnie lie about something like this? Why would her grandma omit this fact from her? She'd ask Pearl for the real story, but for now, she still had questions for the Leto in front of her.

"Do you regret having me?" Sam asked.

Bonnie shook her head. "Depression is a nasty thing. I remember when I had you, I was terrified. I thought I would accidentally drop you, or you'd die in your sleep, or I'd do something wrong. You were this tiny, helpless little thing. I'd gone from high school to being a mom, and I just wasn't ready for any of that responsibility. I had no idea what I was doing. You have a baby, and then they send you home and there's no help. No instruction manual. They just expect you to figure everything out on your own. But it was just me and your grandma."

But Bonnie hadn't been responsible for Sam. She'd given that job to Pearl. Sam decided to also keep that thought to herself, for the moment, at least.

"I got better, I thought. You grew and grew. I mean, you were three years old and up to my belly button. Always so tall." Bonnie shook her head at the memory. "Things got easier. But then I'd get depressed on and off. Some days I could barely leave the house, and your grandma would get so frustrated with me. She couldn't understand why I wouldn't just get out of bed. By the time you were in middle school, you had your own life separate from mine. And I just thought, *Maybe she'd be better off without me altogether.* So I left after you started high school. In hindsight, I realize that was my depression doing the thinking for me."

Sam remembered her mom holing herself up in her bedroom. But at the time, she'd assumed her mom just didn't want to see Pearl, or her. That was how Bonnie had always been—moody, hard to read and in ever-shifting moods. Sam never considered the possibility that it was the result of anything other than Bonnie's wanting to be anywhere else.

Bonnie sniffled, trying to hold back her emotions. "I don't regret having you," she said through a sob. "I just wish I'd gotten help sooner so I could've been the parent you deserved instead of the one you ended up with. Deep down, I always loved you. I hope you know that." Bonnie's hand reached for Sam, but then her mom seemed to think better of it and pulled back.

"Why did you wait until now to come back?" Sam couldn't hide the skepticism in her voice this time.

Bonnie looked out at the sand ahead of them before answering. "When your grandma called to tell me she was selling the house and you were coming back, I just thought that maybe this could be my chance to finally tell you the truth about why I left and how sorry I am. I didn't tell your grandma I was coming, because I was afraid she'd talk me out of it again."

Sam's eyes narrowed as she processed what Bonnie had said. Grandma Pearl had always firmly stood by the fact that Bonnie never reached out, but now her mom was suggesting that she *had* wanted to come sooner.

"That's not true," Sam said. "You didn't reach out at all."

Bonnie stopped walking, which forced Sam to stop walking. She took Sam's hands and said, "It's true that I didn't reach out for a long time. I had to find a therapist, and get on medication and I was so ashamed of both of those things that I didn't feel I even deserved to be your mom. But eventually, when I was sober, and stable and had my own place, I called. I told Pearl I was coming, but she told me you were doing better without me and I don't know, I believed her."

Maybe Sam was getting too much information all at once, but her head felt heavy. She squatted down and put her head in her hands and massaged her temples. This was a lot, too soon, and too fast. She didn't know what to think or believe—either her mom was telling the truth and her grandma had lied, or Bonnie was lying to her now.

"Sam." Bonnie's voice was laced with concern. She dropped down and rubbed a hand over Sam's back. They stayed like that for a good long while, and Sam was surprised to find that Bonnie's hand gently soothing her *was* helpful.

A ping from Bonnie's phone broke the moment, and she said, "Grandma got the all-clear to go into the house so we can get our things. Should we head home? I'm so sorry to tell you all of this. I'm sure it's a lot. We don't have to—"

"Stop," Sam managed to say. "Please, just stop."

"Okay." Bonnie stood and held out a hand, which Sam took. As she stood, she couldn't help but clock the sad expression on Bonnie's face. Maybe sadder than she'd ever looked before.

32

When they got back, Bonnie pushed open the screen door on the back porch. "Mama?" she called out. "Where are you?"

"In the living room!" Grandma Pearl shouted back. "We're going through some of the things we salvaged from Sam's room."

"I can check on them, if you want a little space," Bonnie offered.

"Thanks," Sam said. She pulled out a chair at the kitchen table and plunked down into it.

Bonnie pursed her lips, then headed toward the living room. Sam watched her leave and contemplated her options. Bonnie claimed that Pearl had kept them apart for years. Was it really possible that Bonnie had just decided not to reach out, even when Sam became an adult? Even if that was the case, was she supposed to blindly believe Bonnie? Would the only way to the truth be to confront Pearl? Her grandma had been Sam's support system for so many years that ambushing Pearl with this didn't feel right, either.

"Sammy girl." Grandma Pearl came into the kitchen. "Your mom seems to think this broken CD player might be worth something on eBay. Do you want me to save it or toss?"

Sam's eyes widened at the CD player in Pearl's hand. The CD

player she'd tried to find, but hadn't been able to. And there it was, just waiting for her. She pushed herself up from the table, came around and grabbed it from her.

"I told you she'd want it," said Bonnie. "Your grandma doesn't know how much this nostalgia stuff goes for, but I'm telling you, what's old is new."

"She's here to clean the house out, not keep more junk." Pearl opened the cupboard under the sink and scowled. "Where are my trash bags? Sam, did you move them?"

"But these are *her* things." Bonnie opened cabinets above the sink, and eventually found the box of trash bags that Sam had moved. She peeled one out and handed it to her mom. "The same way my room had *my* things."

Bonnie and Pearl were bickering once again, but Sam was busy trying to turn the player on. She hit the power button, but the screen wouldn't light up. She opened the lid, made sure the CD was placed correctly, then closed the lid. It was still dead.

"What did you do?" she asked.

"If you really wanted your stuff, wouldn't you have come back for it sooner?" Pearl directed at Bonnie; apparently, she hadn't heard Sam.

"Yes, I would have," Bonnie said pointedly.

"Grandma." Sam's voice was loud, and the women turned.

"Yes?" Pearl asked, maybe annoyed.

"It's not working." Sam held the player up to demonstrate her point.

"I know, hon, that's why I assumed you'd want to toss it." Pearl shot Bonnie a look.

"But it *was* working before." Sam was agitated now. "What did you do to it?"

"Huh?" Pearl asked as she shook open the trash bag. "I don't know what you're getting at."

"I listened to a CD on this the night of the storm, and now it's not working. Did you do something to it?" Sam realized then that she was upset. Maybe she should be relieved—after all, the CD player had too strong of a hold on her—but she was claw-ingly desperate to have it light up again. There was one song left, and she needed to know how Damon and Alt-Sam resolved their issues.

"Well, check the batteries," Pearl said as she headed back to the living room. "Maybe the tree hit it or something."

"Can you play the songs on your phone?" Bonnie tried to be helpful, but she just didn't get it. Neither of them did. Not that Sam completely got it, either.

The CD player worked without batteries. It worked after being abandoned for over a decade. But now it'd suddenly just stopped? That didn't make any sense. Maybe she had to be in her room, or close to her teenaged things, or...

"Give me a sec," Sam said as she raced out of the kitchen and toward her bedroom.

"Be careful in there! I think I cleaned up all the broken glass, but you never know," Bonnie called out after her.

Sam's room was darker than usual with the power still out and the boarded-up window in place, so she used the flashlight on her phone to illuminate the floor as she made her way to the bed. There were leaves and broken branches that had been swept to a corner of the room, and various items that had once been on her desk—the *Twilight* books, gel pens and Lip Smacker balms—were now on her bed. The only thing left on her desk was, miraculously, the somehow intact lava lamp. Sam sat on the bed, pushing aside the items from her desk, and furiously hit the play button, but the screen remained blank. She opened and closed the top again, found batteries in her desk drawer and popped them in. She whispered, *Come on, come on, come on*, on a loop as she stared at it.

But there was just...nothing.

Unless that was it, and there were no more visions to be had; Alt-Sam stayed in Tybee and ended up with Myles instead of Damon. Or neither of them. No flight school, just cookie dough ice cream and gummy bears for the rest of her life. And maybe Alt-Sam grew to be happy with that, but Sam was upset that she'd never get to know.

Sam:

The CD player stopped

Rachel:

Good. That thing was probably giving you some kind of radioactive powers that would make you grow a third arm.

Sam:

But this is weird. Why won't it turn on? There's supposed to be one more song on the CD.

Rachel:

Who cares. It was weird that you were seeing things. At least now you're being saved from yourself.

Rachel:

Speaking of which, you need to get back to work, because they've put Steve on as my copilot. No one should have to be trapped in a small cockpit with Steve and his steamed broccoli. He eats the stuff for breakfast, Sam. BREAKFAST BROCCOLI, he calls it. And then he has the nerve to SMILE.

Rachel:

Please get back soon before I forcibly eject him from the plane.

Two knocks on Sam's bedroom door startled her, and she looked over to see Bonnie inching the frame open.

"Are you hungry? The power's back on at Jessie's, and your grandma is going to grab a rotisserie chicken from Publix. Apparently, it's a ten out of ten on their Cluck-Cluck scale, whatever that means." Bonnie gave a small smile, and Sam forced herself to smile back.

"Yeah," Sam said. "Sounds great."

Bonnie held on to the frame, tapped her fingers against it, then said, "Sam, you can ask me anything, you know."

"Okay." Sam would use the opening to do exactly that. "How long are you staying?"

Sam wasn't totally convinced Bonnie would give her an honest answer, but she didn't want her to think she was just welcome to be here for as long as she liked. Not that it was her house or anything.

"As long as your grandma needs me," Bonnie said. "There's a lot to do."

And then Sam just decided to say the damn thing. "Are you here because you think Pearl is going to give you money or something?"

"No, what are you—" Bonnie's brows furrowed.

But Sam plowed forward. "Because whatever she gets from selling the house is staying with her. I'm going to make sure she's taken care of."

"I don't want anything from your grandma," Bonnie said. "But I do want you to try to have a little more faith in me."

"Why would I ever do that?" Sam asked.

Bonnie gave two taps on the frame, then closed the door shut behind her. Sam couldn't be with her mom. And since she couldn't vanish into her music, she turned to the only other safe place she had—Damon.

Sam:

I'm coming over.

33

If Sam had never left Tybee, Damon could've given her his address and she'd likely be able to find her way there without GPS. The island was small, roughly four miles long with just a little over three thousand people living there year-round. During the busy summer months, the population more than doubled with tourists flocking to the white sand beaches. But in hurricane season only locals remained.

Sam wasn't a local anymore, though. Her sense of direction on the island was on par with that of any other tourist. So she relied on her phone to get her back to Damon's. She'd known the route to his childhood home as if it were her own. And even though she'd driven or biked along these very same streets hundreds of times while growing up, traveling down them now left her with an uneasy sense of déjà vu; like she was experiencing someone else's memories instead of her own.

When she parked her rental in his driveway, the uneasiness was replaced with relief. The feeling wasn't dissimilar from the one she'd have when she used to slip her headphones on and zone out to music. Maybe, though, the common denominator there had always been Damon.

She tucked a mesh tote bag over her shoulder. Unlike the last time she'd come to Damon's, this time she'd brought a toothbrush, change of clothes and various other essentials. And he must've heard her arrive, because he opened the door before she had to so much as knock.

"I can't tell if you need a drink *now* or after you tell me what Bonnie did this time." Damon held the door for her as she stepped past him and into the house, like she belonged there.

"She's just making a big show of how much she's changed, and claiming that Pearl kept her from coming back sooner." Sam dropped the overstuffed bag onto the couch.

"She's blaming Pearl now?" Damon shoved his hands into his pockets. "That's a new low."

"I know." Sam cracked her neck to relieve some of the tension that had built up from her chat with her mom. "Are you sure it's okay if I stay here again? You can say no. Jessie will love the excuse to have me sit and model for her."

Damon didn't hear her, though; his gaze was locked on the front pocket of her bag.

"You brought your old CD player?" Damon asked.

Sam had tucked her Lisa Frank notebook and the player into the front pocket, and the headphones dangled out. It wasn't that she didn't trust Bonnie and Pearl with these things, but she didn't want to risk anyone snooping through the notes she'd taken.

"I've been listening to it since I came back, but it stopped working," she said vaguely. She picked the player up and held it out for Damon to inspect. "Which is a real bummer."

Damon reached for the player, and as his hand touched the screen, the same electric shock she'd experienced the first time he'd touched it happened again. Sam pulled her hand away, and he held on to the player.

"Looks like it's working to me." Damon held it and the screen lit up, just the way it used to.

Sam shook out her hand, then approached. The CD player *was* working, and it was queued to track thirteen—the last one. Her jaw went slack and her mouth gaped at the thing. Damon had somehow fixed what she couldn't—a beer-slinging wizard— so all she had to do was put on the headphones, hit Play and...

"Should we listen to it?" Damon asked. "I don't totally remember what I put on this. It'd be cool to hear."

"No," Sam said emphatically. She searched for something, anything, to get her out of a situation where she and Damon listened to a song and were both transported. Was that even possible? She didn't know, but she wasn't ready to test it.

Unable to find the words, she let her fingers trail up Damon's forearm, then biceps, then toward his neck where she brought him in for a deep kiss. It was true that she was taking a page from Alt-Sam's playbook by redirecting Damon to sex instead of the truth. And it worked, as he kissed her back and wrapped his strong hands around her waist. This was a man, not the boy she'd grown up with, and he led her toward his bedroom to remind her of that fact.

Damon gently snored next to Sam, but she hadn't rested at all. She'd been waiting for the right moment to leave the room. She knew she could—and should—stay with him and just be. But she could also slip out of bed, so quietly Damon wouldn't know, grab the CD player and hit Play. It would take three or four minutes tops, depending on the song, and then she'd have the ending to their story.

They were meant to be—Sam had seen that from the start of the playlist—and while they'd clearly hit a rough patch, she knew that Damon could get Alt-Sam through it.

Sam carefully placed one foot then the other on the floor, stood up and snuck out. In the living room she found the player exactly where Damon had dropped it on the couch. When she picked it up, the screen glowed back.

Hello, friend, she said to herself as she stroked the front.

When it came to self-awareness, she was deeply clued in to

the fact that she was talking to an inanimate object. But she felt connected to Alt-Sam and Damon, and she was ready to see them again.

She sat on the couch and glanced out the floor-to-ceiling windows to see the world lit from the moon and stars. Gazing out at the infinite stretch of sky with all of its possibilities filled her with a kind of hope. She'd thought her path was clear, until she saw what could've been if only she'd made one different decision. Life was filled with constant small choices that charted an eventual destination. But maybe in seeing what she could've had, she'd get clarity on a potential way forward.

There was only one more song, so she hit Play.

The air was humid and heavy when Sam opened her eyes. Fat gray clouds overhead signaled that it had just rained. The sky threatened more, but Sam could almost smell it drifting away from where she was on the pier at the beach. The plank under Sam's foot groaned as she took a step forward and looked around. A gull cawed, almost as if it could see her, and maybe it could, but Sam was focused.

Blink-182's "Always" played in her headphones. The song was about persistence, and second chances, and trying to save a relationship, if only the other person would allow for that. This was the moment when Alt-Sam and Damon were going to find their way back to the good place—their second chance.

Alt-Sam's elbows rested on the top of the pier's railing as she peered into the water below, and Damon eyed her as if seeing her for the first time. The ocean churned as Sam walked toward them.

"What if you change your mind?" His voice had an edge. "Am I supposed to wait and see how this all turns out?"

Alt-Sam looked up at Damon through a newly trimmed bob of hair. And then she straightened to her full height so she was eye level with him. Something about this version of her had changed. She seemed more assured in that moment, maybe stronger. So much more familiar to Sam.

"I don't expect anything from you. You owe me nothing." Alt-Sam adjusted her glasses. A plane flew overhead, and she chanced a glance at it. "I just have to do this. If I don't try then I'm going to regret that for the rest of my life."

"And what about us?" Damon cracked his knuckles as he spoke. "You're going to regret losing this."

"Yes." Alt-Sam's lower lip trembled, and she bit it to stop herself. "But if I keep going the way I am, I'll just disappear. There will be no us. Do you understand what I'm saying? I physically cannot keep pretending that I'm okay when I'm not. That's not fair to you or me."

"I just don't get why we can't figure this out together." He reached for her hand, and she let him take it.

Alt-Sam hesitated, then said, "We've been tied to each other for so long that I don't know who I am without you. But being with you has meant that I've slowly begun to vanish. It's not your fault, Damon. I know this is on me. But if I have any hope of figuring out what I actually want, then I need to try to do that. I need time to understand why I feel so broken all the time."

And then Damon began to cry. His body shook and his head fell into his hands, and Alt-Sam wrapped him up tightly in her arms, as a tear rolled down her cheek. "I love you," she told him. "I will always love you. I'll never stop loving you. I'm so sorry. I just can't keep drowning like this."

"Drowning?" Damon pulled back from her. "You think I'm *drowning* you?" He was hurt, as his expression darkened into one of disbelief.

"Of course *you're* not drowning me. I just feel completely over my head with—"

"With what? Having all your bills paid for? Having a free place to live? With me forgiving you even after you…" And then his expression tightened as he took another step back from

Alt-Sam. And Alt-Sam looked down, as if weighing her options, trying to carefully choose her words.

Sam wanted so desperately to have the right answer to fix everything. Wasn't this supposed to end happily for them both? She wanted to make the situation better, but she didn't totally know what Alt-Sam was feeling; much like Damon, she was a little in the dark. Sam had felt the urge to leave Tybee, her house, her life, but to feel like she was drowning? She'd never hit that kind of rock bottom. So she knew that whatever Alt-Sam *was* going through had to be bad. Bad enough to force her to leave Damon so that she could survive.

And then Sam remembered Bonnie. *Drowning.* Wasn't that a word she'd used to describe how she'd felt when she was stuck in Tybee? Alt-Sam was depressed, just as her mom had been, and she was desperately trying to dig her way out of it before it was too late. She *had* to leave. There was no way she could stay.

Sam swallowed down the realization that a part of her now empathized with Bonnie, something she never imagined possible.

"I cheated because I needed to feel something. I know that's shitty to say, but I've been so numb for a long time. Ever since the miscarriage happened, I was just…desperate for something to change." Alt-Sam sniffled.

"Flight school is never going to happen for me because of the…" Alt-Sam pointed to her eyes. "But I can still travel as a flight attendant, and that's where I'm supposed to be right now. Deciding to go has been the first decision I've made that feels really right. I don't want to hurt you. I never have. And maybe that's the problem. Because I've ignored this part of myself so I could be with you. So we could be together. But in doing that I'm just…lost now. I feel totally gone. So I'm doing this— I have to do this. If I don't, then I really don't know what will happen. It scares me to think about it."

And suddenly, it all made sense to Sam—the thing she couldn't quite put her finger on but sensed. While she'd seen Damon making her other self happy, there had also been tenser moments—

when Alt-Sam had her miscarriage, the surgery didn't take and she'd cheated on him. She hadn't been in some coupled-up cocoon of bliss; she'd been missing something. She'd missed the thing that Sam had left Tybee to go and find all those years ago: herself.

Her need to explore was the thing that had and always would keep them apart. Sam wasn't able to just stay in one place. She had to see the world. The heavy stone that had settled in Sam's gut since she'd watched Alt-Sam begin to deteriorate slowly lifted. She saw the whole picture; no matter what she did, her place was in the sky.

"You know I'm not great at expressing myself," Alt-Sam said as she dug her hands into her pockets. She pulled out a folded piece of paper from one of them and handed it to Damon. "I wrote it all here. I feel like this song says everything I can't, because I'm terrible at talking about this. But this is how I feel about you, and us. I know what I'm doing is something I can't take back. But if we're meant to be, we'll find a way back to each other. I want to find my way back to you."

Alt-Sam held out the paper for Damon, but he didn't move. He didn't so much as look at her. And she held it for him, and waited, but there was no change. So she eventually put it in his pocket. She looked up at him and swallowed hard. "I know nothing I've said is right, but I love you. I wouldn't be doing this if I didn't."

And he guffawed, and then Alt-Sam's eyes welled with tears, and she wiped them with the back of her hand. Before saying another word, she walked away from Damon at a pace so fast it bordered on a run. Damon turned, his brow finally creased with emotion, and he watched her disappear like a bird soaring higher and higher.

Eventually, Damon took the paper out and unfolded it. Sam stood on her tiptoes and looked over his shoulder. The song was Blink-182's "Always," the same one she was listening to. And those words, *Always, Always*, drifted from her headphones.

As the last speck of Alt-Sam vanished, Sam was yanked hard and fast back to the present. She quickly readjusted to the feel of the couch cushions beneath her, but her throat was tight and her stomach in knots. What did all of this mean? If it didn't matter what she did and she was always destined to leave Tybee, then what was the point of all this?

The CD player was still in her lap, and while it was lit up, there were no more songs to play. She'd listened to all of them. Sam tried to fast-forward and rewind, but it was stuck on this final track.

Sam reached for her bag and pulled out the notebook.

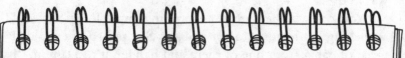

SAM AND DAMON'S MAGICAL PLAYLIST

Track One: "Bring Me to Life" by Evanescence. Other-worldly song about being understood by another human. Tybee High parking lot. Questionable amounts of eyeliner. Alt-Sam kisses Damon. Missing earring is found.

Track Two: "I Believe in a Thing Called Love" by The Darkness. A bop about being head over heels for some-one. Alt-Sam and Damon are officially dating. Myles con-tinues to disappoint. Marissa didn't have an awkward phase in high school. Jansport backpacks are timeless.

Track Three: "Supermassive Black Hole" by Muse. In-arguably the best song and movie scene pairing ever. Damon and Alt-Sam make out during *Twilight* and get kicked out. One too many hickies.

Track Four: "Want You Bad" by The Offspring. A banger

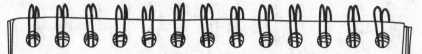

about a bad boy wanting to corrupt a good girl. Myles gets owned by Alt-Sam. Damon skips detention. Alt-Sam skips her extracurricular. I miss Dunkaroos.

Track Five: "Dance, Dance" by Fall Out Boy. A song about a guy meeting someone he likes at a school dance, and the angst of trying to desperately impress them. Damon tries to impress Alt-Sam and they get into A GODDAMN CAR CRASH. Soffe shorts. Condoms from Pearl. Looks like I never get to go to prom.

Track Six: "Fell In Love With a Girl" by The White Stripes. Can I ever hear this song again and not think about Alt-Sam and Damon sneaking around (??) and probably having sex (??). Alt-Sam's vision problems continue AND she's getting a C on an essay?

Track Seven: "Read My Mind" by The Killers, which is all about uncertainty. Makes sense, since in Alt-Sam's high school graduation, I'm not valedictorian and waiting on a surgery to get into flight school.

Track Eight: "Over My Head" by The Fray. Written about a fight, where one person was totally out of their depth. Alt-Sam is pregnant and moving in with Damon. Maybe they're not ready to be parents?

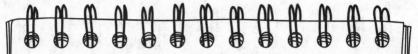

Track Nine: "Maps" by the Yeah Yeah Yeahs. Damon's starting nursing school and not a brewery. Wanting someone to stay is the theme of the song, and maybe Damon wants Alt-Sam to know he'll stay by her side and through the miscarriage?

Track Ten: "The Curse of Curves" by Cute Is What We Aim For. Myles at the ice cream shop being a little too friendly with Alt-Sam, much like the song suggests. Eye surgery set for the next day. Damon and Myles acting like weirdos.

Track Eleven: "My Happy Ending" by Avril Lavigne. Saw anything but a happy scene. Alt-Sam and Damon at Farrah's bar's opening night, big fight. Eye surgery didn't work. Damon asked Alt-Sam to see a therapist.

Track Twelve: "I Write Sins Not Tragedies" by Panic! at the Disco. A vision of Alt-Sam and Myles hooking up. Myles noticed that Alt-Sam was unhappy, and she leaned into his advances. Damon nowhere to be found.

Track Thirteen: "Always" by Blink-182. Instead of a second chance, Damon and Alt-Sam are officially over. Alt-Sam leaves Tybee to become a flight attendant and Damon is left behind...again.

Like many of the emo albums she'd adored, this CD played like a story unfolding. The songs started off with finding love, then falling in love and eventually losing that love. Only she was the subject, and the ending was tragic.

Sam and Damon had already agreed to stop things when she left Tybee, and the CD player showed that she was fated to leave, too. Because how could she choose Damon now without giving up her life or making him give up his? Still, the reality of never getting to be with him—in this life or the alternate one—didn't hurt any less.

34

"What's wrong?" Damon asked. "You haven't touched your mountain of sugar."

Sam glanced down at her plate—thick slabs of French toast homemade by Damon, covered in powdered sugar and maple syrup, sitting untouched.

No, she hadn't eaten any of her breakfast because she had a lot on her plate, both literally and emotionally. While she'd known she couldn't stay in Tybee, her last vision really hammered home the fact that Damon's place was in their hometown, while hers was in flight.

But leaving Damon again seemed wrong, somehow.

Their fate felt unacceptable, she supposed. But that wasn't an easy thing to explain to a man who just wanted her to try his French toast that he'd cooked to remind her of Paris.

"They call this pain perdu," Sam said as she cut off a corner of the sweet-smelling stuff. When she took a bite, the crisp and caramelized edges melted in her mouth and momentarily distracted her. Sam sucked rogue syrup off her thumb. "Did they teach you how to make this in beer school?"

"Yes, Hangovers 101 taught us the basics of breakfast items to bring you back to life," he joked.

Damon wiped a bit of syrup from the corner of her mouth with his thumb, and her breath caught. In a few days she'd leave Tybee, and this man and these moments. Even the visions told her that was what she was meant to do. But a big part of her couldn't imagine just walking away.

"You're giving me the saddest little face right now. What's wrong?" He leaned forward, like he genuinely wanted to know. Because if nothing else, he was Damon, a real friend, so of course he did.

She realized the only real way through was to tell Damon the truth. She couldn't keep this from him any longer.

She brushed powdered sugar off her fingers, turned in the swivel chair and placed her palms on his knees. "I'm going to tell you something, and you're probably going to think I'm making a joke, but it's not a joke."

"Okaaay," he said, extending the word. "I'm listening."

"The CD player I brought with me?"

"Yes." He dabbed at the corners of his mouth with a cloth napkin.

"It's umm…" She scratched her forehead and realized there was no easy way to say this. "When I play the songs from your CD, I see things."

She waited for him to say something.

"You see things?" he repeated. "What do you see?"

"Like, memories of us from high school." Her eye was on the verge of twitching from lack of sleep, the sugary syrup and having to make this confession. "But an alternate version of high school where you and I dated each other."

His gaze went off to a corner of the room as he thought about this. "So you fantasize about that?"

"No." She scratched at her forehead again. "I think the CD player is magic and it's showing me how our lives would've been if we hooked up. But I don't know *why* it's showing me these things. At first, the visions were really cute and sweet. Like, you were a very doting boyfriend, and I seemed happy. But then they got darker, and I didn't go to flight school, and you never got to start the bar with your sister. The one I saw last night—"

"Last night?" he said, apparently not interested in the magic CD part and instead fixated on her sneaking out of his room.

"I got up in the middle of the night and listened to a song on your couch." She let out a big breath and waited for him to respond, but he didn't. "Say something," she warily said.

Damon studied her. "I can't tell if you're just making a joke, like you said."

"It's not a joke." Sam stood up from the stool, walked to the living room where her bag was and pulled out the CD player. She brought it back to Damon.

"See this?" She held the player in front of her, hit the next button, but nothing happened. It stayed locked on track thirteen. "I can't hit Skip. I can't rewind. I can't replay. Any time I listen to a song, it queues up the next one. When I found the CD player, it didn't work. Then you touched it and suddenly it started to play. Explain this to me, Damon. Are *you* a witch?"

She was talking very quickly, and her eye had officially started to twitch. Her index finger gently touched her lid to stop it, but that only seemed to make it worse. And Damon must've realized that this was all a bit too much, because he grabbed her shoulders and said, "Let's just take a breath."

So she did.

"I believe you," he said. "I'm just digesting all of this. It's a lot."

"I know." She put the player down on the counter and sipped her coffee. "I should probably stop drinking that."

He slid his water toward her, and she sipped from that instead.

"Can I listen to a song?" he asked.

She cocked her head and considered that he would either

see a vision just as she had, or nothing at all; which would be worse was debatable. The CD player hadn't worked when Rachel tried to listen. What would happen if Damon tried?

"Go ahead," she eventually said. "But right now it won't play anything except for the last track."

Damon picked up the player and the screen changed to track one. Sam blinked hard to make sure she was seeing clearly and, yup, things were getting weirder.

"Oh, my fucking God." She steadied herself with a hand on the counter. "You saw that, right?"

She might as well have asked Damon if he'd seen a ghost, but as he looked at her, even he seemed to tense. "I did," he hesitantly said.

Then he hit the next button, and Rewind, but the screen was locked on track one, just waiting for him to press Play.

"Should I take a listen?" he asked.

"Okay, based on my experience with this, you should be on the couch, or your bed. There's this kind of fall that happens and it's hard to explain." She stood up and signaled for him to do the same. Damon got up and she led him to the couch, where they sat side by side.

"If you feel scared, don't worry," Sam said. "The visions only last as long as the song."

"Let me just..." And he put the headphones on, readjusting the sides so it fit to his head. He gave her a look so warm and accepting that her anxious breathing slowed. "We'll be okay, Sam-Sam."

"Yeah." She smiled back. *We'll be okay*, she repeated to herself. And most of her believed him. "Ready?"

Her finger hovered over the play button. He nodded his approval, and without much fanfare she pressed it.

35

"Damon?" Sam whispered. She could hear Evanescence's "Bring Me to Life" through the headphones. Part of her didn't want to disturb whatever mysterious forces were at work that made it possible for Damon to listen to the CD.

Damon had closed his eyes, relaxed his shoulders and now he was still. So still, in fact, that she wasn't entirely sure if he was even breathing. She put her head on his chest and heard the frantic *boom boom boom* of his heart, but he wasn't responding to her touch, or her voice.

Was this how she'd been when Bonnie had found her the other night—unresponsive? She poked Damon's shoulder, scratched a fingernail down his beard.

"Woah," she said.

Damon was totally and utterly immersed in the song, or a vision—but either way, he was going through something.

He let out a breath, lurched forward and began to cough uncontrollably. She hurried to grab a glass of water as he took the headphones off. His eyes were wide and clouded as he took the glass from her and gulped it down.

"Well?" she impatiently asked. "What happened?"

He set the glass down and abruptly stood from the couch. "What the fuck was that?"

"You saw it?" She was relieved, and hopeful and over-whelmed from the fact that she wasn't making this up.

"Yeah, I fucking saw it." He pulled on a wad of his hair until it stood up at all angles. "How could you not tell me about this?"

"Believe it or not, I didn't want to frighten you," she said. "But come on, what did you see?"

Damon sat back on the couch and put his head in his hands. He spoke to his lap. "I saw us. High school. The night I asked you…" He drifted off, then looked at her. "But this time, you kissed me."

"Yes, that's what I saw, too!" She was excited. Too excited, because she wasn't alone in this anymore.

Damon, on the other hand, looked like he'd just been punched in the gut. "Why didn't you tell me how bad my hair was with those red highlights and all the gel?"

"*That* is what you're thinking about right now?" Sam chuckled.

Damon swallowed and picked up the player. He rotated it with awe and horror. "What, uh, what *is* this, Sam?"

"I don't know." She threaded her fingers together in her lap. "I've been trying to figure that out. I was hoping you might have an answer."

"So every time you play a song, you get a new…?" he cautiously asked.

"Exactly." She nibbled her lower lip. "It's like, the memories I have from that time are a different version of our life."

Damon exhaled, then leaned back into the couch and put the headphones on. "Again," he said. "Show me another one."

"Are you sure?" Her voice was full of caution, but she still sat next to Damon. "You could take a minute," she said, thinking of how long she'd waited in between songs, and how she'd needed time to process.

"I need to understand. I need to know what you know." He

handed her the CD player. He could've just as easily hit the play button himself. But maybe having Sam there with him was a comfort.

She waited for him to close his eyes and, when he did, she pressed Play.

"Wow, Myles," Damon said after listening to the next track. He pulled the headphones off and wiped a hand down his face.

"I tried to tell you, but you seem to think he's a nice guy." Sam sat cross-legged next to him. Should she warn Damon about Myles, and what she was going to do with him later?

"When you saw this last vision, did you also see…baby Marissa talking to me at the end?" Sam wasn't sure if Damon's vision was exactly as hers, or if he was seeing more through Alt-Damon's eyes.

"Marissa?" He looked off, as if trying to remember. Then shook his head. "No. The last thing I saw was me, or the *other* me, walking away with a big grin."

"Gotcha." Sam opened up her notebook and glanced at the track list. If he was experiencing these visions, but through the lens of his teenaged self, then he may not see all of the details she had. He was present in every single song, up until "The Curse of Curves," when he showed up at the ice cream shop in the middle of Myles flirting with Alt-Sam.

"What's on there?" he asked while reaching for it. She tucked the pad of paper to her chest, though.

"You can have a look once you've seen a few more, otherwise the notes won't make sense," she said.

He sat back into the couch and centered the headphones over his ears. "Then let's play the next one."

Sam put the notebook aside, leaned over and hit Play.

Two hours later, he'd gotten through twelve tracks, with just one more song to go. They'd had to take breaks. Damon had excused himself to the bathroom at one point, emerging red-eyed and sniffling.

"It's not real," she offered, but knew what he was going through. The feeling that it *was* real, and was happening, made it hard to unsee.

Damon wiped at his eyes with the back of his hand as he sat down next to her. "Can I see your notes?"

She pulled the notebook out from behind the couch cushion where she'd hid it, and opened to the page with her thoughts.

"Sam and Damon's Magical Playlist," he said with a smile. The smile faded, though, as he scanned the songs.

"I've been taking notes on everything I saw. I'm not able to replay anything, so this is the only way to keep track of what happened to us."

"We break up?" He'd jumped ahead to number thirteen. Of course he had. She should've thought to warn him.

"We do," she said. "*They* do."

Damon pushed himself off the couch and walked toward the back door. "Give me a minute," he said without looking back. He went onto the porch, pushed his palms into the deck railing and hung his head.

Sam stood to follow, but stopped herself. He'd asked for a minute, and she'd give him that. One minute turned into several, and after a full ten, she decided she'd earned the right to check on him. She slid the door open, and he turned at the noise.

"Sorry, I didn't mean to leave you in there like that," Damon said. "I just feel overwhelmed by all of this."

"Yeah." She stood next to him. A big puffy white cloud blocked out the sun and shaded them, making the air unexpectedly cool. Damon pulled her into his side and attempted to warm her. He smoothed his hand up and down her arm.

"Well, the good news is you're not making this up," he said.

"Thank you," she said. "As you can imagine, there were times when I absolutely worried Pearl was spiking my food with hallucinogens."

A minute, maybe more, passed. "So, we didn't make it," he eventually said.

"No," she said, her voice low and hushed. "I really thought they would."

"Myles would be thrilled with how things turned out." Damon sighed. "He's asked me for your number every time I've seen him. Who knew he had a big crush on you all these years."

"Alt-Sam did." Then she clarified, "That's what I call the other Sam."

"Ah, so then I'm Alt-Damon."

"Or Emo Flame-Tipped Damon," Sam joked. And at least this made Damon crack a smile. "Why do you think we're being shown this?"

Damon looked at her through his dark lashes, so vulnerable and unsure. "I don't know," he said, then his jaw clenched.

But part of Sam already knew why they'd been shown the answer to her biggest what-if: so that there would be no gray area when it came to them. They weren't meant to be together. Even if she did want to be with him, she'd seen what happened when she wasn't living her life's purpose. What happened to Leto women, in general, when they felt stuck. And while she might be a little in love with Damon, their lives were just too different. Nothing would change that.

"Maybe the visions are just telling us the truth." She looked at Damon. "We aren't meant to be together, in that timeline or this one."

Sam swallowed down the sick feeling, pushed off the porch railing and turned to head back inside. She'd quickly get her things and leave before she started to cry.

"Sam, stop." The tone of Damon's voice *did* stop her. And when she saw his chest rise and fall with heavy breaths, his shoulders tense and the way he looked at her, like she was the last life raft on a sinking ship—that stopped her, too.

"What is there left to say?" Her voice was so stoic she barely recognized it.

"You are not just walking away from me. Not again." And then he walked toward her, as if to prove his point, with powerful strides that shook the ground beneath her. "Do you really think I would just let you leave? After everything we've been through then and now, do you actually think that you're just going to leave?"

And Sam didn't really know what to say to any of that. Her mouth fell open, as if to say something, but she couldn't. She'd never seen Damon this forceful with anything, certainly not with her.

He cleared his throat and their eyes met, and she finally felt her body relax under the weight of his gaze. He was annoyingly calming that way. "All those years ago, I thought we'd be together. I really loved you. You broke me when you left. Maybe you don't know that, but you did. I thought what we had was going to be forever. And you left, like I was nothing. Like we were nothing.

"I hoped that you would come back. But then months passed, and years, and I gave up. I gave up on ever seeing you again. But then you did come back. You're here. And when I saw you, I realized that I've been waiting for you all this time. Just standing in this same spot and waiting. I can't just let you go and pretend like there's nothing between us."

Sam realized she hadn't blinked in quite some time, and when she did, the tears she'd been holding back fell quickly down her cheeks. She bowed her head and wiped them away with her fingertips.

"Sam?" Damon closed the space between them, and his index finger gently lifted her chin. "I can take it. I lost you once, and

I can do it again. But you can't just run. You need to tell me you don't want to try."

And he looked like he was bracing himself for the inevitable letdown that Sam always brought with her wherever she went. She'd always, without fail, manage to disappoint Damon. Because while Damon was perfect in every possible way—thoughtful, caring and he loved her—Sam's default was to run. And while she may not want to run from Damon in this exact moment, eventually she would. And she wasn't going to let that happen. She couldn't say yes to him when she knew that she'd inevitably need to leave.

"I don't want to hurt you." She grabbed his wrist and held him there. "You saw what happened in those visions. If we can't work then, why would we work now? I think that's why we're being shown these—a warning that we'd never work out." Sam hated how harsh it sounded; it made her sad, too. But she didn't see any other meaning to the visions. She was always destined to leave Tybee, and Damon was meant to stay.

His gaze fell to the ground and the finger that had lifted her chin fell, too. "If you really think you're going to leave here and never come back, like you did before, then maybe you're right," he said.

She didn't know how to answer him then. Damon loved her. She loved him. It was that simple, and also that complicated. She knew that whatever answer she gave would have to be her final answer. There was no middle road with them, not when both of their hearts were on the line.

Her phone rang and snapped her out of her trance. She pulled it out of her pocket. "That's Pearl," she said.

"Take it," he said.

Sam answered the call. "Grandma?"

"Sam." Her grandma's voice was tight and high.

"What's wrong?" Sam asked.

"I need you to come home," Pearl said. "Hurry."

36

Grandma Pearl was not a woman who asked for help often. Even with trying to sell the house, she hadn't officially asked Sam to come back home. Sam had come because she knew Pearl needed her there.

So when Pearl told Sam to come home in a hurry, Sam did exactly that. And even though Damon had implied he was worried Sam might run again, he didn't stop her. She knew they still needed to talk, but it would have to wait.

When Sam got out of her rental car, Bonnie was on the front porch waiting for her. "What's all this about?" Sam sidestepped a palm frond that had yet to be moved to the street for pickup.

"Pearl wants to tell you herself." Bonnie nodded for Sam to follow. They walked around the side of the house until their feet sank into the flour-like sand and gulls hovered in the sky above them. When they got to the back, Pearl sat in the middle Adirondack chair and patted Sam's chair as a signal for her to sit.

"Are you okay?" Sam quickly asked as she took a seat. "You've got me worried now."

Bonnie sat in the chair on the other side of Pearl. It was the first time the three generations had been in this spot together in years.

Bonnie reached for Pearl's hand and held it. "Your grandma and I had a heart-to-heart this morning."

Pearl tipped the brim of her sunhat lower to shield her eyes from the revealing light. "It's time for the truth."

Sam straightened. She was still emotionally raw from her morning with Damon, and while she didn't know where this conversation was leading, the truth didn't sound light.

Pearl continued, "I made a mistake. Well, I made a few mistakes. And one of them was discouraging your mama from coming back to see you. She wanted to, a few times, but I was worried she'd do more harm than good. So I asked her not to."

Sam's mouth went completely dry. While she'd heard Bonnie tell her this, she didn't actually believe her grandma would do something so cruel. And she was more than a little shocked that Bonnie was the one who'd been telling the truth, in the end. "You kept my mom from me," Sam said. "How could you do that?"

"She was an alcoholic who abandoned you, and I was worried she'd do it all over again. That's how," Pearl said and sat back in her chair.

It was a fair point. But it didn't make what she'd done right. "Grandma, you understand how wrong that was, don't you? You saw how upset I was. How angry I got at my mom. Any of those times you could've told me that she'd tried to reach out. You made me believe she didn't want anything to do with me. Do you know how much that traumatized me?"

Pearl didn't look at Sam, though; she stared out at the ocean. "I was trying to protect you. And as time passed, you got better. You stopped crying. I thought you'd moved on."

"Moved on?" Sam blurted out. "Moved on from losing my mother? No, I didn't move on."

"Well, how was I supposed to know? You keep everything

so bottled up." Pearl shifted in her chair, clearly uncomfortable with Sam's tone, but probably knowing she deserved it. "What do you want me to say?"

"How about that you're sorry for lying to me? Or you're sorry for keeping me away from my own mother? Or you're sorry for making me think she'd completely abandoned me?"

Sam waited. And waited. And finally, Pearl said, "I am sorry for all of those things. I'm sorry. What happened in the past is not great. What *I* did was wrong. But that's the truth about most things in the past that we don't like to remember."

"We can't change what happened," Bonnie offered. "But *we* can change how we approach the future. Your grandma and I want to move on, but you have to decide what's best for you, too."

Grandma Pearl and Bonnie were ready to move on. They had, apparently, worked through their issues. Bonnie was now truthful, and her grandma had lies to apologize for. What had happened to the women she'd known? Suddenly, these two who could barely be in a room together without yelling were holding hands and looking at Sam and asking *her* if she could move on.

"I don't want to die with regrets." A sigh escaped Pearl. "If I didn't tell you the truth, that's something I'd regret. If I didn't make things right with Bonnie, that's something I'd regret. You have to decide if you can live with regrets, or if you want to try to move on from them. That's your choice. I can't make it for you."

Sam snuck a glance at Bonnie, who shifted in her seat. "It's not up to you whether or not I move on," Sam said.

"The hell it isn't. You're my granddaughter, and she's my daughter. We're family. We do dumb shit, we apologize and then we have family holidays where we rehash things after a few drinks." As if to prove her point, Pearl downed the rest of her coffee.

"Mama," Bonnie said. "If Sam doesn't want to clear the air,

then we have to respect that and give her the emotional space she needs."

"I understand you've been to therapy, Bonnie. You don't have to use fancy words to remind us all," Pearl said.

Sam sucked her cheeks in and tried to pretend she was admiring the ocean waves.

But Pearl, of course, wasn't about to let her get off scot-free. "And besides, if we give Sam the time she needs, she'll disappear for another decade and *I'll* be the one who's dead. So, respectfully to both of you, you need to talk this out."

"Look at you Letos!" Jessie's singsong voice sailed over the sand as she walked toward them from her back patio. "Oh, how I wish I could paint this moment." Jessie took a step back and bit her bottom lip as she admired the three of them. She then took out her phone and snapped a photo. "Well, now I can!"

"We're kind of in the middle of something," Pearl told her. "Can you come back later?"

"No, I can't. Because now that I have all three of you here, I have a proposal." Jessie rocked back on her heels. "I want Pearl to live with me. Permanently."

Pearl waved her comment away. "I told you to stop asking me that. I don't want a roommate."

Jessie slid her sunglasses off. "I don't want to visit you at some old-folks home. I want to wake up and see your Hawaiian print shirts all over the house. I need a roommate to help me cover the monthly costs, and you need a place to go. Come to my place. It'll be like *Golden Girls*, Tybee Island edition."

Sam smiled. Now *this* was an idea she could get behind. "We could still sell this place, Grandma, and you could use the money to cover the rent with Jessie."

"We can't even agree on which store has the best rotisserie chicken. Why do you insist on sharing a refrigerator with me?" Pearl sat forward.

"People can change! Sam's near-death experience with the

palm tree really hit it home for me," Jessie explained. "Life is short. Yeah, sometimes we annoy the hell out of each other, and I truly *hate* that white noise machine, but I don't want to lose my best friend. I want to watch her sleep, and then paint her while sleeping."

"You know I love your quirky sensibilities, but if you hover over my bed you'll give me a heart attack. And you know who died from that? Carol Gaines."

"Oh, no, she was my art teacher," Bonnie said.

"Yup." Pearl looked triumphant. "And you know who else is dead?"

"Spoiler alert, it's everyone," Sam said. "Literally every day I've been here there's a new dead person."

"That's because people die, Sam. That's why you have to take your vitamins." Pearl shook sand off her tropical shirt. "And forgive people before it's too late."

"See?" Jessie asked. "How could I possibly go every day without this in my life?"

"What do you think, Grandma?" Sam really hoped Pearl would at least consider the move. She'd feel a lot better about packing up the house if she knew the boxes were headed next door.

Pearl seemed to weigh her options as she sipped her coffee. "Let's discuss," she said to Jessie. "But I'd need to bring my beach signs."

"Of course!" Jessie extended a hand to Pearl.

Grandma Pearl stood from the chair then. "I'm going to get another cup of coffee with my potential new roommate."

Sam watched her grandma and Jessie walk toward the house. Before she talked things out with Bonnie, she had to talk things out with Pearl. "Wait," she said before standing from her chair and following the women toward the house. "Grandma?"

Pearl turned around and motioned for Jessie to continue inside. "Sam, you can't run from your mama anymore."

"No, I want to talk to you. Just us." Sam caught her breath

and continued, "You somehow forgave Bonnie, but I still need to process a lot of things, too."

Pearl gently stroked her thumb along Sam's jawline. "If packing up this house has taught me one thing, it's that it's healthy to let things go. It's time, Sam."

Sam swatted Pearl's hand away and let out a frustrated breath. "You know something? Maybe I *shouldn't* be mad at Bonnie anymore. Maybe I should be mad at *you*."

Pearl's shoulders slumped. "I realize now that I should have told you sooner. But when would have been a good time for that? You never came home. And it wasn't news I wanted to drop over a quick holiday where all you wanted to do was talk about anything *but* Tybee."

"You could have told me," Sam insisted. "You had years to find the right time."

"Well, I didn't." Pearl adjusted her hat and looked off. "Anyway, I'm going to be paying my dues truly alone now, aren't I?"

Sam stopped short. Sure, she had flown Grandma Pearl out to Paris a few times over the years, but Sam never really thought that maybe Pearl was hurt by her fleeing Tybee, too. Pearl had a whole community here—Jessie, the Rochas, Alligator Alice, Byron…she understood Sam had her own life to live, too, right?

"Grandma…" Sam started to say. "I was never running from you. You are the most important person to me. And you getting injured scared me so much. I don't want to leave here again knowing you might be isolated in some retirement home. What happens if Jessie can't visit every day, or you can't access the beach so easily anymore, or get your rotisserie chickens, or—"

"Sammy girl, I'm going to figure it out." Pearl straightened and her expression turned serious. "I always do."

"With Jessie." Sam scratched her eyebrow while she searched for the words to make Pearl see her side of things. "Please say you'll seriously consider her offer."

Pearl turned toward the house and let out a little muffled sound that might have been her getting choked up.

But just through the window, Jessie had a bottle of sriracha and seemed to be squirting some into a coffee cup. Then she poured hot coffee into the mug.

"Hot sauce in coffee," Sam said. "You don't want to miss out on that every morning."

And then Pearl laughed and turned back to Sam and wiped the tears from the corners of her eyes.

"Change doesn't have to be huge for it to be significant, Grandma," Sam offered. "I know that now."

Pearl let out an exhausted sigh as she glanced at Jessie in the kitchen. "I meant what I said about keeping my beach signs, though."

Sam wrapped Pearl in a hug. "Thank you. I love you."

"I love you, too." Pearl hugged her back. Then she grabbed Sam's chin, maybe too forcefully, and said, "You are not perfect, Sam, no matter how much you want everyone to think that. So have a little compassion. Talk things out with your mama."

Sam rubbed the spot her grandma had pinched and turned to see Bonnie watching her. *One more to go*, Sam thought to herself as she made her way back to Bonnie and the beach chairs.

Bonnie clasped her hands in her lap and leaned forward. "I'm not the world's best actress, but if you want me to pretend we worked things out when Pearl gets back, I can do that." Bonnie brought a hand to her chest as if swearing a solemn oath. "I really don't want to force you to have any conversations you don't want to have."

Sam was *not* perfect, that much had become abundantly clear through her trip here. She'd gotten a lot of closure from getting answers out of Bonnie on the beach—answers that were probably hard for Bonnie to give. So maybe Sam could at least try to do the same thing for her mom, even if she maybe didn't deserve it.

"Who knows when we'll be in the same room again after

you leave," Sam said. "Sorry, I didn't mean to sound rude, but who knows. We might as well say what we need to say. But you go first."

Bonnie pressed her palms into her capri pants and looked at Sam. "I want to say that I am sorry for how I left, even if you don't believe that. I regret my choice every single day, and I wish I could go back and change things. But I can't. None of us can. All we can do is learn from our mistakes. And I promise I will do that. I will be here for you, if you ever need me for anything. And I won't leave you to figure out things with Pearl by yourself. She's my mom, and I plan to help sort out what she needs, okay?"

"Okay," Sam said. She wasn't totally sure how her mom planned to help, or if she actually would, but what else could she say? She could grill her mom about the details of how and why, but what would that do, other than remind Bonnie that Sam didn't trust her? "It probably goes without saying, but you leaving me behind was not okay. What you did will never be okay. I am going to try to move forward with you, but if I can't, then you have to respect my decision not to talk to you."

Bonnie licked her lips and considered that. "You're not wrong. I'm asking you to forgive me for something unforgivable."

Sam glared out toward the water. She didn't owe her mom anything, but she had promised to try to move forward. "Grandma has missed having you here. As much as you're trying to mend things with me, you need to mend them with her as well. So if you expect me to give you a chance, you have to try with her, too."

Bonnie cracked maybe all of her knuckles, but said, "I will try to be better with Pearl, too."

Sam slipped her shoes off and dug her toes into the sand for comfort. "So what happens now?"

"Maybe we can start small, you know?" Bonnie shrugged. "Texting. Calling."

Sam nodded. "Let's start small. I can do small. Texting first."

"I would really like that." Bonnie's eyes welled with tears and she dabbed the corners with her fingertips. "I think Grandma would be really proud of us."

"Yeah," Sam said. "She will be."

Bonnie reached her hand across the chairs and toward Sam's. Sam initially stiffened, but then remembered that she was going to try to give Bonnie a chance. So she reached her hand out and held on to her mom's fingertips and they both squeezed each other.

"Are you going to come back to Tybee?" Sam asked.

"Are you?" Bonnie asked back.

"I think I will, yes." Sam pulled her hand away and looked out at the beach and the water and the endless sky. She remembered feeling so much dread on her first day back, but now she had a bit of what Pearl felt when she came out to the water: clarity. "You probably think that's a bad thing. 'Don't end up stuck in this place.'"

"What?" Bonnie looked like she'd been slapped.

"Don't end up stuck in this place," Sam repeated her mom's fateful words.

Bonnie frowned, like she was genuinely confused.

"That's what you told me about Tybee," Sam said, a little annoyed.

"But I didn't say that. That's not—"

"You did," Sam cut her off.

"I *did* often say 'Don't end up stuck in this place,' but I didn't mean that about Tybee. It was about a state of being..." She stopped midsentence. "Being in the mental state that I was. I didn't want to end up in *that* place. And I didn't want *you* to end up like I was. Depression can breed depression, and I didn't want that for you. I didn't want you to end up stuck in the place I was."

"So, just to be clear," Sam started to say, "you were not talking about Tybee?"

"I was talking about a state of being, not the state of Georgia."
Bonnie sat back in her chair.

What was happening here? Sam had built so many of her
choices around that warning, and how her mom had behaved,
and now Bonnie was suggesting she was…wrong about everything? Sam leaned forward in her chair, trying to sort through
the unfamiliar feeling of trusting what her mom was saying.

"I've been so scared that you'd repeat my mistakes." Bonnie dusted something from the arm of her chair into the sand.
Then she readjusted herself to look right at Sam. "But the truth
is, you never have. You've charted your own path, despite what
I put you through. And for what it's worth, Damon is a good
man. He's successful, and he loves you—I could see that as clear
as the blue sky above us."

Sam was surprised to hear Bonnie say something nice about
Damon, let alone acknowledge that he loved her. The kind-
ness was so unexpected that she said, "Thanks, Mom." It was
the first time she'd called Bonnie "mom" as an adult, and she
found it felt more natural than expected.

Talking to her mom had freed something up inside her.

Damon was her home. Wherever he was, Sam wanted to be.
And maybe he felt the same way. She would never be stuck in
Tybee, because Damon wouldn't force her to be somewhere that
made her unhappy. Sam had been on autopilot for so long—
believing coming home would destroy her—when the truth was
she'd been running from the one person who accepted her for
exactly who she was. And now it was time to go fight for him.

Bonnie had changed. The mother she'd been was not the person she was now. Even Grandma Pearl was willing to change—
she'd apologized to Sam. She was agreeing to move in with
Jessie.

And what if Sam could change, too? Not everything about
her life, but the parts that were willing to bend to make space

for something magical. What if opening herself up to someone she trusted unearthed a new adventure?

"I need to go do something," Sam told Bonnie.

"Do you need any help?" Bonnie was practically already out of her chair, and she gave Sam a look as if she genuinely would help.

So Sam, despite everything, decided to give her mom a chance. "Yeah, actually, I might need all of the Letos on board for this one."

37

The neon guitar sign for Band Practice Brews flashed bright as Sam pulled into the parking lot with Pearl in the passenger seat and Bonnie and Jessie in the back. Fallen palm fronds were draped around the parking lot like obstacles in a game of Mario Kart, but Sam managed to find a spot close to the front that hadn't been claimed by Hurricane fallout.

"It looks open," Sam said, surprised.

"After a hurricane, people need somewhere to eat and drink," Jessie said. "Smart of Damon to open the place up."

Sam inhaled a steadying breath. She'd run from Damon once, but now it was her turn to prove she would never run from him again. She opened the mirror on her visor. Heavy black eyeliner? Check. Purple shimmer eyeshadow? Double check. Black lipstick? Check, check, check. "Okay, let's go, Letos."

Sam opened the car door and, in some ways, felt like the cooler version of her high school self. She'd parsed through her throwback closet and put on a pair of fishnet tights, a black pleated miniskirt and white button-down shirt with a plaid vest. She'd topped her look off with a skinny tie, Doc Marten combat boots and a skull necklace.

As she walked to the entrance with her mom, grandma and her grandma's new roommate, she felt confident. Like the lead of a teen rom-com who'd taken off her glasses to reveal how hot she was. Only, in Sam's version, she'd basically done the opposite, reverting to who she'd been in high school. But those were just details.

"Vampire girl!" Myles called out as Sam walked through the door of the bar.

Sam definitely felt like she was back at Tybee High. But now she knew who she was, and where she was going. So no assholes were about to stop her. "This vampire bites!" Sam called back, and hissed as she walked right by him.

Myles held up his hands in surrender, but Sam didn't really care what he did, because the person she wanted to see wasn't in the room.

"He's not here," Pearl said.

"He's probably outside." Jessie glanced out the back.

"He'll be here," Bonnie reassured Sam. And she smiled back at her mom.

"Is everything ready?" Sam asked her team of senior citizen assistants.

"The music is setting up," Jessie confirmed.

"And I will get us the beers." Pearl didn't wait for further instruction as she approached the bar.

"You've got this, honey." Bonnie gave Sam a little fist pump in the air.

Sam nodded to reassure herself. She hoped she did have this—the *this* being Damon. But now it was the moment of truth, and there was only one way to find out if he'd jump out of the plane to see where they'd land.

When she went to the back patio, the tables were full of people eating and drinking, but Jessie found one empty high top and went to grab it. Sam scanned the crowd in search of a dark swoop of hair, but instead of Damon, she saw Marissa.

And Marissa most *definitely* saw her, as her mouth hung open at the mere sight of Sam. Sam gave a small wave. The confidence she'd had shrank a little at the sight of the in-real-life Disney Princess gaping at her. But she also realized that she owed Marissa an explanation, and maybe an apology. Sam moved through the people milling around tables until she reached Marissa's.

Marissa sat with a handful of other women, all of whom eyed Sam like she was the most obvious Where's Emo Waldo. Sam figured it was on her to cut the tension. "Hey, Marissa," she said. "Good to see you."

"I barely recognized you," she said with a laugh. "But now I totally remember you from high school."

"Yeah." Sam held up her hands and let them fall down the length of her. "This is me."

"I'm not sure where Damon is, if that's who you're looking for." Marissa crossed her arms, not exactly happy about that statement.

"I just wanted to say I'm sorry for how that ended between you two," Sam said. "I never meant—"

"Oh, don't be." Marissa took a sip from her beer. "I want to be with a guy who looks at me the way he looked at you."

"You will," Sam quickly said. "I'm serious. You smell like glitter, if that's even possible."

Marissa chuckled. "Thanks."

And then, just behind Marissa, the dark swoop of hair appeared. Sam's mouth opened to call out his name just as he clocked her. A surprised grin crossed his face as he came out from the bar and onto the back patio.

"Sam-Sam," he said as he reached her. "I thought I might be having a vision there for a second."

"I'll take that to mean I *look* like a vision." She grabbed his hand and led him toward the stage where Fall Out Troy had performed. When they got in front of the stage, she turned to face him. "You asked me if history was going to repeat itself.

And while I'm dressed in my old clothes, I want you to know that you're the only person who's ever really known me. You loved me even when I wore these stockings." Sam pulled at a piece of the fishnets for emphasis. "You're the only one I've ever wanted to be with. And when I saw you again, I realized that I'd been waiting for you all this time. We were always meant to be together, Damon. We just had to become who we are now before we ever stood a chance."

He brought his hand up and she pressed her cheek into his palm and he stroked his thumb along the line of her cheekbone. "Are you sure?"

She nodded and reached for his hand, and he squeezed her back. She wasn't having one of her visions of being in high school, but her stomach still flipped, the way it always had for Damon. "This reminds me, I've been meaning to tell you that there's a song you should add to the playlist."

"Oh, yeah?" he asked curiously.

Sam waved to Jessie, their secret code. And Jessie let out a wolf whistle so loud that the entire outdoor patio went silent for a few blissful seconds. In those moments, Troy of Fall Out Troy took the steps up to the stage. "Hey, everyone," he said into the waiting microphone. "I'm Troy. I don't have my band with me tonight, but I got a last-minute request for a very special song."

Damon opened his mouth, a kind of delighted confusion overtaking him. "What have you done?" he asked.

Sam let go of Damon's hand and made her way to the steps on the stage. She'd never done anything quite like this, but as she stepped in front of the microphone, she gave Troy a nod. He strummed a few initial times before launching into the song Sam had asked him to play. "One, two, one, two, three, go," Troy said to her.

And then Sam began to sing an acoustic version of "Still Into You" by Paramore. The words were etched into her brain from memory. But still, she stumbled over a few of the lines as she looked up from the mic and into the crowd at Damon. He watched her, with one hand over his mouth, maybe in shock. The lyrics were sentimental and about still being head over heels in love with someone, even after such a long time together, which felt true to their relationship.

She wasn't a singer, but Sam sang each word and line like they were a poem written just for them. And Damon held her gaze as she unlatched the mic from the stand and continued to sing to him as she walked down the steps and into the crowd. Sam met Damon in front of the stage, and as she sang the final lines of the song, he began to sing them back to her, too. They were having the duet he'd asked her for, just in a different way than planned.

When the song ended, the crowd at the bar erupted into applause. Sam glanced around, but when she looked back, Damon watched only her.

"Of course," he said as he brushed hair out of her face, "you'd pick a sappy love song to add to the playlist."

Sam laughed. "This is a love song, yes, but it's not sappy. Now, me dressing in our old emo clothes and serenading you? That's a bit sappy."

Troy continued to strum the instrumentals to the song in the background. So Damon took Sam's hands and wrapped them behind his neck, and he began to slow dance with her. Sam let her head rest against his shoulder as they both swayed.

"We never did get to go to prom, in this life or the other one," Damon said.

Sam looked up and gave a knowing smile. "We were way too cool for it anyway."

When the song ended, Damon's index finger gently lifted her chin, and they kissed. And while she knew they were in the present, she felt inextricably pulled back in time. Like she was still in high school and it was the first time they were kissing all over again. She'd never left, and Damon had always been part of her life, and would continue to be. What was between them was electric and alive and pulsing.

Eventually, Pearl shouted, "Get a room!"

Sam pulled back and touched her fingers to her lips. She wanted more, but then Damon asked, "What now?"

And she knew the definitive answer to his question. "We get to figure out the rest of our lives together," she said.

38

There were hardly any waves as Sam and Damon stared out at the water. They'd spent the night on the beach, cuddled on a striped blanket as they talked through their hopes for their futures—together and individually. Sam wanted to continue operating as an international flight pilot, and Damon wanted to take his small-town beer and distribute it globally. Sam needed to spend more time with Grandma Pearl that didn't involve her having to travel, and Damon would need to be in Tybee regularly to continue operations at the brewery.

But they would live together. They'd spend six months in Paris, then six in Tybee, to start, and reevaluate from there. While Sam flew, Damon would travel to new European locations to make relationships with restaurants and distributors to introduce them to Band Practice Brews. When they were based in Tybee, Sam could still fly out of the Atlanta hub, but make use of her time off to spend with Pearl and Damon. They had an initial flight plan and, maybe more importantly, they had each other.

There was something between them, though. More specifically, it was the CD player. "I don't think I've ever been so torn about a CD," Damon said.

"Not sure that's true. Remember when Farrah got pissed at you for eating all of her Cocoa Puffs and then broke your New Found Glory CD in half?" Sam cringed at the memory of Damon's face when he found it.

Damon bit his lip, perhaps remembering the same moment. "That was my favorite CD. She knew that."

"I remember tears." Sam let her head rest on his shoulder. "And you refused to throw it out. It just sat on your desk, snapped in two, like a memorial."

"I don't think I ever did throw it out. It's probably still somewhere in my parents' house."

They hadn't intended to catch the sunrise, but the warm light sliced across the top of the water as Sam dug her toes into the sand. Soon after, Byron made his usual trek down the beach, whistling the same wakeup call he'd soon play.

"Morning to ya," Byron called out to them, and Sam waved back.

The silence stretched comfortably until Byron placed his lips on the bagpipes and began to play. Sam nestled herself against Damon, rubbing her forehead on his arm like a cat looking for pets. He obliged by tucking her in close to his side.

When she'd arrived in Tybee, her whole body had buzzed from the lack of control she felt over her situation. But now she found herself humming pleasantly from the closeness to Damon and the rhythm of this place.

Byron finished his set by saluting the sun, then turned and walked back up the beach. Sam would miss waking up to the sound of his music.

"Don't worry," Damon said with a squeeze to her shoulder. "I recorded the whole thing on my phone so we can play it when we wake up in Paris."

"You did not." She sat up with a smile. "I wonder if he knows we're his biggest fans."

"The man has many fans, Sam. Of course he doesn't know."

Then, like the elephant in the room that it was, they both glanced at the CD player. On the one hand, this was the thing that had shown Sam a way back to Damon, and Tybee, on her own terms. On the other hand, it was possessed and had to be destroyed.

"Okay." Sam tucked her hair behind her ears. "So our options are burn it, bury it, lock it in a safe or sell it on eBay."

"Do you know how many hours I spent making that CD for you?" He leaned back in the sand, and the sun made him glow, and Sam hoped she would never forget the way he smiled out of the side of his mouth at her.

"Putting 'Want You Bad' on the mix was a little forward," she said.

"You noticed that, huh?" He raised a playful eyebrow.

And then she had an idea. Sam popped open the lid of the player and gently removed the CD. It had once been the thing that marked the end of them, and now destroying it would mark a new beginning.

"You remember those friendship necklaces that were a broken heart, and one person got the half that said *best* and the other got the half that said *friends*?"

"Vaguely," he said.

"Maybe this could be our version." She handed the CD to Damon, and he took it. "Our *more than friends* CD. You always keep one half, and I'll always keep the other."

"I like it," he said. "But what about the player?"

Damon pushed himself up and held his hand out for her. She took it, and the warmth and strength in just his palm reassured Sam that she didn't need this CD anymore. It was a thing that only showed the past, and she was ready to embrace her future with Damon.

"Maybe we keep it as a little reminder of what brought us back together." She tucked the CD player under her free arm and held on to Damon's hand as they walked the short distance down the beach. Their toes reached the point where water met earth, and the cool waves lapped gently across their feet.

"You can hold one side, and I'll hold the other?" Damon pinched one side of the CD and held it out to her.

She grabbed the other side. "Let's count to three, and we'll snap it, okay?"

Sam rolled out her shoulders, ready to finally say goodbye to the what-if playlist.

"One, two, three," they said together, then snapped it in half. There was Damon's handwriting, and his drawings, cracked down the middle, forever changed.

He raised the broken half of the CD and slapped it against his open palm. "Now we have to make a new playlist."

"I think we've seen what happens when we make music together." Sam cringed at her own bad joke.

Damon raised an eyebrow. "I sure hope that's the innuendo I think it was."

Sam rolled her eyes.

"I'm serious, though." Damon slung an arm around her. "Let's start fresh, with new music, new meanings, and it can be a mix you can listen to when you're flying and missing the hell out of me."

"You really think I'll be missing you when I'm forty thousand feet up and cutting through the clouds?" Sam said.

"Yes, I do." He smiled broadly.

"Yes, I will," she confirmed.

Damon shook out the beach blanket, and a spray of sand flew in the air. "How about Paramore's 'Still Into You' for the first track?"

"I'm thrilled to hear my performance moved you so deeply." Sam helped him fold the blanket. "What about 'With Me' by Sum 41?"

"Yeah." Damon squinted against the brighter light. "But since this is a love album, I think we also just need a Celine Dion banger. Like, 'My Heart Will Go On,' just to round it out."

"Nah," Sam said. "If we're doing a Celine song it's 'I Drove All Night.'"

"'I drove all night,'" someone loudly sang.

Sam and Damon turned to see Alligator Alice power-walking behind them and singing the song's title.

"Love that song!" Alligator Alice widely smiled. "Great morning for a walk, isn't it?"

"Absolutely," Sam said, holding back a chuckle.

Damon gave a cocky smile as he pulled Sam in toward him. "Making you this CD was the best thing I ever did, as it turns out."

"And avoiding you for over a decade only to return and discover it was haunted was the best thing *I* ever did." Sam started back up the beach.

Damon closely followed. "Sam?"

She turned at his voice, and he grabbed her hand. "Should I get the red-dyed tips again?" he asked, all serious.

"They're coming back now, I hear." Sam was equally serious.

Damon bent his head slightly, and she reached up toward him. Their lips met and Sam knew he would be her home, no matter where she went.

epilogue

When the wheels touched down in Morocco at Casablanca Airport, Sam was certain it had been her smoothest landing yet. Not a single bump, and the runway sailed beneath like a steady ocean breeze.

"Now *that* was a landing," Rachel said, genuinely impressed.

Sam gave a satisfied little exhale. She loved her job.

"Captain Leto?" Flight attendant Ashley's voice came through the intercom. "What are the results of the 'What If' game?"

"We're about to touch down," Sam responded into the mic.

Touch down was code for ending the game. Which meant Sam would have to leave the cockpit to see who'd won this round.

They opened the door to the main cabin to do their traditional farewell to the passengers. But as Sam glanced in the first row, she was only looking for one passenger in particular. Her *what if*.

Damon was packing up his carry-on bag. He wore a Band Practice Brews sweatshirt, and his hair had the smallest hint of red-dyed tips, which she'd dared him to bring back and, true to his word, he had. They were going on their first vacation together, and it was to Morocco—a place neither of them had been, and would allow Sam to complete her travel bingo card.

He glanced up and clocked her there, and an instant smile crossed his lips. He pulled out his AirPods and gave a slow and steady clap while looking at Sam. She crossed her arms and leaned against a wall of the cabin.

"So, you have to settle a bet for me. What song were you listening to?" she asked.

He cocked his head. "Our playlist," he said. "'The Glory of Love' by New Found Glory."

"Dammit," Sam said.

Ashley gave a closemouthed smile and held out her hand. "Pay up."

Sam reached into her back pocket and handed over twenty Moroccan dirham. "I hope you know I was going to spend that on a souvenir for my grandma," she told Ashley.

"I hope you know I'll be using it to buy some ghriba cookies for myself." Ashley snapped the paper currency, as if for emphasis. "Thanks, One C."

Damon frowned, but Sam came into his aisle and patted his shoulder to reassure him.

"I messed up, huh?" he asked, slinging the backpack over his shoulder.

"I think you just made Ashley's day." She put her arms around his neck, and he rested his easily around her waist. "Do you have it?"

Damon pulled out a booklet from his carry-on bag. It was the bucket list bingo card he'd made her in high school.

Explore Casablanca

That was the last item on her list to check off. He handed her the paper and the sheet of stickers. "Ready, Sam-Sam?" he asked.

But she handed him the sticker sheet back. "We're doing this together. Why don't you have the honors?"

So Damon pulled a small gold sticker off and placed it next to the open square. They both admired the page, dotted with gold and crinkled from overuse.

"We made a new x, and now we'll have to make a new card," he said.

"As long as we make it together, I'm in." Sam grinned, and he gave an easy smile back. She pulled him in, and as they kissed, she felt like she was already experiencing the biggest adventure of her life.

★ ★ ★ ★ ★

Scan the QR code to listen to

SAM AND DAMON'S MAGICAL PLAYLIST

and other music from The Backtrack

acknowledgments

Since listening to music fueled this book, I think I'd like to organize my dedication as I would a playlist. Happy listening!

Track one: "Still Into You" by Paramore—this song goes out to my husband, Eoghan, who I am forever trying to impress. Thank you for telling me this is your favorite book of mine so far. I hope you say that about every subsequent book, and mean it.

Track two: "A Thousand Years" by Christina Perri—to Lynn Raposo, my fellow Twi-hard editor. I hope we get to work together for a thousand years, because I just adore you! Thank you for cheering this book on, giving fabulous notes and sharing in the emo joy with me.

Track three: "Do Better" by Say Anything—this one is for my fabulous agent, Jessica Errera. Now, hear me out—this is a song about pushing yourself to do better, and that is exactly what you do for me, Jess. I hope you know how much I appreciate your feedback and wisdom in all things. And let's keep pushing each other forward!

Track four: "Teenage Dirtbag" by Wheatus—to every single person at Canary Street Press... I often have to pinch myself about how lucky I am to work with your team. I am floored by how wonderful you've all been to me on this journey, and let's just say you are my "Noelle" and I am the teenage dirtbag lucky enough to be in the same room as you. Thank you for making my dreams come true!

Track five: "In Too Deep" by Sum 41—as a mom of two young kids, writing is made possible with the help of a lot of people, particularly childcare. Thank you to our nanny, day care and grandparents for giving me time to write and be the best mom I can be! And to Three Sisters Coffee in Burbank, your lattes fuel me. Thank you!